The Motor Rally Mystery

BY

John Rhode

CONTENTS:

CHAPTER I

THE British Motor Car Rally of that year, organised by the Royal Automobile Club, was generally voted to have been a huge success. But it proved a bitter disappointment to Mr. Robert Weldon, one of the competitors. He owned a luxurious 20hp. Armstrong Siddeley Saloon, the performance of which entitled him to expect to win one of the coveted prizes. But his luck was against him. He never finished the course, owing to circumstances which were no fault either of the car or her crew.

The task set to the competitors was this: They had to cover a course of approximately a thousand miles at an average speed of twenty-five miles per hour. This course finished at Torquay, where subsequently a series of tests to determine the efficiency of the competing cars was held. The competitors were distributed over nine separate starting points and each was allotted his own time to start. To Bob Weldon was assigned the official number, 513. His task was to leave Bath at 8.45 pm on Tuesday, March 1st, and proceed to Torquay via Norwich, Kendal, Droitwich and Moorchester. At each of these towns Controls were established, where competitors had to produce their route books, sign them and have them stamped. Since the shortest possible distance by this route was 1005 miles, Bob Weldon's finishing time at Torquay was 12.57 pm on the 3rd.

All went well at first. Bob had taken a pretty efficient crew with him. Richard Gateman, an old friend of his, was acting as second driver. Since a map reader was also desirable, Richard had suggested an acquaintance of his, Harold Merefield, and Bob had fallen in with this suggestion. The three of them started from Bath at the appointed time and ran steadily enough for the first twenty-four hours, keeping well ahead of the schedule which they had prepared.

But their luck turned shortly before the midnight of the 2nd, when they were about two-thirds of the way between Droitwich and Moorchester. They ran into a bank of fog, which seemed to fill the valleys with a sort of fluid cotton wool. Their speed dropped at once and on several occasions the car had to be stopped while Harold got out and tried to decipher the signposts with his torch. Eventually they lost their way completely, and spent much valuable time in getting back to the right road.

They left the fog belt behind at last, but the experience had told upon all of them. This was their second night on the road, with only such snatches of sleep as they

3

could get by turns in the back of the car. Bob was driving; Harold, schedule in hand, was sitting beside him; Richard, who had been relieved at the wheel a few minutes before, was dozing in the back.

"How are we getting on?" asked Bob, without taking his eyes from the strip of illuminated road in front of him.

"Not very well, I'm afraid," replied Harold. "We lost a devil of a lot of time in that confounded fog. As far as I can make out, we're still twenty miles or more from Moorchester, and it's long after four o'clock already."

Bob grunted. "What fools we were to take this job on!" he exclaimed. "If this is your idea of pleasure, it isn't mine. I'm pretty well played out, but Richard's no better, so there's no point in changing over again. What time were we due at Moorchester?"

"2.25," replied Harold. "We're running something like a couple of hours behind time."

Bob's reply was to press gently on the accelerator. Tired out as he was, nothing would have induced him to give up. The speedometer needle crept over the dial as the car gained speed, till she settled into her stride at something over fifty miles an hour. This was the utmost speed at which Bob dared to travel, even on the straight stretches. A few thin wisps of fog still hung about, appearing like puffs of steam in the beam of the headlights, and the frequent bends in the road made it necessary to slack up every half-mile or so.

Neither of the two in front felt inclined for conversation. Bob's whole attention was concentrated upon the road in front of him. Only by a supreme effort of will could he keep at bay his overmastering desire for sleep. An instant's relaxation, and he found himself plunging headlong into the void of unconsciousness. Harold, free from the responsibility of driving and lulled by the luxurious movement of the car, dozed fitfully. At one moment he saw the road in front of him, white and unreal, like the highway of a dream. At the next his eyelids had closed of their own weight, only to start open as his subconscious self reminded him of his duty to watch the route and direct the driver if necessary.

At last, after an interminable period, as it seemed, a faint glare began to soften the darkness ahead. Lampposts began to appear and they felt rather than saw that scattered houses fringed the road on either side of them. The road became a street, the silent and unlighted houses flanking it like endless walls. Bob slackened speed and turned sharply as a painted board, "To the R.A.C. Control," caught his eye. A couple of minutes later he pulled up in the courtyard of the Imperial Hotel.

Several cars were standing in the courtyard, presumably belonging to the control officials. None of them bore the flag and official number which showed that they were competing in the rally. All these must have passed through long ago, and by now were well on their way to the finishing point. Harold noted this at a glance, then shouted over his shoulder, "Wake up, Richard! Moorchester Control!"

Urging their weary limbs to action, they descended from the car and entered the hotel. In a comfortable room reserved for their use they found a group of control officials. Richard blinked in the brilliant illumination and looked about him. "My word!" he exclaimed. "I like the way you fellows make yourselves comfortable in the best pub in the town, while we go hurtling across England. Any chance of a drink? I'm dying of thirst."

The officials laughed. "You're Number 513, I suppose?" said one of them. "We were wondering what had become of you. There's some cold tea on that table over there, if that's any good to you."

"Oh, never mind him," interrupted Bob impatiently, as he came forward, route book in hand. "He'll stay here all night if you encourage him. And we haven't a minute to spare."

"You've only just saved your bacon as it is," replied the official, glancing at the clock. "The control closes in ten minutes and then we are off home to bed. All the other Bath cars are through. What happened to you? Did you have a breakdown, or something?"

"Breakdown?" said Bob scornfully. "No, fog — ran into it about midnight and couldn't get clear. We'd have been here hours ago but for that. Still, we'll do it all right if we don't strike another patch."

He signed the book with shaking fingers, his usually firm and bold signature looking like that of an old man. The other two, their fingers numb with sleep, followed his example. The official stamped it with a rubber stamp and handed the book back to Bob. "Off you go, and better luck to you on this stage," he said.

Outside in the courtyard they held a hurried council of war. "It's now three minutes past five," said Harold, consulting the schedule. "We're two hours and forty minutes behind time. We're due at the finishing line at 12.57 and we've got 225 miles to go; that means we've got to average about twenty-eight miles an hour."

Bob patted the bonnet of the car affectionately. "She'd do that on three wheels," he said cheerfully.

"It's easy, if only we can manage to keep awake. Feel like taking a spell, Richard?"

"How you fellows manage to do sums in mental arithmetic at this hour of the morning, I can't think," replied Richard, with his mouth full. "Have a cold hard-boiled egg; you've no idea what wonderful things they are for keeping you awake. I can't offer you any salt. I spilt it all on the floor of the car yesterday evening; or was it a week ago? It seems like it. I believe we're dead and gone to hell, and our punishment is to ride in this bus for the rest of eternity."

"Oh, shut up, Richard!" exclaimed Bob. "Yes, I'll have an egg, it you haven't eaten them all. And if you look in the left-hand pocket of the car you'll find some lukewarm coffee in a thermos. Now, are you going to drive, or aren't you?"

Richard shook his head. "I'd rather you kept on a bit longer if you can manage it, Skipper," he replied. "You know this part of the world and I don't. We daren't risk losing our way again. I'll take over as soon as you strike the main road."

"All right, but it'll be your fault if I go to sleep and ditch her. Look sharp! Jump in; we don't want to hang about here till daylight!"

"What about petrol?" asked Harold, as they settled themselves into the same positions as before.

Bob glanced at the gauge. "We've enough for a hundred miles," he replied. "We'll stop at the first garage we see open after it's light. He flicked the pre-selective gear with his finger and touched the clutch pedal. The car glided softly out of the courtyard and began to gather speed. "5.5," remarked Harold, as he pencilled in the time on his schedule.

"Good enough!" exclaimed Bob. "Bar accidents, we'll be in Torquay to the minute and have time for breakfast on the way into the bargain. You see if we don't."

The few minutes at the control and the mouthful of coffee he had swallowed seemed to have roused Bob for a while. He swung the car through the deserted streets of Moorchester until he gained the open road, the bonnet of the car pointing westward. It was pitch dark, with only a few frosty stars twinkling overhead, but mercifully a faint breeze had sprung up, driving before it the last vestiges of fog. The steady beam of the headlights shed a hard, cold ray upon the road ahead of them.

It could not be described as a fast road. For the first few miles out of Moorchester it was narrow and winding, with an irritating succession of sharp corners, necessitating constant checking of speed. But the car responded nobly to Bob's driving. The brakes acted smoothly but powerfully; at a touch on the accelerator pedal the car gathered speed again like a live thing. At last the road seemed to make up its mind to keep a constant direction. It became comparatively straight, running like a ribbon across a stretch of flat country, with deep ditches on either side.

Bob took advantage of this at once and the speedometer needle settled at a steady sixty. But it was obvious that he had come to the end of his tether. More than once the car edged towards the grass alongside the road, to be corrected by an almost convulsive clutch at the wheel. Harold endured this as long as he could, but at last, when the near wheels actually mounted the grass, he could not contain himself any longer. "Steady, Skipper!" he exclaimed. "You'll have us in the ditch if you're not careful!"

"Sorry," said Bob dreamily, "I'm so tired I can hardly keep my eyes open. The only thing I can see are the trees by the side of the road, and they persist in making faces at me. Give Richard a hail, and as soon as he's properly awake he can take over."

Harold was about to turn his head for the purpose, when he caught sight of something in the road ahead of them. "Look out!" he said. "There is a red light in front there — the road's up, as likely as not."

Bob nodded. "I see it," he replied. Harold turned to wake Richard, a feat which he accomplished with some difficulty. By the time he was facing the road again, the car had slowed down and the red light was no more than a hundred yards or so ahead. "Hallo!" he exclaimed. "That's the rear light of a car, and, by jove, he's in the ditch, by the look of it!"

Bob pulled up the Armstrong Siddeley a few yards from the red light, which seemed to glower at them like some evil eye. "He's in the ditch, all right," he said. "We'd better have a look, I suppose, before we go on."

There was no doubt about the car being in the ditch, which, as Harold had already noticed, was particularly wide and deep. The car had apparently swerved to the right, the off-front wheel was right in the ditch, and the near front wheel was just on the edge of it. The car had not overturned, though it had a dangerous list, only the rear part remaining on firm ground.

The crew of the Armstrong Siddeley got out and hurried towards the derelict. "Hallo!" exclaimed Bob. "It's a rally car. The flag is still fixed to the radiator cap. A two-seater Sports Comet, by the look of it. Did anybody think of bringing the torch along?"

The torch was obviously necessary. Although the rear light was still burning with an ominous red glow, the side and headlights were smashed and nothing in front of the car could be seen. Harold produced the torch, walked a couple of yards up the road and turned the light on to the radiator of the Comet, revealing a plate with the official number, 514.

"Hallo, the next number to us!" exclaimed Bob. "He must have started from Bath soon after we did. I wonder what's become of the driver and his passenger?"

"I remember the car now," said Richard. "It was standing next to us in the starting park. There were two fellows with it, and I remember thinking that they'd be jolly miserable before they finished in an open car like that. I expect —"

But he was interrupted by a horrified cry from Harold. "Good Lord, look there!"

The beam of his torch was directed upon a point on the farther side of the ditch, about a couple of yards beyond the radiator of the Comet. The beam moved to and fro in his shaking hand and it was a second or two before the others understood the cause of his exclamation. Then, simultaneously, they made out the figures of two men lying in horribly contorted positions between the ditch and the hedge beyond it.

A sudden sense of disaster shocked them into instant wakefulness. Richard, the most agile of the party, took a running jump at the ditch and cleared it. The others followed him more deliberately. As Harold threw the light of his torch upon the nearest figure, they started back instinctively. His leather coat was covered with blood, and a dark patch spread over the grass round the upper part of his body. Fragments of broken glass scattered round about told their own story.

"He must have gone straight through the windscreen," said Bob, in a shaky voice. "Poor chap! Is there anything to be done for him?"

Harold, who had some knowledge of medicine, put his fingers hesitatingly upon the wrist of one outstretched arm. After a second or two he shook his head. "He's gone, I'm afraid," he replied. "Look at the blood he's lost."

"What about the other fellow?" asked Bob, his voice sounding harsh and broken.

The second man, also wearing a leather coat, lay like the first, on his face. Though he also was spattered with blood, no pools of it lay round him. But he showed no sign of life, and once more Harold shook his head. "He doesn't seem to be cut about like the other one," he said. "More likely his neck was broken when he was thrown out."

"Well, it's all pretty ghastly," remarked Richard. "It's plain enough what happened. The driver went to sleep and ran off the road when he was travelling at high speed. I suppose we'd better get these poor chaps into the Armstrong and find the nearest hospital?"

"I don't think we can do that," replied Harold, hesitatingly. "I'm pretty sure there's nothing to be done for either of them and if they're dead we mustn't touch their bodies."

"Then it's a job for the police," said Bob, with decision. "Where the devil are we? I've lost count of time and direction."

Harold produced a map from his pocket and consulted it by the light of his torch. "I reckon we've come about fifteen miles out of Moorchester," he said. "If that's so, there's a place called Westernham about three miles ahead."

"I've driven through it," replied Bob. "It's a small market town and there's bound to be a police station there. Look here, Richard, you're the freshest of us. Take Harold with you and drive like the devil. I'll stay here. I don't like the idea of leaving these poor fellows alone. It's good-bye to our chances of finishing, I'm afraid."

For an instant they stood in silence, staring with horrified faces at the figures at their feet. To their sluggish senses, blunted by exhaustion and lack of sleep, the tragedy which had confronted them suddenly as a bolt from the blue seemed strangely unreal. They were as men in a dream, half conscious that they must awake from this ghastly nightmare.

Richard was the first to pull himself together. "Right, Skipper!" he said. "Come along, Harold. Better leave the skipper your torch."

Followed by Harold, he clambered over the ditch on to the road. They took their seats in the Armstrong and drove off, leaving Bob Weldon to his lonely vigil.

CHAPTER II

"WHAT a beastly thing to happen!" exclaimed Richard, when they were well under way. "I can quite understand it, though. I've driven one of those Comets myself, and they're none too easy to keep on the road when they're travelling really fast."

"And those two fellows can't have had much sleep in an open car like that," replied Harold. "It's been quite different for you and the skipper. You've both had an hour or two of comfort in the back of this most luxurious car. What's more, she practically steers herself. Yet all the same, I don't mind telling you that the skipper frightened me more than once as we came along just now."

"One nod on a Comet and you're off the road. That's what happened, beyond a doubt. It's queer that they went off on the right-hand side, though. The instinct of most English drivers, at least, is to pull in towards the left. They must have been travelling some when it happened. Did you notice that the whole front axle was knocked right back?"

Harold made no reply. He was intent upon watching the road. They seemed to be nearing a town. A pavement sprang up to one side of them and the glare of the headlights was reflected in the windows of houses ahead. A big notice board appeared — "Westernham. Narrow streets. Please drive slowly."

Before they had gone much farther, they saw a blue lamp burning over the door of a severe-looking building. "This'll be the police station," said Richard, as he pulled up. "Slip out and see if there's anybody about."

Harold descended from the car. As he did so, he noticed that the ebony blackness through which they had driven for so many hours had softened to a dull grey. Objects were becoming dimly visible, seeming monstrous and misshapen. The stars were no longer bright and hard and seemed less plentiful. Those that remained showed as pale and sickly points in the sky. He mounted the steps leading to the police station and rang the bell. A muffled clangour, harsh and threatening, rang out inside the building.

Then there was silence, intensified by the utter stillness of the sleeping town, until at last it was broken by the sound of Richard's footsteps as he rejoined his friend. "Seems as if the local constabulary were plunged in slumber," he remarked.

"Looks like it," replied Harold. "Hold on, though, I believe I hear somebody moving about inside."

They listened, and a sound, as of heavy boots pacing a stone passage, came to their ears. There was the groan of a bolt and the door was flung open, revealing a massive form in shirt sleeves. "Well, and what do you gentlemen want?" asked a deep, bass voice.

"There's been an accident on the road, about three miles from here," replied Richard. "A car in the ditch and the driver and passenger killed, by the look of it. One of the rally cars; the driver must have gone to sleep —"

His voice trailed off as he caught the policeman staring at him curiously, then he realised that he was swaying as he stood and made a spasmodic effort to steady himself.

"An accident, eh?" said the policeman suspiciously. He came a step nearer and began sniffing, as though suddenly afflicted with a violent cold. "I should like to see your driving licence, please," he said sharply.

"It's in the car," replied Richard. And then as the absurdity of the policeman's action dawned upon him he laughed mirthlessly. "We're not drunk — only dog-tired," he explained. "We were competing in the rally, too, and we've been some thirty-three hours on the road. None of us have tasted a drink since we started — I can promise you that."

"Oh, so that's it!" exclaimed the policeman, somewhat mollified. "Well, some folks have queer ways of enjoying themselves, that's all I can say. Did you see this accident happen?"

"No, we didn't," replied Richard wearily. "We saw the car by the roadside and stopped to investigate. But hadn't you better come and see for yourself? You can ask all the necessary questions later. We'll run you to the spot."

The policeman grinned. "Perhaps you're right," he said. "Come inside a minute while I get my coat and telephone to the doctor. You're sure the people you saw were dead and not merely stunned?"

"I had a look at them without disturbing them in any way," said Harold. "I couldn't find any signs of life about them."

The policeman nodded and disappeared through a doorway. They heard his voice as he used the telephone in the charge room. Then he came back fully clad, and they saw that he wore a sergeant's stripes. And to Harold's astonishment, he had a camera in his hand.

"I'll have your names, please, gentlemen," he said, producing a notebook. "Mine is Showerby — Sergeant Showerby, of the County Police. I've rung up Dr. Mason and asked him to come along. He'll be here in his own car in a minute or two. Mr. Richard Gateman? Thank you. And yours, sir? Mr. Harold Merefield? And which of you gentlemen is the owner of this car?"

"Neither of us," replied Richard. "We've left the owner with the other car, the one that's had such a smash."

It seemed to Richard that the sergeant's eyebrows lifted for an instant. "And what is the gentleman's name?" he asked.

Richard told him, and he closed the note-book and replaced it in his pocket. "That will do for the present," he said. "We had better get into the car, so as to be ready for Dr. Mason when he comes."

Richard and Harold walked out to the Armstrong and got in. "Jump in at the back. Sergeant," said the former. "I'll turn her round ready to start when the doctor comes."

But Sergeant Showerby seemed to be in no hurry. Instead of getting in by the door nearest to him, he walked slowly round the car, staring at it as though a motor was a wholly unfamiliar form of transport. "What's he up to?" asked Richard impatiently, his foot on the clutch pedal.

"Looking for the damage," replied Harold softly. "He suspects us of having run into the other fellow. Haven't you spotted that yet? You can't blame him — he's only doing his duty."

At that moment the sergeant opened the door and climbed in. Richard reversed the car, and for a few minutes they waited in silence. Then the lights of a second car shone out behind them and drew alongside. The sergeant leaned out of the window. "That you, Doctor? Well, will you follow us? These gentlemen say it is about three miles along the road."

"All right, go ahead," replied Dr. Mason. The Armstrong started off, closely followed by the other car. The three miles were covered in silence and Richard pulled up beside Bob Weldon, who was waiting for them by the roadside.

By now it was getting light, that deceptive half-light in which, though objects cannot be clearly discerned, the most powerful headlights seem feeble and irresolute. The wrecked Comet, tilted at an unnatural angle, seemed utterly abandoned and forlorn. And beyond it were the two motionless figures in leather coats, the blood about them like sullen patches of deep black.

Without a word. Doctor Mason scrambled across the ditch and knelt beside them. Sergeant Showerby stared at the wrecked Comet and then turned suddenly to Bob. "You're the owner of this car, I understand," he said, nodding towards the Armstrong. "Do you know who owns the one in the ditch there?"

"I don't," replied Bob curtly. "But if you want to know the names of those two poor fellows there is an easy way of finding out. Their route book will be in the car somewhere and you'll find their signatures in it."

"Perhaps you wouldn't mind looking for it, sir," said the sergeant. "You know what it looks like."

As Bob stepped towards the Comet, Harold had an uncomfortable feeling that the sergeant was not anxious to let any of them out of arm's reach. Instead of awaking he was going from one nightmare to another. Inanimate objects about him seemed endowed with mysterious movements in the deceptive half-light. They seemed to threaten him, to converge upon him as though to overwhelm him. He staggered and recovered himself with an effort as Bob came back from his search of the car, route book in hand.

Bob switched on his torch as he handed the book to the sergeant. "You'll see their signatures at each control," he said, "together with the times they reported."

Sergeant Showerby opened the book. "15hp. Comet, Sports Model," he read aloud. "Official number, 514, entered by A. Lessingham. Yes, that's what the first signature looks like. I can't make out the other quite, but I think it is T. Purvis. They seem to have left Bath at 9 pm on the 1st, that's the day before yesterday. Where did you gentlemen start from?"

"We started from Bath, too," replied Bob. "Our official number is 513, the next before theirs. We started at 8.45 pm. — a quarter of an hour in front of them."

"And yet you found this car in the ditch as you came along?" said the sergeant quickly. "They must have been in front of you, then?"

"Of course they were," replied Bob, with a hint of irritation in his voice. "You wouldn't expect us to keep the same distance apart over eight hundred miles odd, would you? We happened to be delayed by fog and perhaps they escaped it."

A new idea seemed to strike the sergeant. "You have a route book similar to this, Mr. Weldon?" he asked.

"Yes. Every competitor in the rally carries one. Slip over to the car and fetch it, will you, Harold? It's in the cubby hole in the front."

Harold fetched the route book and smiled as he saw the eagerness with which the sergeant inspected the names inscribed in it. Apparently satisfied that they corresponded with those he had already been given, he turned to the record of the Moorchester Control. "Your time is given as 4.56 am this morning," he said. "Mr. Lessingham's is given as 4.32 am. He was twenty-six minutes in front of you, then?"

"You can't tell exactly. Those are the times at which the books were presented. They may not have left immediately afterwards. Though we signed in at 4.56, we didn't actually leave till 5.5."

"So that Mr. Lessingham's car may have been only a short time ahead of you? Not more than a minute or so, perhaps?"

"It must have been a good deal more than that. It had left the control before we arrived there. No other car with the rally flag and number was in the courtyard of the Imperial Hotel."

"But still, you might have overtaken it between Moorchester and here?" persisted the sergeant.

"I can only assure you that we saw no signs of it in front of us until we found it as you see it," replied Bob firmly.

Their conversation was interrupted by Doctor Mason, who rejoined them at that moment. "They're both dead," he said tersely. "One of them has a jagged gash right across the jugular, and must have bled to death in a very short time. I can't say off-hand how the other man died. He appears to have escaped the broken glass and, so far as I can see at present, no bones are broken. Some internal injury, no doubt. They had better be taken to the mortuary, Sergeant, and I will communicate with the coroner."

"Can you say how long they have been dead, Doctor?" asked the sergeant, taking out his note-book once more.

"Not to within a few minutes, naturally," replied Doctor Mason. "Somewhere round about an hour, I should think. The indications seem to show that the man with the gash in his throat died first, if that's any good to you. I can't do any more here, and I'm off back home. I'll see you later in the morning."

Harold looked at his watch as the doctor was speaking. He stared at it for an instant, then held it to his ear. No, it had not stopped; yet it was incredible that the time should be no later than twenty minutes past six. Only an hour and a quarter since they had left Moorchester! It seemed an eternity! He nudged Richard and showed him the watch. Obviously, Richard was equally incredulous. He fumbled in his pocket and produced his own. The two watches agreed to the minute.

"By jove, I thought it was hours later than that!" he muttered. "I say, we might do it yet!" Then he turned to the sergeant. "Anything more we can do for you, Sergeant?" he asked nonchalantly. "If not, we'd better be getting along."

Sergeant Showerby's lips widened in a grim smile. "I'm afraid I shall have to ask you gentlemen to stay here for the present," he replied. "One moment, Doctor. Would you mind calling at the police station on your way home and asking them to send a constable out here on a bicycle at once?"

Doctor Mason nodded, got into the car and drove away. By this time it was really light. The eastern sky was flecked with pink and the stars had completely disappeared. For the first time Sergeant Showerby was able to observe the group that stood before him.

It struck him that their appearance was scarcely prepossessing. Their unshaven faces were haggard and drawn, stained with the grime of the fog through which they had passed. The heavy coats and mufflers which they wore did not improve matters.

13

Bob Weldon was the eldest, a man of forty-five, or thereabouts, with a shrewd, half-humorous expression. Richard Gateman, between thirty-five and forty, was slighter and shorter. He wore glasses and his expression was one of eager alertness. He moved restlessly, as if the whole affair bored him and he longed to be done with it. Harold Merefield, the youngest of the party, was tall and powerful, but had the face of a man who spends most of his time indoors.

The sergeant's face, as he glanced at them each in turn, was inscrutable. "I should like to see your driving licences, please," he said.

Bob and Richard produced theirs and the sergeant noted the particulars in his book. Then he turned to Harold inquiringly.

"Sorry, I haven't got a licence," said Harold. "I wasn't driving — merely time keeping. You'll have to take me on trust, unless you like to ring up my employer."

"We'll see about that later," replied the sergeant curtly. "Now your occupations, please?"

"Manufacturer," said Bob Weldon. "I own a pottery works at Clayport — Weldon & Company."

"And I suppose I can be described as a manufacturer's agent, can't I, Skipper?" said Richard. "I manage Mr. Weldon's London office for him, in Upper Thames Street."

The sergeant took down these particulars and glanced at Harold. "Secretary," said the latter. "My employer's name is Dr. Priestley, and he lives in Westbourne Terrace, London."

Evidently the sergeant was a man of method. He next noted the registered numbers of the cars. That of the Armstrong was QK1773, and of the wrecked Comet ZV9694. Once more he examined the Armstrong Siddeley closely, then turned his attention to the Comet. The damage to the latter was now clearly apparent. The impact of striking the farther side of the ditch had bent both dumb irons and driven the front axle heavily back towards the gear box. The radiator was apparently undamaged, but only a few jagged spikes of glass remained where the windscreen had been. So far as could be seen from the road, there was no blood inside the car, but the bonnet was spattered with drops. One of the spokes of the steering wheel was broken and the column was bent forward. The front seats had fallen from their normal positions and were lying on the floor, beneath the dash. The rear portion of the car was undamaged.

While the sergeant was noting these details, the figure of a policeman on a bicycle appeared from the direction of Westernham, pedalling furiously towards them. He dismounted, breathing heavily, and saluted. Sergeant Showerby took him aside and gave him a few brief instructions in a low tone.

The sergeant then opened his camera. The sun had risen by now and, though the shadows were still long, the light was at least passable. He took several photographs

14

of the wrecked car and of the bodies lying in front of it, trying to get his pictures from as many different points as possible. Then he turned his attention to the road itself.

During the night a certain amount of dew had fallen, covering the smooth surface of the Tarmac road with a thin film of moisture, which was already beginning to disappear in thin vapour under the sun's rays. But enough remained to show distinctly the wheel tracks of the Armstrong and the Comet. The former, being the most recent, were the clearest. They led up to the scene of the tragedy in a fairly straight line. Only occasionally did they trend gently towards the left-hand side of the road and back again. In several places they crossed the tracks of the Comet, which were thus obliterated at these points. Finally, they showed no trace of skidding or of the wheels having locked, where the car first drew up, showing that the brakes had been applied normally.

Up to about thirty yards from its present position, the Comet had left very similar tracks. They were even straighter than those of the Armstrong, running without deviation along the centre of the road; but suddenly this regularity ceased. For a few yards the front wheels had left a serpentine track, as though the steering wheel had been wrenched violently first in one direction then another. Finally, the steering wheel seemed to have been turned hard over and the tracks led abruptly to where the car stood now. And, throughout the whole of these contortions, there were marks where the wheels had been momentarily locked and then released.

Sergeant Showerby changed the spool in his camera and took a series of photographs of the tracks. This done, he turned to the waiting group, on which the constable had been keeping a watchful eye. "I'm sorry to have kept you waiting, but I thought it best to take these photographs in your presence," he said weightily. "It will, I am afraid, be necessary for you to remain at Westernham for the present. You all appear to need a rest, and if you will get into your car, the constable will show you the way to the White Hart, where, I am sure, you will be quite comfortable."

Under other circumstances, they might have questioned Sergeant Showerby's authority for disposing of them thus summarily. But, as things were, there seemed no alternative to compliance. By the time they could appeal to the sergeant's superior, it would be far too late to continue their journey with any hope of arriving within the specified time.

They all realised this and resigned themselves to the prospect of the White Hart. After all, sleep was what they all craved and here was a chance of getting it. Without protest, they entered the Armstrong, taking the constable with them. Under his guidance, they reached the hotel, where they made the just-roused staff understand that they wanted a wash and somewhere they could sleep undisturbed.

CHAPTER III

BOB WELDON was the first to wake. He did so with a start. How was it that the car was not moving? Had they reached a control? Then as he opened his eyes, he saw that he was lying on a bed in an unfamiliar room, and recollection of the events of the early morning returned to him. A chambermaid, a stolid girl, who looked as though nothing was likely to perturb her, was standing by his bedside. "Beg pardon, sir," she said, as soon as she saw that Bob was awake, "there's a police inspector asking for you downstairs. He says he'll come up here if you don't want to go down."

"Oh, I'll go down," replied Bob hastily. "What time is it?"

"Just gone one, sir, and there's some lunch on in the coffee-room, if you'd care for it."

"Just gone one!" He would have been over the finishing line at Torquay, if this confounded business had not interfered with his plans. For an instant he regretted the impulse that had led him to pull up and investigate the ditched Comet. But the thought of its occupants flung out lifeless beside it recurred to him. He could not have gone on and left them untended.

"Lunch," he said. "Yes, rather! I'll have some as soon as I've finished with this inspector chap. Tell them to keep me some at all costs. And if you're going down you might tell the inspector I shall be with him in a couple of shakes."

The chambermaid departed and Bob sprang out of bed. He had only thrown off his outer garments and he was quickly dressed. As he caught sight of his face in the mirror he paused. He was certainly a ghastly spectacle. Why shouldn't his visitor wait while he had a shave? No, better not; perhaps there would be time for that later.

He walked downstairs with legs that had a curious feeling, as though they did not belong to him. As he reached the hall, a tall, pleasant-faced man of about his own age came towards him. "Mr. Weldon?" he asked. "I am Inspector Harraway from Moorchester. I am very sorry to disturb you, but I am anxious to obtain information regarding the accident which happened to Mr. Lessington's car this morning."

"I should have thought that Sergeant Showerby could have given you full particulars," replied Bob. "He asked enough questions last night, or, rather, this morning. Still, I'm ready to tell you all I know. Is there anywhere here where we can sit down and talk?"

"The landlord says we may use his office," replied Inspector Harraway. "There's nobody there at this time of the day, and we shan't be disturbed. It's just through here."

He led the way to a small but comfortably furnished room and the two seated themselves. "I'm afraid that, you must have thought Showerby a trifle officious," began the inspector, apologetically. "But you must realise that he was bound to collect what information he could, and to take every possible precaution. He's really a most intelligent and painstaking man, and a very good fellow at heart."

"I'm sure he is," agreed Bob dryly. "I had evidence of his thoroughness, anyhow. I wouldn't have minded if he hadn't so obviously suspected us of being responsible for the smash."

Inspector Harraway smiled. "He was bound to consider the possibility, you know," he replied. "In fact, I think he's still got it at the back of his mind that your car had something to do with it. Now, I'll be perfectly frank with you, Mr. Weldon. For my own part, I don't believe for a moment that you know anything of the cause of the accident. But I'm bound to make certain inquiries. In the first place, I want to be quite clear as to the details of this rally. As I understand it, each competitor had to cover a distance of approximately a thousand miles, at an average speed of twenty-five miles an hour. Both you and Mr. Lessingham started from Bath during the evening before last?"

Bob nodded. "That's right," he agreed. "Competitors were given the choice of nine starting places. They had to start between six and nine o'clock, and each was allotted a separate starting time. Our time was 8.45 pm and we were the last but one to start from Bath. The Comet followed us at nine o'clock."

"I gather that your course was marked out for you, and that you had to report at various controls en route?"

"We had to report at Norwich, Kendal, Droitwich and Moorchester, in that order. Competitors starting from other points had a different set of controls. But, as long as we reported at those controls, we were free to choose the route to follow between them. No doubt different drivers choose different routes."

"I see. Just one more point, Mr. Weldon. Each competitor was given a route book on starting, which he had to produce at each control to be stamped with the time of his arrival?"

"Exactly. When the route book was produced, all the occupants of the car had to sign it in the presence of the officials."

"Thank you, Mr. Weldon. Now, I have been comparing your route book with Mr. Lessingham's, and there are certain discrepancies which perhaps you can explain. I have made a summary of them on a piece of paper. Here it is."

The inspector handed Bob a piece of paper, drawn up as follows:

Control 513 (Weldon) 514 (Lessingham)

Bath 8.45 pm. 1st 9pm. 1st

Norwich 3.12 am. 2nd 3.21 am. 2nd

Kendal 12.7 pm. 2nd 9.52 am. 2nd

Droitwich 7.31 pm. 2nd 4.2 pm. 2nd

Moorchester 4.56 am. 3rd 4.32 am. 3rd

"Now." continued the inspector. "There are one or two things I can't quite make out. On the first section, from Bath to Norwich, you and Mr. Lessingham seem to have kept your relative positions. He started fifteen minutes later than you and arrived nine minutes later. That means that you both travelled at about the same average speed?"

"Probably we did." replied Bob. "Our route from Bath to Norwich was 208 miles by speedometer. We took six hours and fifty-seven minutes to cover this distance. Got a pencil and a bit of paper on you?"

The inspector tore a leaf out of his note-book and handed it over, together with a pencil. Bob did a rapid calculation. "That works out at an average speed, including stops for traffic, change of drivers and petrol, of thirty miles an hour. That's what we were aiming at. We meant to travel at that average speed throughout the trial."

"It was not in any sense a speed test?" inquired the inspector.

"Only in so far as the average speed had to be maintained. There was no point in driving too fast. Competitors were penalised if they crossed the finishing line more than five minutes before their time."

"You say that you intended to maintain an average speed of thirty miles an hour, Mr. Weldon. Mr. Lessingham seems to have started with the same intention. But during the second stage of the journey, your times begin to vary. He arrived at Kendal two hours and a quarter before you. How do you explain that?"

"I can explain it best if I fetch our schedule, which is in the car," replied Bob. "Will you excuse me for a moment?" He went to the hotel garage, into which he had driven the Armstrong that morning and brought back with him a board on which was pinned a piece of paper.

"This is a table of times and distances, prepared beforehand," he explained. "You will see that it shows the distances between important points on the route, with the times at which we should pass them if our average speed is maintained. In pencil against these figures is marked our actual time. You will see that we arrived at the Norwich control at 3.12, which is the time registered in our route book. But we did not leave at once. We had some hot coffee and filled up with petrol. This took us fourteen minutes, and we did not leave Norwich till 3.26. Then, again, we had breakfast at Doncaster, which took thirty-seven minutes. The route book shows eight hours and fifty-five minutes between Norwich and Kendal, but fourteen minutes plus thirty-seven minutes, or fifty-one minutes, must be deducted from this. This stage was 249 miles by speedometer, and we covered it in eight hours, four minutes actual running time. Let me work that out. Thirty-one miles per hour near enough.

"Now, Mr. Lessingham possibly did not stop long at Norwich, or for breakfast, en route. If we allow him ten minutes off his route-book time, he covered the distance in six hours, twenty-one minutes, or at the rate of 39 miles per hour. It is pretty good going, but not beyond the powers of a sports car, built for speed, especially as he had daylight for more than half the way. In fact, I daresay we could have done it ourselves had we wanted to."

"I am much obliged to you for your information, Mr. Weldon," said the inspector, as he pored over the summary he had made. "Mr. Lessingham seems to have pushed on as fast as he could. But what was his object, since you have just told me that he would be penalised if he arrived at Torquay before his time?"

"By the look of his route book figures, he intended to get as far ahead as possible by yesterday evening," replied Bob. "I know that this was the intention of several of the competitors. Their plan was to snatch a few hours' sleep at Moorchester last night. Look here, he seems to have taken over twelve hours between Droitwich and Moorchester — 186 miles by the route we took — which is absurd. We were held up by fog and lost over two hours in consequence, but we took less than nine hours and a half."

"You think it possible that Mr. Lessingham slept at Moorchester last night?" asked the inspector quickly.

"I think it extremely probable. Judging by his average speed over the previous stages, he should have arrived at Moorchester about ten or eleven o'clock last night. The Moorchester control did not open till 12.42 am this morning, so he could not present his route book then. He probably took a room at some hotel, slept till half-past four, then presented his book for stamping and started off at once. He would have plenty of time. Since he started from Bath fifteen minutes later than us, his finishing time at Torquay would be correspondingly later, or 1.12 pm to-day. He thus had eight hours and forty minutes in which to cover approximately 230 miles — an average of twenty-six and a half miles per hour."

But the inspector's attention seemed to have wandered. He made no comment upon Bob's calculation, but sat for a moment frowning thoughtfully. "What is your explanation of the accident that happened to Mr. Lessingham's car, Mr. Weldon?" he asked suddenly.

"Why, it seems simple enough to me," replied Bob. "The driver went to sleep at the wheel and the car ran into the ditch. That very nearly happened to me on the same stretch, as Harold Merefield, who was sitting beside me, can tell you."

Inspector Harraway nodded and looked at his watch. "Why, it's half-past one!" he exclaimed. "You must be very hungry, Mr. Weldon. I don't suppose you had much time for food while you were driving?"

"I haven't had a decent meal since breakfast yesterday," replied Bob. "I told the people here that I should have lunch as soon as you had gone."

"How thoughtless of me! I would not have kept you from your lunch for the world. For that matter, I am feeling a bit peckish myself. How would it be if we went into the coffee-room and had lunch together?"

Bob agreed to this readily enough. They adjourned to the coffee-room, where they chose a table at which their conversation would not be overheard by the other occupants of the room. The meal, having been ordered, the inspector began to talk in a conversational tone.

"I should imagine that this rally was a test of endurance for drivers as well as cars," he remarked. "Forty hours, inducing two nights, on the road! You must have been pretty well dead beat by this morning, Mr. Weldon."

"I confess I was. The first twenty-four hours wasn't so bad. We managed to get quite a lot of sleep at intervals in the back of the car. Not that it was real sleep as far as I was concerned. I was always conscious of the motion of the car. I found myself waking up every few minutes wondering how we were getting on. But I was driving most of last night and this morning I couldn't have gone on another mile. I was in that state when everything seems unreal. You'll understand what I mean when I tell you that I could see huge faces grinning at me by the roadside. In fact, we were going to change drivers when we pulled up."

Inspector Harraway nodded sympathetically. "I've felt like that myself when I've been a long time without sleep," he replied. "It's a queer sensation, isn't it? How do you feel now?"

"Fresh as paint and ready to start all over again," replied Bob confidently. "Those few hours' sleep I've had have put me completely right again."

"You got here about seven o'clock this morning, I believe," said Inspector Harraway thoughtfully. "It was not long after one when you came downstairs. Say at the most that you had four hours' sleep. And you feel quite capable of driving a car now?"

"Perfectly. I could drive for several hours on end, if necessary."

"Yes. I suppose four hours' sleep would be sufficient to refresh anybody. By the way, you remember those photographs Sergeant Showerby took? They came out wonderfully well. Photography is Showerby's hobby, and he's awfully keen on it. He married the sister of the local photographer here a year or two back. I don't know whether the hobby was responsible for the marriage or the marriage for the hobby. Anyhow, these photographs are excellent. He showed me the negatives and he's having them printed by his brother-in-law this afternoon. You ought to get him to show them to you when they are ready. The ones he took of the tracks of Mr. Lessingham's car are particularly good. But since you saw the actual tracks for yourself, perhaps you wouldn't be as interested as I am."

It dawned upon Bob that the inspector had been watching him closely throughout this apparently irrelevant conversation. He frowned slightly as he realised that there was something behind it which he had not perceived. "Look here. Inspector Harraway," he said quietly. "As one man to another, would you mind telling me exactly what it is you're getting at?"

The inspector smiled. "I was hoping that you would see that for yourself," he replied. "You told me just now that you believe the accident to Mr. Lessingham's car to have been caused by the driver going to sleep at the wheel. From your own experience, you regard such a thing as quite possible. But there is one thing you have quite overlooked. You say that you are perfectly fit to drive now after four hours' sleep. But Mr. Lessingham and his passenger, if your deduction from his route book is correct, had at least that amount of sleep at Moorchester."

Bob whistled softly. "If they had, it is not in the least likely that they went to sleep fifteen miles out," he said.

"Exactly. But until we have verified that they did actually get this sleep, we cannot base any argument upon it. But there's another thing — Imagine yourself driving Mr. Lessingham's car with Mr. Gateman beside you. You are feeling very sleepy and constantly doze off. What would happen?"

Bob laughed. "I can tell you exactly what did happen in my car this morning," he replied. "More than once I did doze off, for a fraction of a second. On the last occasion I did not recover my senses till the wheels of the car were actually on the grass. I daresay it was the slight jolt that wakened me.

"On which side of the road did you go on to the grass?"

"On the left. It's one's natural instinct. It's curious that the Comet should have gone in on the right."

"That's one of my points. Imagine that you were in that car, dozed off and didn't wake in time. What would have happened then?"

"If Richard had been beside me and awake, he would probably have snatched the wheel and got the car back on the road before we hit the ditch. If he had been asleep, we should have gone into the ditch as the Comet did."

"In that case, what would be the appearance of the wheel tracks of the car?"

"They would have shown a gradual tending towards the left, until the car came to a stop in the ditch."

"That is just my opinion, and I am very glad you have confirmed it. If you will recall the appearance of the tracks of Mr. Lessingham's car, you will remember that they were very different. Before the car took the final swerve to the right into the ditch, there was a very well-marked wobble from side to side, and as soon as that wobble commenced, the brakes were applied. Is it possible that the application of the brakes caused the wobble and the final swerve? I should like your opinion as an expert driver."

"I suppose it would be possible if the brakes were very badly out of adjustment," replied Bob thoughtfully. "I have known cases of cars with badly adjusted brakes tending to one side or another when the brakes were applied. But I can't imagine any adjustment being so bad as to cause the extreme wobble and the sudden swerve that the tracks showed. There was no question of a skid. The tracks showed no sideways movement of the wheels."

"Did you form any theory to account for the behaviour of the car as shown by the tracks?"

"I can't say that I did. For one thing, I was too sleepy, and for another, I took it for granted that the driver had gone to sleep, and didn't think any more about it. But now after what you've said, I see the objections to that. The only thing I can think of is that the driver somehow lost control of the steering wheel while retaining hold of the brakes. I admit that I don't quite understand how that could have happened."

"Well, Mr. Weldon, it's my business to find out how the accident did happen, and I am going to ask you to help me. I'm not a motorist and want someone at hand who is, and who can explain the details of the rally. We shall want your evidence at the inquest in any case. I hope that you will consent to remain here till that is over."

"I understand from Sergeant Showerby that we're as good as detained, as it is," said Bob with a smile.

"Oh, never mind about Sergeant Showerby. We can't make you stay here if you don't want to, of course; but I should be very grateful if you would stop and help me with expert advice."

"I may as well, I suppose," replied Bob. "I wasn't expecting to get home till Saturday, in any case. There are some further trials to be held at Torquay to-morrow."

"I'm very much obliged to you, Mr. Weldon. To begin with, I wonder if you would be good enough to drive me in your car to Moorchester, after we've finished lunch?"

Bob stared at the inspector, then burst out laughing.

"You want to experiment and see if I'm really capable of driving, I suppose?" he said. "All right. I'll take it on."

CHAPTER IV

LUNCH over, Bob went upstairs and looked into the rooms occupied by Richard and Harold. They were sleeping like logs, and it seemed a pity to disturb them. He shaved and made himself look more presentable and then rejoined Inspector Harraway in the hall.

They got out the Armstrong. Bob regretfully removed the rally flag and official number and they started off in the direction of Moorchester. The inspector sat beside Bob, very much on the alert. "There's nothing much the matter with your driving now, whatever it may have been like early this morning," he said. "But my object in asking you to take me out wasn't only to test that. I want you to help me with some inquiries in Moorchester, if you will. The control there was established at the Imperial Hotel, I know that. Where did competitors leave their cars while they were reporting?"

"I don't know what the others did. We were so late that they had all gone on by the time we arrived. We parked in the courtyard, under the instructions of an R.A.C man who was there. I expect the others did the same."

"We'll try and find that R.A.C man. He may be able to tell us when Mr. Lessingham arrived and put us on his track. I'm very anxious to find out if he did actually put up anywhere in Moorchester last night."

Bob nodded. That seemed reasonable enough. And at that moment he recognised the spot that he remembered so well. The Comet had disappeared and the only trace of the tragedy that remained was a break in the regularity of the ditch.

"We had the bodies taken to the mortuary and the car towed to a garage for expert examination," explained Inspector Harraway. "Sergeant Showerby's photographs show exactly how things were, so there was no point in leaving the car here. We may be able to discover some defect that led to the accident. At present it's all very puzzling."

They drove on towards Moorchester, until, at a crossroads about three miles outside the town, they found an R.A.C man on duty. "Let's pull up and have a word with that fellow," said Inspector Harraway. "He may be able to tell us who was on duty at the control last night."

It turned out that this was the very man they wanted. "I was on duty at the Imperial Hotel myself, sir," he said, in reply to the inspector's questions, "I came on at midnight, and stayed till five o'clock this morning, when the control closed."

"Had any competing cars arrived before you came on the scene?" asked the inspector.

"Yes, sir, about half a dozen of them. They were standing in the courtyard. Their drivers were inside the hotel, I expect, waiting till the control opened at 12.42."

"Do you happen to remember if there was a two-seater Comet sport, painted grey, among them?"

"Yes, sir, there was. I remember it because it was the only open car there. The rest were all saloons."

"Do you know when it left the control?"

"Yes, sir. A lot more cars came in and drove away after I got there, but this particular Comet didn't move. In fact, I wondered what had become of the driver. About half an hour before the control closed it was the only competing car left; and then a couple of gentlemen came running out of the hotel, jumped into it and started off. I heard one say to the other something about having overslept themselves. I thought that must be the last of the rally cars, but quarter of an hour after these had gone, an Armstrong-Siddeley, exactly like the one you're in now, sir, arrived at the control. Three gentlemen got out of it, went into the hotel and came out again almost at once. I thought to myself that if they'd been a few minutes later they would have found the control shut. I remember the official number. It was 513."

"This is the very car," remarked the inspector. "It has been unfortunately prevented from finishing the course. Don't you recognise either of us?"

The R.A.C man peered at Bob and the inspector. "I can't say that I do, sir," he replied. "It was very dark in the courtyard and I couldn't well distinguish faces. It's bad luck that you weren't able to finish, sir."

"Then you wouldn't recognise the gentleman who got into the Comet if you saw them again?" asked the inspector.

"No, sir, I'm pretty sure I shouldn't. But they were both wearing leather coats, and the shorter of the two was at the wheel when they left the control. He started off as if he was in a terrible hurry, too."

The inspector thanked the man for his information and they drove on towards the town. "Your theory appears to be correct, Mr. Weldon," remarked Inspector Harraway.

"I thought something of the kind must have happened when you showed me their control times," replied Bob. "They evidently arrived at the control before midnight and went to sleep somewhere — probably in the Imperial Hotel itself, since they left their car in the courtyard. I should try there first, if I were you."

Again Bob proved to be on the right track. Inquiries at the Imperial Hotel revealed the fact that Mr. Lessingham had engaged a room there for the previous night. The letter in which he had done so was produced. It was headed: " 14 Cawdor Street, W.I." and was written in a careless, untidy hand. "Please reserve a room with two beds for me on the night of March 2nd. — Aubrey Lessingham."

"That's the address given on his driving licence, and the signature is similar to the one in his route book," remarked the inspector, aside to Bob. Then, addressing the reception clerk, to whom he was apparently well known, "I'll keep this letter for the present. Now, can you tell me if Mr. Lessingham actually occupied the room?"

"Oh, he occupied it all right. He and his friend. They were driving in the rally, you know, and they stayed here for a few hours to get some sleep."

"Did you actually see them?" the inspector asked patiently.

"No, I didn't see them myself. I left instructions with the chief night porter that they were to be shown into Number 212. You see, I go off duty at ten o'clock, and they hadn't come by then. And by the time I got here at ten o'clock this morning they had gone. They paid the chief night porter, and he handed the money to me before he left this morning. The hotel was busy all night with people coming and going."

"I expect it was. Did the porter tell you what time they arrived?"

"Oh, yes. Theirs was the first of the rally cars that he was expecting to turn up. It was just about half-past ten. Mr. Lessingham gave his name and he showed them up to Number 212. They looked very tired, he said, and they must have been, for they didn't wake when they were first called. It was like this, you see, Mr. Harraway. They asked the porter to call them at a quarter to four, as they wanted to get away by four o'clock, sharp. So he sent a man up to wake them then. He didn't think any more about it for a time, he was so busy with all those people continually coming and going, and wanting this and that. But half an hour later it occurred to him that he hadn't seen them about, and he sent up to their room a second time. Do you know, Mr. Harraway, they had both gone to sleep again!"

"Not altogether surprising under the circumstances," replied the inspector, with a glance in Bob's direction.

"What happened then?"

"Oh, they came tearing down, asked the porter for the bill, paid him, went into the control room and were gone, all inside five minutes, so the porter told me. And I suppose in the bustle he forgot to tell Mr. Lessingham that there was a telegram for him. It's very annoying, for it may be important, and I don't know what to do with it. It's no good sending it to his London address if he's on the rally, and I don't know where he is staying in Torquay."

"Don't let that worry you," replied the inspector. "I'll take charge of the telegram for you."

Apparently the reception clerk had infinite faith in the resources of the police, for she handed over the telegram at once. "That's very kind of you, Mr. Harraway," she said.

"Oh, not at all," replied the inspector gallantly. "It's the least I could do, after the information you have been kind enough to give me."

He put the telegram in his pocket and he and Bob left the hotel and returned to the car. "Don't go on for a minute," said the inspector. "Let's see where we stand first. I'll interview the night porter this evening and get him to confirm at first hand what that girl told us. I don't suppose there's any reason to doubt her story. What do you make of it?"

"Why, that Lessingham had planned beforehand to drive as hard as he could for the first twenty-four hours and then put in as much sleep as he had time for here. I know that several people started with that idea. It's not a bad plan, but the objection to it is that it doesn't allow much margin for possible mishaps on the final stage from here to Torquay."

"Well, that's as may be. I think we've established that Mr. Lessingham and his friend did actually get a certain amount of sleep last night and that, in my opinion, finally disposes of the theory that the cause of the accident was the driver going to sleep. Perhaps the experts will discover some defect in the car to account for it. Meanwhile, I'm going to open this telegram. It may tell us something that we don't already know about Mr. Lessingham."

He tore open the envelope and took out the telegraph form. Having read it, he handed it silently to Bob. It had been handed in at 6.12 pm on the 2nd, the previous day. The office of origin was South Kensington and the message was as follows: "Lessingham, Imperial Hotel, Moorchester. Cannot meet you at Torquay as we arranged. — Love."

"I don't know that that's particularly enlightening," remarked Bob, as he handed the telegram back. "Except that it shows he had spoken beforehand of his intention of stopping at the Imperial Hotel, which you knew already from his letter."

"Oh, it tells us a lot more than that," replied Inspector Harraway. "It tells us that the sender was a woman. For one thing, no man would put the word 'Love' at the end of a wire. And there's another thing: the address and the message proper took eleven words. Now, nearly everybody likes to send twelve words, and so get full value for their shilling. But the average person, having a word to spare, would add his name — Tom, Dick or Harry. To put in the word 'Love' is a regular woman's trick. I wonder if Mr. Lessingham was married? I don't think that there's much more we can do here, for the present. Suppose we get back to Westernham?"

As they drove over the now familiar road, Bob could no longer restrain his curiosity. "It seems to me, Inspector, that you're spending a lot of time and trouble over this business," he said. "Do you always do this sort of thing in the case of a pure accident?"

"Our instructions are to investigate very carefully the circumstances of any fatal accident," replied the inspector. "Besides, the coroner will want to know all about it, you may be sure. And, to be quite frank with you, Mr. Weldon, there are points about this particular accident that I don't understand. I'm hoping that the examination of the car may throw some light upon it."

"Perhaps it will, and perhaps it won't," replied Bob doubtfully. "With the front of the car smashed up like that, it will be the deuce of a job to discover any defect which existed before the accident. Look here. Inspector, it's none of my business, but who is carrying out that examination?"

"The people at the Central Garage at Westernham. We got them to send out and fetch the car."

"Well, without any disrespect to them, I doubt if they will be able to tell you much, unless the defect which you suspect is still very obvious. You see, they are not likely to be expert in this particular make of car, and they might not recognise any unusual adjustment. If I were you, I'd get on to the Comet people and get them to send one of their engineers down. If any defect existed, he'd be more likely to find it than anyone else."

"I'm much obliged to you for the hint, Mr. Weldon," said the inspector gratefully. "If the garage people haven't found anything by the time we get back, I'll put a call through to the Comet people. I've already asked the Metropolitan Police to call at the addresses given on both Mr. Lessingham's and Mr. Purvis's driving licences and inform their relatives. That's always the worst part of it. That reminds me of another thing I want to ask you. Why, if Mr. Lessingham lived in London, should he have started on the rally from Bath?"

"I couldn't say, off-hand. Competitors were given the choice of nine starting places, of which London was one. The routes by which they had to reach Torquay differed in each case. The controls for those who started from London were Harrogate, Edinburgh, Buxton and Cambridge. I personally started from Bath because it was the nearest starting place to where I live. Mr. Lessingham may have chosen it because he knew the roads on the Bath route better than any of the others."

"I think you told me, Mr. Weldon, that within certain limits competitors could choose their own time of starting. Why did you hit upon 8.45 pm.?"

"I asked to be allotted as late a starting time as possible. You see, the later one started, the more hours of daylight one got during the following forty hours. You may take it that it is dark from 6 pm to 6 am at this time of year. A car starting at 6 pm would have twenty-four hours of darkness and sixteen light, while one starting at 9 pm would have twenty-one hours darkness and nineteen light. I was told that the latest starting time — 9 pm. — was already allotted, presumably to Mr. Lessingham, but that I could have 8.45 pm."

"The same idea must have occurred to Mr. Lessingham," remarked the inspector. He said nothing more until they reached Westernham, where, after thanking Bob for his assistance, he left him at the White Hart.

Bob found Richard and Harold up and gorging themselves upon an excellent tea. "Hallo, Skipper!" exclaimed Richard. "We thought you'd bolted from the clutches of the law. They told us that you'd taken out the car and driven off and we were hoping to see the face of our estimable friend. Sergeant Showerby, when he heard you'd given him the slip."

"Showerby has been superseded as far as we're concerned," replied Bob. "I've spent a most interesting afternoon in the company of his superior, Inspector Harraway."

"The devil you have!" exclaimed Richard. "And he didn't lock you up at the end of it? Are we still supposed to be the bold bad boys who forced the Comet into the ditch? It strikes me that these local sleuths are pretty thick-headed. It's perfectly obvious that those poor fellows went to sleep and crashed in consequence."

"Don't you run away with the idea that the inspector's a fool," replied Bob. "He's anything but that. And what would you say if I told you that Lessingham and his passenger had nearly six hours' sleep at the Imperial Hotel in Moorchester last night?"

Harold was the first to see the implication. "Six hours' sleep!" he exclaimed. "Then, by jove, they aren't likely to have gone to sleep at the wheel!"

"You're an apt pupil of Dr. Priestley, I can see that," replied Bob. "Then, if they didn't fall asleep, how did the accident happen? That's what the inspector wants to know."

"Well, if he does, it's his job to find out," Richard put in. "How long are we to be kept hanging about here? I don't see what it's got to do with us."

"We needn't hang about here, as you call it. But we shall have to turn up at the inquest, which will probably be to-morrow, so we may as well stay where we are till then."

Richard groaned. "I don't find a small provincial town particularly exhilarating, myself," he said. "It would be different if this was Clayport and we were at the Unicorn. What on earth does one do here? I say, I've an idea. Let's drive over to Moorchester and spend the evening there."

"You always were a restless devil, Richard!" said Bob. "I don't feel in the least like spending the evening in riotous living. I'm going to bed as soon as I can after dinner. Meanwhile, a little exercise wouldn't do any of us any harm. What about walking along the road to where the smash happened, and having another look at things?"

Harold agreed eagerly, and neither he nor Bob paid any attention to Richard's protests. In the end, all three set out, Bob explaining the situation as he went.

"I confess that I don't understand what happened," he said. "If those fellows had as much sleep as it appears, they weren't in the least likely to fall asleep half an hour later. I was pretty well played out this morning, as Harold knows, but after four hours' sleep I could have driven for another couple of hundred miles at least. The inspector's theory is that some defect developed in the car, presumably in the steering."

"That's possible, I suppose," replied Richard. "But it's a very unusual thing to happen in a modern car. Look here, what if their lights failed suddenly? All at once, I mean — sidelights and headlights together. That could happen if the main lead to the battery broke or came adrift."

"Yes, I've had something like that happen to me, once," agreed Bob. "But I've two objections to that theory in this case. The first is that the road is dead straight where it happened. You'd think, even if they were suddenly left in the dark, they would have been able to keep the car straight and pull up. The second is that the rear lamp was burning when we came on the scene. I don't quite see what could have happened to extinguish the front lamps and leave the rear one burning."

"That sounds reasonable enough," remarked Harold. "It's my turn to make a suggestion. What if the driver lost control trying to pass something on the road? Not another car, of course, or we should have seen its tracks, or a pedestrian, either, for that matter. He or she would hardly have gone on their way and left them in the ditch. But a stray cow, or something like that."

"There may be something in that," conceded Bob, "but again I've an objection: They must have been travelling at least sixty miles an hour. Although they put on their brakes, as the tracks show, they hit the ditch hard enough to pitch them both out and smash up the front axle. Nobody in their senses would try to pass a cow on the road going at that pace."

"They may not have seen it until they were right on top of it. It may have jumped over the hedge, or come out of the ditch just as they reached the spot."

"Do cows lurk in ditches at night and pounce out upon the unsuspecting wayfarer?" inquired Richard. "I don't know — I'm not an expert upon bovine habits. Anyhow, apart from the classical instance of the cow that jumped over the moon, and that's probably symbolical or connected in some way with a solar myth, I know of no instance of a cow behaving like a steeplechaser."

"Oh, shut up, Richard!" exclaimed Harold. "I'll admit that cows may not jump over hedges, but horses can and do."

29

"All right, I'll allow you to transform your cow into a horse," replied Richard. "But what became of Pegasus after the event? He must have been a bit startled by the crash, and I'll wager he pranced about a bit. And if he did, we should have seen the marks of his hoofs on the road."

"Not if he kept to the grass at the side," remarked Bob. "Well, here we are. We may as well look and see if we can find any traces of Harold's quadruped."

But, though they searched very thoroughly, they could find nothing of the sort. And, upon inspection, Harold was bound to confess that his theory of any animal leaping the hedge into the road was improbable. The hedges on either side were six feet high and wide in proportion. Further, the fields beyond them were under cultivation, and there were no signs of any large animal having passed over them.

In the end, they were constrained to return to the White Hart, without having formulated any theory which would account satisfactorily for the mystery.

CHAPTER V

BOB WELDON'S intention of going to bed soon after dinner was frustrated. He had barely finished that meal when a telephone message came for him from Inspector Harraway, asking him if he could come over to the police station. He consented, with as good a grace as he could, and walked down the street to the building with the blue lamp.

There was no sign of Sergeant Showerby, and Bob was taken straight into the presence of the inspector, who immediately rose to greet him. "It's very good of you to come over, Mr. Weldon," he said. "I would have come to the White Hart, but I was afraid that we might not find an opportunity of an uninterrupted conversation there."

"It might have been a bit difficult," agreed Bob. "I'm at your disposal, if you have anything to ask me."

Inspector Harraway smiled. "As my expert adviser, I think you should know that the garage people report that they can find no defect in Mr. Lessingham's car which would account for the accident."

"That's very much what I expected," replied Bob. "You're satisfied that they made a thorough examination?"

"I think we can assume that they did. They've sent a pretty full report, anyhow. Perhaps you'd like to see it?"

The inspector handed over a couple of sheets of closely typewritten paper, which Bob read carefully.

"Not very helpful, is it?" he remarked, as he handed it back. "Plenty of details of the damage caused by the accident, but that's about all. I see that they report that the car seems to have had very little wear, and that the speedometer reading is only just over five thousand. You wouldn't expect a serious defect to develop in a modern car after it had run only five thousand miles."

"Well, can you suggest any other cause of the accident?" asked the inspector.

"I'm not sure," replied Bob thoughtfully. "We did a little detective work on pur own this afternoon. I'll tell you about it." He described their visit to the scene of the accident and the theories that had been put forward. "I'm not sure that there may not be something in the stray animal idea," he concluded. "Although we can't find any traces of it."

"And I'm inclined to agree with you, Mr. Weldon. Had you been in Mr. Lessingham's place, what would you have done if an animal had suddenly appeared in the road just in front of you?"

"It depends on the animal," replied Bob. "If I'd thought it was big enough to wreck the car, I should have done my best to avoid it, and I might have run into the ditch easily in the process. If it was anything smaller, I should have gone straight on, rather than risk the lives of my passengers and myself by a sudden swerve."

Inspector Harraway nodded. "That seems logical," he replied. "I'll bear that theory in mind. By the way, I've had reports from London about Mr. Lessingham and his passenger. Mr. Lessingham had rooms in Cawdor Street. A man-servant was in charge there, who said that he had been with him for several years. He also said that the only relation his master had, so far as he knew, was his cousin, Thomas Purvis."

"Who was killed with him," observed Bob. "I wonder who the lady of the telegram can have been?"

"I don't think it will be necessary to inquire into that," replied the inspector hastily. "Mr. Purvis's address turned out to be a private hotel. They knew very little about him there. He had only been there for a week, and they believed that he was home on leave from somewhere in the East, where he held an appointment of some kind. At all events, neither of them appears to have any near relatives. The London police got the name of Mr. Lessingham's solicitor from his man, Farrant, his name is. He promised to come down here first thing to-morrow morning. The inquest is at eleven, by the way. I shall serve you and your friends with notices to attend, but I expect it will be sufficient for you to give your evidence. The coroner probably won't require anything further."

"Oh, we'll attend," said Bob. "It won't be the first time we've been to an inquest together. By the way, are you satisfied with the report on the car, or are you going to call in the Comet people?"

"I should have been satisfied but for what you said this afternoon, Mr. Weldon," replied the inspector. "As it is, I got on to the Comet people and they are sending a man down to-morrow morning. I described the car to them, and they told me it was one they had delivered to Mr. Lessingham early last month."

Bob nodded carelessly, and then something seemed to strike him. "Early last month and his speedometer registers five thousand miles!" he exclaimed. "Lessingham must have been exceptionally fond of driving. His mileage must have been over four thousand before he started on the rally. That means that he must have driven that distance during February, or more than a thousand miles a week. He wanted to run the car in thoroughly, I suppose."

Shortly afterwards, Bob took his leave and went back to the White Hart. It was settled that, as soon as the inquest was over, he should drive home to Clayport, while the others returned to London by train.

Next morning, at a few minutes to eleven, they arrived at the police station, where a room was used as a coroner's court. It was bare and chilly, with a few forms and a table hastily put in place. It struck them that there was an informal, almost apologetic look about the whole scene. They were shown to a bench near the table and asked to sit down. The general public was represented by a sprinkling of men and women, who were presumably there because they had nothing better to do. Doctor Mason strolled in, closely followed by a middle-aged man in glasses. And finally, five minutes late, the coroner appeared, accompanied by Inspector Harraway.

It was not until he had taken his seat and muttered a few inaudible words that Bob realised that the inquest had begun. The absence of a jury, the complete lack of interest evinced by the representatives of the public and the press, seemed to render the proceedings all the more informal.

Charles Farrant was the first witness called. The middle-aged man in glasses stood up. He explained that he was the head of the firm of Farrant and Farrant, solicitors. He had visited the mortuary, and had there been shown two bodies. The first, the smaller of the two, he identified as Aubrey Lessingham, aged 32, a client of his, of independent means. The second was that of Thomas Purvis, Aubrey Lessingham's second cousin, aged 29. He had known Aubrey Lessingham for many years. Although he had not seen Thomas Purvis for some three years, he had no hesitation in identifying him. Thomas Purvis had been in the Malay States during that period, employed by one of the tin mining companies, and, to the best of his belief, had only recently returned to England.

The parents of both men were dead, Thomas Purvis had been Lessingham's next of kin, and vice versa. Neither had any near relatives and he could not say at present who was now the next of kin. Mr. Lessingham had never made a will, though on more than one occasion he (Mr. Farrant) had urged him to do so. He could not say whether any will of Mr. Purvis's existed. This concluded the solicitor's evidence, and he sat down.

The coroner nodded towards Sergeant Showerby, who stood up and recited his evidence in a dear voice. Acting upon information received — and here he glanced at the three friends — he had proceeded to the spot on the Moorchester road. And so on and so forth. Nothing that threw any fresh light upon the matter.

Inspector Harraway bent down towards the coroner and whispered a few words in his ear. "Ah, yes. Certainly," he said. "I understand, Sergeant — ah — Showerby, that you took some photographs of the accident."

"Yes, sir," replied the sergeant importantly. "I have them here, sir. They are numbered —"

But the coroner cut him short. "A most commendable precaution," he said. "Lay them on the table; they can be admitted as evidence if necessary." He consulted a piece of paper. "Robert Weldon."

Bob stood up and gave a brief account of the finding of the wrecked car and of the steps that had been taken, to which the coroner listened impatiently. "Both you and the deceased were taking part in a contest, I believe?" he inquired. "Was there any question of a race between you?"

"None whatever, sir," replied Bob. "The rally was not a race in any sense. It was —"

Again the coroner interrupted, this time waving his hand with a gesture of irritation. "I do not wish to hear any details," he snapped. "In the absence of any other evidence, I must take your word for it that the two cars were not actually racing. It is hard to believe that a race of some kind was not in progress. I was awakened several times that night by the noise of cars passing through Moorchester at excessive speeds. I am surprised that the police should countenance a contest which causes such inconvenience to the residents of places through which the competitors pass. Inspector Harraway!"

Bob sat down. The inspector took his place and described the result of his investigations. In his opinion, the deaths of Mr. Lessingham and Mr. Purvis were due to purely accidental causes.

"Of course, accidents will happen if people persist in driving at reckless speeds in the dark along the public roads," commented the coroner. "It is to be hoped that no members of the general public have been killed in the course of this contest." Once more he consulted the list of witnesses. "John Meacher!"

John Meacher stood up. He explained that he was the proprietor of the Central Garage, Westernham. At Inspector Harraway's request he had proceeded with a breakdown lorry to the point on the Moorchester road described by a previous witness. Here he had found a Comet car, with the front portion in the ditch beside the road. Having examined the position in which the car stood, he had taken steps to haul it back on to the road, and had then conveyed it to his own garage.

There he had examined the car very carefully, with special attention to the steering gear and the adjustment of the brakes. Considerable damage had been done to the car by the accident itself. But he had been unable to discover any previously existing defect in the car which might have caused the accident.

The coroner snorted. "Do you consider yourself an expert on the subject of motor cars?" he asked.

"Well, sir, I've been in the trade for twenty years," replied Mr. Meacher, with a suggestion of indignation in his voice.

"Very well, at what speed would you estimate this car to have been travelling when the accident happened?"

"It is very difficult to say, sir. The brakes had been applied, but the car must have been travelling at at least thirty miles an hour when it struck the ditch."

"Then it must have been travelling at a considerably greater speed a short time previously. Do you consider such a speed to be safe at night?"

"With a suitable car and lights, such as the car I examined, and on a straight and open road, I should consider it perfectly safe, sir."

"Indeed! In my opinion it is most unsafe. Perfectly reckless, in fact. You may stand down. Doctor Mason!"

Doctor Mason proceeded to give evidence as to the cause of death. When he had arrived upon the scene of the accident, he had found two bodies, identified by a previous witness as those of Mr. Lessingham and Mr Purvis, lying a few feet in front of the car. Their attitudes suggested that they had been flung from the car when it came to a sudden stop.

Dealing first with the body identified as that of Thomas Purvis. In this case there could be no doubt of the cause of death. Mr. Purvis, who appeared to have been sitting beside the driver, had presumably been thrown head first through the windscreen, the glass of which had severed the principal blood vessels of the neck. A very large quantity of blood was found on the ground beside him and on the bonnet of the car. No blood had been found within the car itself. Mr. Purvis had probably been stunned by his fall and had no doubt bled to death within a few minutes of the accident.

The case of Mr. Lessingham was not so obvious. He, apparently, had been driving. The sudden stoppage of the car had flung him violently against the steering column. The column was bent forward and the steering wheel was damaged. Examination of the body had revealed extensive abdominal injuries, which might or might not have been fatal.

But, as was shown by the position of the body when found, the steering column had not arrested its movement. Mr. Lessingham had also been flung out, but with less violence than Mr. Purvis. The latter was considerably bruised about the head and shoulders, whereas in the case of Mr. Lessingham the bruising was hardly noticeable. He must, however, have struck the ground with sufficient force to have caused considerable shock. Examination had revealed that Mr. Lessingham's heart was in a condition which a sudden violent shock might render fatal.

The coroner listened to Doctor Mason's evidence with growing signs of impatience. At this point he could contain himself no longer. "Are you prepared to state whether death was due to the abdominal injuries or to shock?" he asked.

"It is very difficult to decide," replied Dr. Mason. "On the whole, I am inclined to the opinion that the injuries, though they would probably have proved fatal, would not have been immediately so. It is therefore probable that the immediate cause of death was shock."

"Then, since it is a matter of no practical importance, I shall record a verdict to that effect." The coroner glanced at his notes. "The evidence I have heard leaves no doubt as to the cause of the deaths of these two unfortunate young men. I have no option but to record a verdict of accidental death in both cases. The technical reasons for the accident having taken place do not concern me, as coroner. As I have remarked before, it must be obvious to any sane man that such so-called accidents are bound to occur if motor cars are allowed the uncontrolled use of the public highways as speed tracks.

"I feel it to be my duty to express my opinion very strongly upon this point. I hope that the police will take a lesson from this most unfortunate occurrence and exercise in future the powers that they possess to put a stop to contests which menace the life and limbs, not only of those foolish enough to take part in them, but of the general public as well. These two young men have fallen victims to the craze for speed which has become such a distressing feature of modern life. It is devoutly to be hoped that their deaths will serve as a warning to others."

Then, after a pause to assure himself that the reporters had got his words correctly, the coroner closed the proceedings and left the court.

The witnesses did not follow immediately. Doctor Mason was about to make his way out when Mr. Farrant interrupted him. The solicitor seemed in a great state of excitement, and spoke so loud that Bob could not help overhearing much of what he was saying. It seemed to concern the exact time of Lessingham's death. Mr. Farrant took off his glasses and waved them in the air as he spoke.

"You understand, Doctor, that it is a most important point," he was saying. "Aubrey Lessingham was a young man of considerable means. He inherited an estate from his father, which was valued for probate at over a hundred thousand pounds. It has depreciated somewhat since then, but the sum involved is still considerable."

Doctor Mason, who seemed to be in a hurry, tried to get past. "Quite," he replied vaguely. "Quite; but I don't altogether see —"

"Perhaps I have not expressed myself with sufficient clarity," said Mr. Farrant, adroitly barring the lines of escape for Doctor Mason. "In the course of my evidence I remarked that Aubrey Lessingham had not made a will. Now, as you are doubtless aware. Doctor, in cases of intestacy, the deceased's estate passes to his next of kin. Aubrey Lessingham's next of kin was Thomas Purvis, who would then normally have inherited the estate."

"Well, in any case, he can't do that, since he is dead," replied Doctor Mason impatiently. "Excuse me, Mr. Farrant, but I have a most urgent visit to make."

"I shall not detain you more than a few minutes, Doctor," said the solicitor, without budging an inch. "I assure you that this matter is of the greatest importance. It will become a leading case if it is necessary to refer it to the court. The point is this: Did Thomas Purvis inherit the estate, or did he not? You said in your evidence that Purvis bled to death a few minutes after the accident. In other words, he was alive during those few minutes. Aubrey Lessingham, you say, may have died immediately from shock. In that case, he predeceased Purvis, and Purvis became his heir. The estate, therefore, devolved upon Purvis and became his to dispose of. If he also has died intestate, the estate will descend to his next of kin.

"On the other hand, if Aubrey Lessingham died of his injuries, he may have outlived Purvis. In that case, failing Purvis, already deceased, the estate passes to Lessingham's next of kin —"

At that moment, Inspector Harraway came up to Bob. "I wonder if you would mind coming with me to the Central Garage, Mr. Weldon?" he asked. "The man from the Comet company arrived just before the inquest began, and I should like to hear his report. And I should be grateful if you would come with me to explain technicalities."

"I'll come like a shot," replied Bob. "But I thought that the coroner had ruled that the technical reasons for the accident were of no importance?"

Inspector Harraway looked over his shoulder hastily. "Between ourselves, Mr. Weldon, the coroner is an ass," he said. "He's got an exaggerated idea of his own importance and he hates cars like the plague. I believe that it is his proud boast that he has never driven in one. He always carries on in that way when there is an inquest on a road fatality. Anyway, his verdict was sound. He is quite capable of having found that those two poor fellows committed suicide."

They walked round to the garage together, where they found the engineer from the Comet company. He had put on a suit of blue overalls and was staring at the wrecked car with a puzzled expression on his face.

"Well, have you discovered anything?" asked the inspector.

"I have made a very remarkable discovery, but probably not in the sense you mean," replied the engineer. "This is not the car of which Mr. Lessingham took delivery at our works on February 3rd last, although in outward appearance it resembles it exactly, being one of the same series and colour."

"Not Mr. Lessingham's car?" exclaimed the inspector. "I don't quite understand. He was certainly driving it."

"Very possibly, but it is not the car of which he took delivery. The chassis number of that car was 431722 and the engine number 63208. The chassis number of this car is 431673 and the engine number 62141. I am sure of the numbers of Mr. Lessingham's car, for I looked them up before I left the works this morning. Curiously enough, however, the registration number, ZV9694, is that of Mr. Lessingham's car. Also the R.A.C official number 514 is that allotted to Mr. Lessingham for the rally."

The inspector frowned, but said nothing. Bob stared at the official number and the rally flag, which had not yet been removed. And then he had a sudden inspiration. "Have you examined the back axle?" he asked.

The engineer turned to him. "No. Why?" he replied.

"I was a competitor in the rally," said Bob, addressing the inspector as well as the engineer. "My official number was 513 and both Mr. Lessingham and myself started from Bath. Every competitor's car was inspected before the start. At the conclusion of the thousand miles test, certain slow running, accelerator and braking tests were to take place. In order to ensure that competitors should use the same gear ratios throughout, the back axles of their cars were painted with a stencilled monogram. My back axle was so marked at Bath, and Mr. Lessingham's must also have been, or he could not have been issued with a route book."

The engineer knelt down on the floor of the garage and crept under the wrecked car. In a minute or two he emerged. "There is no painted mark of any kind on the back axle of this car," he reported.

CHAPTER VI

WHEN Harold Merefield reached London that afternoon, he was lucky enough to find his employer. Dr. Priestley, in an exceptionally good humour.

The cause of this was immediately apparent. Dr. Priestley had just received the proofs of a paper, in which he had demonstrated, with his usual ruthless logic, that a certain eminent scientist had been guilty of a grave blunder. The matter involved was so severely technical that only very highly trained minds could possibly understand it. But the perusal of the proofs had evidently caused Dr. Priestley the utmost satisfaction.

He listened graciously enough while Harold recounted his adventures, but expressed his disappointment when he learnt that he had been prevented from finishing the course. "I had hoped for the opportunity of examining you before you had slept," he said. "I should have been interested in applying certain tests to ascertain the effect of fatigue upon the mental processes. However, it is not your fault. This accident that you speak of could not be foreseen. I inferred that something of the kind had happened when I received a telephone message from Westernham yesterday morning."

"You received a telephone message from Westernham yesterday morning, sir?" Harold exclaimed,

"Yes, from a person who described himself as Police-Sergeant Showerby. He wished to know whether you were employed by me. I assured him that you were and asked him if any accident had happened to you."

"And what did he say, sir?"

Dr. Priestley allowed himself one of his rare smiles.

"He said that you were perfectly safe, and added that you were, in fact, under his own eye."

Harold laughed. "That wasn't far from the truth, sir. The sergeant had an idea that we were somehow responsible for the accident. He sent us to the local hotel in charge of a constable."

"Were there any grounds for supposing that the disaster was not purely accidental?" asked Dr. Priestley.

"Not then, sir. But, as it turned out later, there was a very queer circumstance connected with the car that was wrecked. But by that time the inquest was over, and a verdict of accidental death returned. The coroner was an irritable and not over-intelligent man, who struck me as having made up his mind before he had heard the evidence. But after his verdict, even Sergeant Showerby displayed no further interest in us."

"What was this very queer circumstance to which you refer?" inquired Dr. Priestley.

"I should like to tell you the whole story, sir, if you're not too busy to listen," replied Harold. Dr. Priestley nodded encouragingly, and Harold described to him the engineer's discovery and the absence of the R.A.C.S stencil on the back axle of the Comet.

Dr. Priestley listened attentively, in his favourite attitude, the tips of his fingers together and his head thrown back so that his eyes were fixed upon the ceiling. He said nothing till Harold had come to an end of his story and even then his comment was not immediate. It was only after a considerable pause that he spoke. "And what are your deductions from these facts, my boy?" he asked abruptly.

"There's one thing that can safely be deduced, I think, sir," replied Harold cautiously. "The car in which Lessingham and his passenger were killed is not the one in which they started from Bath at the beginning of the rally."

Dr. Priestley frowned. "That is an assumption, not a deduction," he said severely. "I will point out some of the fallacies involved in your argument. It does not follow that Lessingham started in the car which had been delivered to him a month previously. Nor is the isolated fact that the stencil was not found on the back axle of any significance by itself. It might have been erased — accidentally or purposely. Finally, the fact that two men are found dead by a wrecked car is not logical proof that they were driving in it before the wreck. However, presuming your assumption to be correct for the moment — could Lessingham have gained any advantage by changing his car en route?"

"That's just what's been puzzling me, sir. An advantage might have been gained in this way: If a competitor owned two cars, exactly similar in outward appearance, he could have fitted one, which we can call A, with an ordinary back axle and a normal gear ratio. The other, B, he could have fitted with an axle giving very low ratios, which would be advantageous in the slow running tests. If he covered the thousand miles in A and changed to B before the finish he would gain an advantage.

It was to prevent this type of fraud that the cars were stencilled. If Lessingham was trying some dodge like this he must have overlooked the fact that his car would be examined for the stencil at Torquay."

Dr. Priestley's eyes twinkled. "Given an accomplice, there would be a very simple means of evading that precaution," he said. "The accomplice would enter car B for the rally and would actually start, preferably from a different starting point. He would thus secure the necessary stencil marks. Having started, he would abandon the contest and drive to some prearranged point near the finish, where he would await the arrival of A. The transfer would be effected and the official and registered numbers interchanged. But this is of purely academic interest. Your contention is that Lessingham changed his cars without having taken the precaution I have mentioned."

"It certainly looks very like it, sir. I've thought of this. Lessingham lived in London and, I suppose, garaged his car somewhere near his rooms. The route between Droitwich and Moorchester passes close to London. Lessingham would have had plenty of time to go to his garage and change the cars. He took approximately six and a half hours to cover 180 odd miles, which is an average of less than twenty-eight miles an hour."

Dr. Priestley shook his head. "I do not think that the reason for the change of cars, if a change actually took place, is to be found in that direction," he said. "I imagine that steps are being taken to trace the origin of the wrecked car?"

"I expect so, sir. The Comet people would know who took delivery of the car bearing that chassis and engine number."

"When that is known, the circumstances will probably be explained. Conjectures in the present state of our knowledge would be useless. But even then, I fancy, many points of interest will remain."

And with that, Dr. Priestley abandoned the subject.

But it was recalled to his notice sooner than anyone had expected. That very evening he received a visit from Superintendent Hanslet of the Criminal Investigation Department, Scotland Yard. The two were old acquaintances. Long ago the superintendent had discovered Dr. Priestley's love for an intricate problem, and since that time he had frequently consulted him upon the various criminal cases in which he had been engaged.

Dr. Priestley's good humour had persisted, and he greeted his visitor cordially. "To what do I owe the pleasure of this visit?" he asked. "I do not flatter myself that you have come here merely to inquire after the state of my health."

Superintendent Hanslet laughed. "Which means that I only come round when I want your advice, Professor," he replied. "But it's not quite that, this time. I'm investigating quite an ordinary case-car stealing, certainly. But I don't want to trouble you with that. I want a few details from Mr. Merefield, if you've no objection."

"So it was a case of theft?" said Dr. Priestley thoughtfully. "No, I have not the slightest objection. By all means ask Harold any questions you like."

"Thank you, Professor," replied Hanslet. "It's this way, Mr. Merefield. We have had a telephone communication from a place called Westernham. Our informant was a certain Inspector Harraway. Among other things he told us that you had been present when a Mr. Lessingham was found dead beside his wrecked car, and that you could provide us with a detailed account of the circumstances. If you can, I should very much like to hear it."

Harold smiled. "I've already told Dr. Priestley all about it," he said. "If you like, I'll go over it all again."

Hanslet listened while Harold repeated his story, putting in questions here and there. "Thanks very much," he said at last. "I only had the outline over the telephone. The next question, of course, was the ownership of the wrecked car. If it was not the one which had been delivered to Lessingham, it must have been delivered to somebody else. Harraway communicated with the Comet Company, who informed him that the car bearing that chassis and engine number had been delivered to one of their agents in December last."

"Ah, that accounts for it!" exclaimed Harold.

"Accounts for what?" inquired the superintendent quickly.

"Why, for a point which puzzled Bob Weldon, and which he told us he had mentioned to the inspector. You see, the speedometer showed a total of about five thousand miles. Allowing a thousand for the rally, he must have covered four thousand miles in a month if this had been the car of which he took delivery on February 3rd. But if the car was actually delivered in December, the mileage becomes more reasonable."

Hanslet nodded. "That's a good point," he said. "The agents to whom the car was delivered were the Supremacy Motor Company of Kingston. They gave instructions that the number plates should be painted with the registration number, UG1754. The agent's driver took delivery at the Comet works in North London on December 10th last year.

"Harraway then got on to the Supremacy Motor Company. They confirmed the statement of the Comet people. They had used the car as a demonstration car until last month. They had then found a purchaser for it. The car was overhauled, repainted and put in condition as new. Their customer, Mr. Chalk of Byfleet, drove it away on February 17th.

"At this stage Harraway got on to us, asking us to get in touch with Mr. Chalk. He should, of course, have communicated with the Surrey Police. But, as it happened, his mistake saved time, for we had been informed that a grey two-seater sports

Comet, registered UG1754, owner's name Chalk, had been stolen on the night of March 1st."

"If it was stolen on the night of March 1st, Lessingham can have had nothing to do with it," said Harold. "His route book, signed by himself, shows that he could have been nowhere near Byfleet that night."

"But it wasn't stolen from Byfleet. Mr. Chalk had gone that evening to dine and play bridge with some friends of his. I've got the statement which he made when he reported the loss of the car — 'I live at Byfleet. At about half-past six on March 1st, I drove to the house occupied by my friend Mr. Catesby, near Denham, Middlesex. There was no room in Mr. Catesby's garage, so I left my car just inside the drive leading to his house. This must have been at about half-past seven. The distance between the two houses is twenty-seven miles, by my speedometer. I stayed with Mr. Catesby and his party till shortly before 1 am. I then prepared to drive home, but when I reached the place where I had left the car, I found that it had gone!' Short and to the point, isn't it?"

But Harold made no reply. He was rummaging in a drawer, from which he produced a road map of Southern England. This he opened and spread out on a table.

"Just look here a minute, Mr. Hanslet," he said. "Here's Bath and here's Norwich. That was the first stage of the rally for Lessingham and ourselves. You can see by the map that there are two reasonably direct routes. The first, and probably the shortest, is by Chippenham, Swindon, Oxford, Bedford, Cambridge and Newmarket."

"Yes, I see that," said Hanslet. "But what's that got to do with this car of Mr. Chalk's?"

"Nothing whatever, but wait a minute. That road, though shorter than the one I am going to show you, is winding in places, and not too easy to follow in the dark. We decided upon a longer, but faster and more certain road. We kept along the Bath road towards London till we reached Slough. Then we turned to the left and came round by Rickmansworth, Watford and St. Albans till we struck the Great North Road just south of Hatfield.

"Now that road took us close to Denham, though not actually through the village. Here is our schedule which I kept myself. From it you will see that we reached Rickmansworth at 11.58 pm. Lessingham was approximately a quarter of an hour behind us. If he followed the same route that we did, he would have passed by Denham somewhere between 12.10 and 12.15 am."

"The dickens he did!" exclaimed Hanslet. "How do you know that?"

Harold explained the routes followed by the rally competitors and the times of the Armstrong and the Comet, as revealed by the route books. Hanslet listened carefully, a puzzled frown upon his face, "Upon my word, that's very queer!" he exclaimed. "You're suggesting, I suppose, that Lessingham saw this car standing inside the drive, as Mr. Chalk describes it, and decided to change over, transferring the number plates when he did so?"

"And the R.A.C official number, which was printed on a piece of stout cardboard and attached to the car. That and the flag which was carried by all competitors. It wouldn't take him more than a few minutes to do so."

"But why, in heaven's name, why?" asked Hanslet. "And how did he dispose of his own car?" He turned to Dr. Priestley, who had been following the conversation with close attention. "You're good at solving problems, Professor," he continued. "What is the answer to this one?"

"I make it a habit never to attempt to solve a problem until I have the necessary data," replied Dr. Priestley quietly.

"Necessary data!" exclaimed Hanslet. "That's all very well, but where are we to get it from? Lessingham and his passenger are both dead, so we are told. And I don't suppose that they took anybody else into their confidence."

"Surely, Superintendent, you are jumping to conclusions," said Dr. Priestley. "You have no evidence that Lessingham passed by Denham that night. He may have taken the alternative route which Harold outlined." Dr. Priestley rose from his chair and leaned over the map. "In which case, his nearest point would seem to be Oxford, nearly forty miles away."

"I don't know so much about jumping to conclusions, Professor." replied Hanslet indignantly. "The car was found in Lessingham's possession, after all; and it isn't so very far-fetched to consider the person found in possession of stolen property as the thief."

"That person might be a conscious or unconscious receiver of stolen goods," remarked Dr. Priestley mildly. "There is reason to believe, from a conversation overheard by one of Harold's friends after the inquest, that Lessingham was a man of considerable means. He was already the possessor of a Comet car. Why should he wish to steal a similar one?"

"If you don't mind my saying so, Professor, that's no argument. He may have made a business of stealing cars. It has become a regular profession, I can tell you. In that case, the rally was his opportunity. It strikes me that the flag and the R.A.C number was a very ingenious way of camouflaging a stolen car. That the cars had been changed would never have been discovered if he hadn't had that smash. You take it from me, he had a confederate hanging round Mr. Catesby's house, who drove Lessingham's car away afterwards. He ran no risk, for he could prove it was Lessingham's car."

Dr. Priestley shook his head. "Will you explain the system of stencilling cars, Harold?" he asked.

Harold did so. "You see, Mr. Hanslet, the car Lessingham was driving would have been examined at Torquay," he concluded. "When the stencils were not found, he would have been called upon to explain why."

Hanslet slapped his thigh and roared with laughter. "Why, man alive, you don't suppose he meant to turn up at Torquay, do you?" he exclaimed. "Not he. Look here, will your friend Mr. Weldon be called upon to explain why he did not finish?"

"Well, no, I suppose not," replied Harold reluctantly. "It will be assumed that some breakdown prevented him completing the course. Until the actual facts become known, that is."

"There you are, you see — Lessingham would have gone on sufficiently far as he thought necessary, for appearance's sake. He would then have driven the stolen car to some quiet place he knew of and faked it so that it could not be recognised. That is one of the tricks of the trade, I may tell you. If any questions had been asked, he would have produced his own car, with a defective magneto, or something like that, which would have accounted for his being unable to finish."

"In order to prove that to have been his intention, you will first have to find his own car," remarked Dr. Priestley.

"I'll see what can be done in that direction," replied Hanslet confidently. "I'm going to make inquiries myself about this Mr. Lessingham. I shouldn't be surprised if this accident led to the exposure of one of the gangs of expert car thieves which are infesting the country. By the way, Mr. Merefield, Harraway said something about a telegram addressed to him. Do you know anything about that?"

"Only what Bob Weldon told me," replied Harold. "It was waiting for him at Moorchester, but he never got it. Somebody had wired him to say they could not meet him at Torquay as arranged and ended the telegram with the word 'Love.'"

Hanslet nodded. "Yes, and Harraway thought it must have been a woman in consequence. That was the impression it was intended to create, of course, if anybody but Lessingham saw it. Depend upon it, it was a code, really — as likely as not, a message to say that Lessingham's own car had reached its destination, wherever that was. I've asked Harraway to send me up that wire. It may help in running Lessingham's associates to earth."

"An undertaking in which I hope you will be successful, Superintendent," said Dr. Priestley gravely.

Hanslet glanced at him. There had been something in his tone which suggested a lack of sincerity. But his impassive face baffled the superintendent's scrutiny. "I'll have a good shot at it," replied Hanslet, with rather less confidence than before. "Now I'm going to ask you something, Professor. I may want somebody at hand who knows the details of this rally business. I wonder if you could spare Mr. Merefield for a day or two?"

Harold glanced anxiously at his employer. He had already been away for three days, and he was afraid that Dr. Priestley might have some urgent but dreary work for him. Rather to his surprise, the professor's eyes twinkled. "Certainly, Superintendent," he replied, "on condition, that is, that Harold is allowed to report progress to me from time to time."

"Then you are interested in all this, Professor?" asked Hanslet in some surprise. "I'm afraid you will be disappointed. There's no suggestions of any serious problem arising. It's simply a matter of exposing Lessingham's organisation."

"Possibly, possibly," replied Dr. Priestley. "I shall be interested in your progress just the same."

Hanslet shrugged his shoulders and turned to Harold. "The first thing to do is to visit Lessingham's rooms," he said. "There seems to be a man in charge there, and we'll see what he's got to say for himself. Will you meet me at the comer of Dover Street and Piccadilly at nine sharp to-morrow morning?"

Harold agreed to this, and the superintendent, after bidding farewell to Dr. Priestley, took his departure. The professor smiled as he left the room, and Harold marvelled anew at his unusual cheerfulness. "It's very good of you to let me go off again like this, sir," he said gratefully.

"My compliance with the superintendent's request was not influenced entirely by altruism," replied Dr. Priestley. "I anticipate deriving a certain satisfaction from the result of his investigations. We shall see, we shall see."

CHAPTER VII

BOTH Superintendent Hanslet and Harold were punctual at their rendezvous the following morning. They walked to Cawdor Street, a quiet backwater of Mayfair, and Hanslet rang the bell of Number 14.

It was answered, after a short delay, by a man faultlessly attired in a black suit. He was the typical gentleman's servant, with a quiet, deferential manner. His face was flat and not over intelligent, but it was relieved by a pair of sharp, almost cunning eyes. It struck Harold at once that few things would escape his observation.

"Mr. Aubrey Lessingham lived here?" inquired Hanslet brusquely. "I'm Superintendent Hanslet of Scotland Yard."

The man's face expressed no particular emotion at this announcement. "Yes, sir. Mr. Lessingham's lived here," he replied. "Will you come in?"

He stood aside respectfully while the two entered the house, then closed the front door behind them. "Mr. Lessingham's rooms are on the first floor." he continued. "If you will come this way, sir —"

"Half a minute," Hanslet interrupted. "Let's have a few particulars first. "What's your name, to begin with?"

"Orchard, sir. William Orchard. I was an officer's servant in the war, and —"

"Never mind that. How long have you been with Mr. Lessingham?"

"Five years, sir — five years next June — ever since Mr. Lessingham took these rooms. I'm a widower, sir, without children and I've got my own quarters on the top floor."

"We'll have a look at them later, Orchard. Now then, go ahead and show us Mr. Lessingham's rooms. I may as well tell you at once that I have a warrant entitling me to search them."

Harold, watching Orchard intently, saw an expression on his face which he interpreted as indicating puzzled surprise. "A search-warrant, sir?" he replied, almost reproachfully. "I hope that will not be necessary, sir. I am sure that Mr. Farrant would wish me to show you everything that you cared to see."

"Mr. Farrant? Who's he?" Hanslet inquired.

"Mr. Lessingham's solicitor, sir. He was here yesterday evening. He told me about the inquest on Mr. Lessingham and Mr. Purvis, and told me to remain here for the present until arrangements had been made for letting the rooms."

Hanslet nodded. By this time they had reached the first floor and Orchard opened a door, bowing them in. They found themselves in a fair-sized room, of which the principal features were a thick carpet and a couple of luxurious armchairs standing before an open grate. Beyond these there was a table or two, looking rather bare, a few chairs and a writing desk. The walls were covered with a fairly good collection of sporting prints.

The superintendent glanced round the room. His eyes rested for a moment on the writing desk, then he sat down in one of the armchairs. "Now then, Orchard," he said. "When did you last see Mr. Lessingham?"

"On Tuesday morning, sir, when I gave him his breakfast. He started soon after that to drive to Bath where he was to begin the rally."

"He left here as early as that, did he?" remarked Hanslet, with an inquiring glance at Harold.

"He would have to report at the Bath control between four and five," the latter explained. "Bath is about a hundred and ten miles from here. He wouldn't want to hurry himself going down."

"Was he alone when he left here?" asked the superintendent.

"Yes, sir. He had arranged to pick up Mr. Purvis at his hotel. They were to drive down together."

"You seem to know all about his arrangements, Orchard. The rally finished at Torquay on Thursday. When did you expect him back?"

"To-day, sir. That's when Mr. Lessingham told me to expect him. He said that I could have leave till then, if I wanted to go away. But I had nowhere particular to go, so I just stayed here, sir, and had a thorough turn out of the place."

"When did you first hear of Mr. Lessingham's accident?"

"When the police came round on Thursday morning, sir. It came as a great shock to me. I couldn't understand it, for both Mr. Lessingham and Mr. Purvis were expert drivers. It was then that I referred the police to Mr. Farrant, sir."

"Yes. Let's get back to Mr. Lessingham's plans. Who did he expect to meet at Torquay?"

Harold fancied that Orchard's eyes flickered for a moment. "I am not aware that he expected to meet anybody, sir," he replied quietly.

"Aren't you, Orchard?" said Hanslet. "Didn't Mr. Lessingham explain why, although the rally finished on Thursday, he wouldn't be back here till Saturday?"

"He did explain that, sir. I understood him to say that though the thousand miles run finished on Thursday, there were to be some trials at Torquay, which might take all day Friday, sir."

The superintendent glanced at Harold, who nodded. He took a telegram from his pocket and spread it out before him. "Listen to this, Orchard," he said. "This is a wire addressed to Mr. Lessingham, at Moorchester, and handed in at South Kensington at 6 pm on Wednesday. It says 'Cannot meet you at Torquay as we arranged. — Love.' Who sent that telegram?"

Orchard shook his head. "I cannot say, sir," he replied. "Mr. Lessingham never mentioned to me that he was to meet anybody."

"It's not a bit of good trying to bluff me," said the superintendent sternly. "It's pretty obvious that this wire was sent by a lady. Which of Mr. Lessingham's lady friends would be likely to go down and stay with him at Torquay? You say you've been with him for five years, so you ought to know all about his private affairs."

Orchard's face assumed a shocked expression. "I am quite sure that Mr. Lessingham had no lady friends of that type, sir," he replied virtuously. "I have never had any reason to suspect anything of the kind." And then a light dawned in his eyes. "If you will allow me to say so, sir, I think you are suffering under a misapprehension," he said.

"Perhaps I am," said the superintendent slowly, with his eyes fixed upon Orchard. "Possibly that wire was not sent by a lady, after all."

"That is just my opinion, sir," replied Orchard respectfully. "Mr. Purvis was lunching here with Mr. Lessingham on Monday, and I overheard a conversation which may explain that telegram, sir."

"Oh, you did, did you? Well, I'll trouble you to repeat it as closely as you can."

"Well, sir, the two gentlemen were discussing the rally. Mr. Lessingham was saying that he would leave Torquay early this morning and drive straight back here. Mr. Purvis said that would be too late for him. He said he had an appointment in London on Friday morning and would have to leave Torquay on the previous evening. Mr. Lessingham seemed rather upset at this. It would leave him without a passenger, and he was bound by the rules of the rally to carry one during the trials on Friday."

The superintendent glanced at Harold, who nodded. "That's all right, Mr. Hanslet," he said.

"The two gentlemen discussed the matter, sir, and at last Mr. Lessingham arranged to get someone in Mr. Purvis's place. 'If you really can't stop, Tom, I'll have to get someone else. I know what I'll do. I'll ring up George Love. He'll come down like a shot.' I expect this gentleman agreed to take Mr. Purvis's place, but was prevented at the last moment, and sent the telegram, sir."

Superintendent Hanslet became scarlet in the face from suppressed fury. "And where does this George Love live?" he asked with dangerous calmness.

"That I could not say, sir," replied Orchard impassively. "I'm not acquainted with him. But I have heard Mr. Lessingham mention his name once or twice previously."

Suddenly Hanslet changed the subject. "How did Mr. Lessingham usually spend his day?" he asked abruptly.

"Well, sir, he did not get up very early. He rarely breakfasted before eleven o'clock. Then he would sit in here and read his letters and papers. Sometimes he would have a friend, like Mr. Purvis, to lunch here, but more often he went out. After lunch he usually went somewhere or other in his car. He nearly always dined out, and did not usually come back before midnight, usually much later."

"Restaurants and night clubs, eh? But look here, Orchard, about going out in the car — he only got it last month, did he?"

"This particular one, yes, sir. But he had several cars before that. Mr. Lessingham never kept a car for very long, sir. He was always exchanging the one he had for another."

"Is that so?" remarked Hanslet meaningly. "Where did he keep his car?"

"He rented a lockup garage in Cawdor Mews, just at the back here, sir. He took the garage at the same time as he took these rooms."

"All right, that'll do, Orchard. You can wait upstairs in your own quarters till we ring for you."

As soon as Orchard had departed, the superintendent set to work silently and methodically. He turned his attention first to the writing desk, going through its contents with a dexterity which aroused Harold's admiration. But he found nothing there to interest him except an address book, which he glanced at rapidly and slipped into his pocket.

Having completed his search of the sitting-room, Hanslet proceeded to examine the other rooms of which the suite consisted. He went swiftly through the dining-room, the bedroom, the bath-room and the tiny kitchen. But in none of them did he find anything that cast light upon Lessingham's occupations. Finally, as a measure of precaution, he went through Orchard's quarters, which were situated in an attic at the top of the house. Here, too, he drew a blank, and after warning Orchard to let him know if any visitors came to the rooms, he and Harold left the house.

Hanslet hailed a taxi and gave the driver the address of Mr. Farrant's office in Bedford Row. During the journey, he studied the address book intently. There were quite a number of entries. Lessingham seemed to have had a wide circle of acquaintances; but the pages devoted to the letter L were blank — the name of George Love did not occur.

Having arrived at their destination, Hanslet sent in his card and they were immediately shown into the presence of Mr. Farrant, who stared hard at Harold. "We have met before, I think," he said. "Let me see, now. Were you not at the inquest upon Mr. Lessingham at Westernham yesterday?"

"That is so, Mr. Farrant," replied Harold. "My name is Merefield. Allow me to introduce Superintendent Hanslet."

"Since you come in company with Mr. Merefield, I take it that your visit is concerned with the unfortunate event to which I have referred?" said the solicitor, turning to Hanslet.

"Exactly, Mr. Farrant," replied the superintendent. "I am hoping that you will be able to give me certain information. I am endeavouring to trace the owner of the car which Mr. Lessingham was driving when the fatal accident occurred."

"I cannot tell you that. It seems to me most extraordinary, so much so that I am tempted to believe that some mistake must have been made. Inspector Harraway told me, before I left Westernham yesterday, that the car was not the one belonging to Mr. Lessingham, though exactly similar to it."

"So I am informed. Mr. Farrant. I have already questioned Mr. Lessingham's man, Orchard, but have learnt nothing from him. It seems to me that if I could get in touch with one of his friends, he might be able to help me."

"I am afraid that I know none of his friends, except, of course, Mr. Purvis, his cousin, who was killed with him. Although he and his father before him had been my clients for years, we have never moved in the same circle. Mr. Lessingham, like most young men of means, cultivated a different type of society to that of an elderly family solicitor."

"I can quite understand that, Mr. Farrant. But perhaps his relatives would be able to put me on the right track."

"His relations!" exclaimed Mr. Farrant. "If you can find his present next of kin you will save me an infinity of trouble, Superintendent. I have just drafted an advertisement, which I hope may prove effective. My position is very difficult, since Mr. Lessingham died intestate. In the ordinary course of events, Mr. Purvis would have been his heir. But up till now I have been unable to obtain any evidence as to whether he outlived Mr. Lessingham. I fear that it will be an extremely difficult question for the Court to decide."

"Meanwhile, Mr. Farrant, I understand that Mr. Lessingham changed his cars very frequently. Perhaps he did so immediately before the rally. It's a point which I am most anxious to clear up."

But Mr. Farrant shook his head. "I am afraid that I can give you no assistance whatever. Mr. Lessingham never consulted me upon such matters."

"Had Mr. Lessingham any definite occupation?" asked Hanslet innocently.

"He had not. Privately, I have always been of the opinion that it was a pity. In my opinion all young men, whatever their position in life, should have some definite object in view. But Mr. Lessingham held that his income was sufficient to justify him in leading a life of idleness."

"Didn't he even have some hobby?" The superintendent's face wore an air of polite interest.

"He had none whatever," replied Mr. Farrant emphatically. "I happen to know that, for I asked him that very question when I last saw him, as recently as last week. He came here to consult me upon some question concerned with the lease of his rooms, and when our business was finished I ventured to suggest that some hobby would be good for him. He told me that his only hobby was driving a car, and that he managed to enjoy life well enough as he was."

"Some people are like that," said Hanslet, rather vaguely. "We mustn't waste your time any further, Mr. Farrant."

As they left Bedford Row the superintendent chuckled. "I didn't think we should get much out of Mr. Farrant," he said. "In my experience, getting information out of a solicitor is like trying to get a cork out of a bottle with a pin. I didn't dare tell him that the car had been stolen and that we suspected his client of having stolen it. He'd have shut up like an oyster."

"Naturally," replied Harold. "I tell you what it is, Mr. Hanslet. I'm not altogether sure that that chap Orchard was telling us the truth, the whole truth and nothing but the truth."

"Oh, so he struck you that way, too, did he? He gave me the impression of being a most accomplished liar. First of all he said that Lessingham was not expecting to meet anybody at Torquay. That was true enough, since he didn't mean to finish the course. Then I produced the telegram and he faked up that yarn about George Love. George Love, indeed! I'm willing to bet that no such person ever existed. But it was ingenious, I'm bound to confess. I think, before we go any further afield, we'll call on the Comet people. We may pick up a crumb or two there."

They took a taxi to Great Portland Street and interviewed the sales manager of Comet Motors, Limited. "I'm from Scotland Yard," said Hanslet, introducing himself and Harold. "We've already been in touch with you over the telephone. It's this business of the car that Mr. Lessingham was driving when he was killed."

"It is the most extraordinary affair altogether," replied the manager. "I do not profess to understand it. I knew Mr. Lessingham personally. He came here several times and talked to me before he decided to buy one of our cars."

"Could you give us a general idea of his conversation?"

"Certainly. He came here first early in the New Year and said that he thought of entering for the rally, if he could find a suitable car. From what he had heard of our new 15hp sports model, he thought that it might suit him. We gave him a trial run and he expressed himself as thoroughly satisfied. To cut a long story short, we eventually persuaded him to buy one, and he took delivery of it on February 3rd."

"During February he brought the car back to our works on more than one occasion for minor adjustments. He explained that he wanted it tuned specially for the requirements of the rally, and, naturally, we were anxious to do all we could for him. He came here a few days before the rally started and thanked me for what we had done for him. He then seemed very keen and confident that he would win a prize."

"The car that he was driving was similar in every way to the one he bought?" asked Hanslet.

"Exactly similar. Unless our customers specify any particular form of body, or other alteration, all the cars of this particular series are built to standard. They are even painted the same colour, which we call comet grey. They were first exhibited at the motor show last November, and I may say that they have proved most successful."

"Would you mind telling me, in strict confidence, how many you have sold since then?"

"We have actually delivered between a hundred and twenty and a hundred and thirty. In addition to that, we have orders for future deliveries from our agents extending over the next twelve months."

"Could you give me any idea of what proportion of these have been delivered in the neighbourhood of London?"

"Fully fifty per cent, I should think. I couldn't say more accurately without consulting my figures."

Hanslet thanked the manager for his information, and they left the show-rooms of Comet Motors, Limited. "The next thing is a spot of lunch," he said. "What about Pagani's? It's close handy."

During lunch, the superintendent outlined his plans for the immediate future. "I've had a message sent to Mr. Chalk that we are coming to see him this afternoon," he said. "He doesn't know that his car has been found yet. After we've had a chat with him we'll have a look at Mr. Catesby's place at Denham. There'll be a car waiting for us at the Yard, and I thought you might drive it. I hate taking a uniformed driver — it's apt to give a wrong impression."

"I'll drive it for you right enough," Harold replied. "I say, doesn't it strike you that Lessingham went to a lot of trouble to steal one car? All that palaver with the Comet people, I mean."

"It strikes me that that was only the beginning of his scheme," replied Hanslet. "Entering for the rally and buying a car specially for it put him in a sense above suspicion. I believe he meant to specialise on one particular type of car. As the manager told us, all that series of cars are as alike as so many peas. Lessingham knew that, and saw his opportunity. As soon as he saw one of them about he or his accomplices found out who it belonged to and where it was kept or regularly parked. I'll bet he knew exactly where to find Mr. Chalk's car on Tuesday night.

"His first effort was to pinch that. But I don't for a moment suppose he meant to stop there. If he hadn't been killed he'd have carried on in the same way. Cars of this type would have been stolen, one after another. There's just one thing: To steal a car is easy enough. But to dispose of it profitably afterwards is another matter. Now we've got on Lessingham's track, we ought to be able to find out his method of disposal. Orchard knows all about it, I'll warrant. Do you know, I've a pretty shrewd suspicion that Orchard had been round those rooms and destroyed everything compromising before we got there. Somebody had, I'll swear. But I'll catch Orchard out — don't you worry."

And the anticipation of Orchard's discomfiture gave the superintendent a relish for his meal.

CHAPTER VIII

SUPERINTENDENT Hanslet and Harold found Mr. Chalk awaiting them when they reached Byfleet. He was a youngish man, apparently in affluent circumstances. He dispensed liquid hospitality, and insisted upon them making themselves comfortable before he referred to the object of their visit.

It was, in fact, the superintendent who broached the matter. "It's about your car, Mr. Chalk," he said. "You'll be glad to hear that it has been found, though in rather a badly damaged condition, I'm afraid."

"Splendid!" exclaimed Mr. Chalk. "The fact that it's found, I mean. As for the damage, I suppose that's a matter for my insurance company. I congratulate you, Superintendent. Where did you find it?"

"The credit is not mine, I'm afraid," replied Hanslet. "Mr. Merefield here can tell you more about the finding of it than I can. He saw it in the ditch about three miles on the Moorchester side of Westernham, with the driver and his passenger lying dead beside it."

"Westernham!" exclaimed Mr. Chalk. "Why, that's where the accident happened to those fellows who were driving in the rally. I was reading about it in the paper this morning. Lessingham was the name of one of them, wasn't it? And, by jove, weren't they driving a Comet? What an extraordinary coincidence!"

"Did you know Mr. Lessingham, or his passenger, Mr. Purvis?" asked Hanslet.

"Can't say that I did. I never heard their names until I read about the accident. But it's a queer thing. I thought at one time of entering for the rally myself. I probably should have done if I had been able to get away in the middle of the week. But I'm in business in the city, and I drive up and down to my office every day but Saturday."

"It is curious that you should not have known Mr. Lessingham," said Hanslet, "for the car in which he met with the accident was yours, Mr. Chalk."

"Mine!" exclaimed Mr. Chalk incredulously. "How could it have been? The rally started before my car was stolen. Are you quite sure that there is no mistake?"

"You can decide for yourself, Mr. Chalk. Do you know the detailed particulars of your car?"

"I've got them written down in my pocket-book. Here you are; 15hp. Comet Sports two-seater, painted grey. Registration number, VQ1754, Maker's number chassis 431673, engine 62141. Six cylinders, bore —"

"That's enough to be going on with, Mr. Chalk. The maker's numbers you have just mentioned are those found on this car by the representative of the Comet Company. The registration number plate had been changed, for it bore the number ZV06Q4."

"Well, I can't make that out at all. It certainly seems to be my car, though. I bought her from the Supremacy Motor Company at Kingston. She was their demonstration car. I had another car, which they took in part exchange. This was only about a fortnight ago, February 17th, to be exact."

Hanslet nodded. "Yes, that confirms what we have already been told," he said. "Now, if you've no objection, Mr. Chalk, I should like to ask you a few questions. You will understand that we are very anxious to lay our hands on the man who stole the car. I have seen the statement you made when you reported the loss. What steps did you take when you found that the car was missing?"

"I was at Jack Catesby's place near Denham. He's my partner and we've been excellent friends for years. He has a regular bridge evening every Tuesday, and my wife and I nearly always drive over to it. Usually we dine with him first, as we did on this occasion."

"Do you always leave your car in the drive, Mr. Chalk?"

"As a rule. You see, Catesby has two cars, and they just about fill his garage. There is a covered yard in front of it, but if it is a fine night, as it was on Tuesday, I don't trouble to go round to it. I just put up the hood, chuck a rug over the radiator and leave the car inside the gate. I shan't do that again, though."

"Once bitten, twice shy, eh, Mr. Chalk? Were there any other cars left in the drive?"

"Not when we arrived. But after dinner several people turned up for bridge. You see, it's a sort of informal club, of which any members who can come along do so. I suppose there are twenty or thirty of us altogether. On Tuesday I suppose a dozen people were there, besides ourselves and the Catesbys."

"Were any of them strangers to you?"

"Oh, no. We knew them all. Not intimately, but through meeting them at Catesby's previously. I can't say that I remember all their names at the moment. We stopped playing about midnight and after yarning a bit we got ready to go home. We were the first to make a move, I remember. I went out to bring the car up to the door, and when I had got to the place where I had left her, I found she wasn't there."

"Were there any other cars in the drive then?"

"Yes, three or four. They were all nearer the house than mine. I had purposely left my own car near the gate, for easiness in getting away. I couldn't make it out at first. The only thing I could think of was that Catesby's chauffeur or somebody had taken it round to the garage yard. I went up to have a look, but it wasn't there. Then I went back into the house and told Catesby.

"They all thought I was joking at first, but when they saw that I meant it they all turned out and we started a search. I suppose we spent half-an-hour looking in every possible and impossible place. But it wasn't a bit of good, and at last it was quite obvious that the car had gone. The only thing we could learn about it was from Catesby's chauffeur. He had been to the pictures or something, and had come back up the drive soon after eleven. He swore that the car was there then.

"Catesby rang up the local police and they sent a man round, to whom I gave full particulars. There was no means of getting back here that night, so my wife and I stayed with the Catesbys. And since then I've been going to and from the city by train."

"A most irritating occurrence, to lose a car like that, Mr. Chalk. Now, without meaning to be impertinent, I should like to ask whether your car was the most valuable of those standing in Mr. Catesby's drive that night?"

Mr. Chalk laughed good humouredly. "No, certainly not," he replied. "There was a Rolls and a big Daimler, I remember. But mine was the easiest to steal. For one thing, she was nearest the gate. And for another, I had turned her round when I came in, so that she faced towards the road. The others were all facing the house. They would either have to back out or drive up to the house and turn there."

"You say that you are in the habit of going to Mr. Catesby's every Tuesday evening. That was generally known, I suppose?"

"Oh, yes. Everybody knew it. All my friends round about here, for one thing. They know it's no use dropping in on us that night. And everybody who belongs to Catesby's bridge circle, for another. In fact, all my friends and acquaintances are sure to know of it."

"So that anybody might have known where your car was to be found on Tuesday nights. They might even be aware that you were in the habit of leaving it in the drive. Do you habitually leave it unattended in any other place, Mr. Chalk? Where do you keep it in the daytime, when you are in the city?"

"In a garage — never in a public parking place. And when she's here, she's always in my own garage, which is part of the house. But you don't think that someone had marked my car down as their particular prey, do you?"

"I think it very probable," replied Hanslet. "Expert car thieves very rarely steal cars at random. Now, Mr. Chalk, your car is at the Central Garage at Westernham. If you communicate with the police there and produce the registration book, they will let you have possession of it."

Mr. Chalk glanced at the dock. "I think I'll go down there at once," he said. "I'm sure I'm very much obliged to you both. Sure you won't have another drink? Well, then, I won't detain you."

As they drove from the house, the superintendent's face expressed a certain satisfaction. "It's all working out very much as I thought it would," he said. "A car left unattended regularly once a week in the same place — wonderful opportunity for an expert car thief. Chalk couldn't have made things easier for him if he'd tried. Even the way Lessingham got to hear of it presents no difficulties. Chalk and Lessingham have a mutual acquaintance, no doubt, though Chalk isn't aware of the fact."

"Yes, that's all very well," replied Harold doubtfully, "but it seems to me there's a snag in the argument. Chalk says that he only took delivery of the Comet on February 17th, which was a Wednesday. The following Tuesday was the 23rd and the one after that March 1st. It was therefore only the car's second visit to the Catesbys' when it was stolen."

But this reasoning did not daunt Hanslet in the least. "You don't realise the thoroughness with which men like Lessingham work," he said loftily. "Lessingham decides to specialise in Comets, probably because he knows of a market where he can dispose of them. He therefore keeps his eyes open for likely ones to pick up and tells his accomplices to do the same. Now, Chalk has owned a car for some time. He mentioned that the Supremacy Motor Company had allowed him something for his old one, you may have noticed.

"Well, one of Lessingham's people comes to him and tells him that he knows a man who has just bought a Comet. What's more, he says that he knows where the car will be left every Tuesday evening. I wouldn't mind betting that on February 23rd Lessingham went to have a look at Mr. Catesby's house and saw the Comet standing in the drive. This was jam for him. He could pass close to Denham on the following Tuesday night without putting himself out in the least. And, by jove, this business gets clearer the further we go. Why did you say he chose to start from Bath at nine o'clock?"

"Because the later he started the more hours of daylight he'd get." replied Harold.

"Don't you believe it! He started at nine o'clock for two reasons: first, because that would bring him to Denham at a convenient time for pinching Chalk's car; and second, because he would be the last starter and there would be no fear of anyone coming up behind him while the transfer was taking place. What do you make of that, eh?"

"It certainly sounds as if there might be something in it," replied Harold cautiously.

They drove into Denham village, where they inquired as to the whereabouts of Mr. Catesby's house. Following the directions given them, they came to a place just off the road from Denham to Rickmansworth, along which the Armstrong had passed on the first night of the rally. A gate in a trim wooden paling led into a drive, a couple of hundred yards long, at the farther end of which stood a fair-sized modern house.

"That's the place, right enough," remarked the superintendent. "I don't think we need call on Mr. Catesby. He can't tell us much more than we know already. All Lessingham would have to do would be to change over the number plates, official number and flag. He had Purvis with him and another accomplice, Orchard, perhaps, standing by, ready to drive his own car away. How long would the job take the three of them?"

"Not more than ten minutes at the most,' replied Harold.

"The point is, what did they do with Lessingham's own car? Drove it straight to Lessingham's depot, wherever that may be. It's still there, I expect. Lessingham meant to drive Chalk's car there on Thursday and change his own number plates back again."

"The problem seems to be to locate this depot, as you call it," remarked Harold. "At present, you've no clue to it at all."

"We shall locate it, without any clues," replied Hanslet confidently. "That's where Orchard is going to help us. I've arranged for him to be kept under observation and followed wherever he goes. In the same way, any visitor to the rooms will also be followed. I've also arranged for a record to be made of any telephone calls he may put through. He's bound to lead us to the place, sooner or later."

After a good look round the vicinity of Mr. Catesby's house, they drove back to London and Harold made his way back to Westbourne Terrace.

But it was not until after dinner that Dr. Priestley betrayed any interest in his adventures. He listened attentively to Harold's account of his day's work, then relapsed into his favourite position, finger tips touching, eyes fixed upon the ceiling.

"This experience should provide you with a very instructive lesson in the art of deduction," he said acidly. "Consider the facts first, apart from the conjecture with which they have become surrounded. I say facts, for there are only two occurrences which have been definitely proved, so far. The first is this: Two men, identified as Lessingham and Purvis, are found dead under circumstances which suggest that they have been killed in a motor accident. The second one is this: The car found on the spot is not the one registered in Lessingham's name. I think we may go so far as to say that it is not the car Lessingham was driving when the rally started.

"Inspector Harraway, quite rightly, was primarily concerned with the cause of the accident. He kept an open mind and his methods of deduction were perfectly sound. In the light of your own experience you and your friends leapt to the conclusion that the accident was caused by the driver falling asleep. The inspector's inquiries show that this, to say the least of it, was unlikely.

"Other theories to account for the accident were then put forward, none of them, apparently, capable of proof. An inquest, conducted most unscientifically, was held. It was apparently obvious to everybody present that an accident had occurred. The exact manner of which the accident took place became of secondary importance. A verdict was given accordingly, and the inspector pursued no further his inquiries concerning the first fact.

"The second fact comes into prominence, and is considered without any relation to the first. It turns out that the car had been stolen, and our friend, Superintendent Hanslet, takes the matter in hand. Now, the superintendent's mind suffers from a defect which has very frequently led him astray. Instead of keeping an open mind, he is apt to form a theory upon insufficient evidence. And once this theory is formed, all his efforts are devoted to proving it. He is, I gather from what you have told me, convinced that Lessingham stole the car from Mr. Catesby's drive during Tuesday night?"

"I think he is quite convinced of it, sir. He believes that he completely understands Lessingham's methods."

"Just so. Now, looking at the matter logically, he is acting upon pure conjecture. Reverting to the first fact for a moment, there is no real proof that Lessingham was driving this car when he was killed. Even if he were, the fact does not prove that he stole it. As I pointed out to the superintendent, he may have been merely a receiver of stolen property. That is a point worth bearing in mind. The essential fact, to my mind, is that at some moment between the time that the car was stolen and the time when you came on the scene on Thursday morning, one car was substituted for the other."

Dr. Priestley paused and Harold ventured a remark. "You'll admit, sir, that it is a curious coincidence that Lessingham could have been passing close to Mr. Catesby's house at the time the car was stolen?"

"My dear boy, you ought to know by this time that I never allow coincidence to influence my reasoning. In this case, you cannot prove that Lessingham chose that route. All you can say is that, since you did, he may have done. I am not denying that the substitution may have taken place at that time. I merely suggest, with all deference to Superintendent Hanslet, that it may have taken place at any time and place during the next twenty-four hours or so.

"Let us try and estimate the available time more exactly. Mr. Catesby's chauffeur saw the car in the drive soon after eleven. It was not there when Mr. Chalk went to look for it shortly before 1 am. It was stolen, therefore, between those times. What time was it when you reached the scene of the accident?"

"As nearly as possible half-past five on Thursday morning, sir."

"That leaves a period of thirty hours during which the cars may have been substituted for one another. I can see nothing to prove that Lessingham was the actual thief. Mr. Chalk's car may have been driven to any point on the route followed by him subsequently. I can, I think, illustrate what I mean. It is unnecessary to assume that Mr. Chalk's car was driven far from the spot whence it was stolen. Get out the map of your route and let me see it again. Also the table of Lessingham's and your own control times."

Harold laid them on the desk and Dr. Priestley studied them for some moments in silence. "I see that on the stage between Droitwich and Moorchester you passed within ten miles or so of Denham," he said. "We may take Windsor as a convenient point. What time did you pass through that town?"

Harold consulted his schedule, which he had brought home with him. "11.13 pm on Wednesday, sir," he replied.

"Very well. Lessingham's time at the Droitwich control was three-and-a-half hours ahead of yours. Assuming that he maintained this lead, he could have passed through Windsor at about a quarter to eight. It would then, of course, be dark. I maintain that it is as probable that the substitution took place, then, in the neighbourhood of Windsor, as that Lessingham stole the car himself on Tuesday night."

"That may be, sir. But, even if it was the case, it does not greatly affect the superintendent's problem. The only way in which he can solve it is to find out where Lessingham's car is now, and who drove it there."

"Not the only way, perhaps, but still a fairly promising one. How does he propose to proceed?"

"He seems pretty sure that Orchard's movements or actions will reveal the hiding place of the car, sir."

Dr. Priestley permitted himself one of his rare smiles. "Much of the superintendent's personal charm lies in his incurable optimism," he said. "But try to free your mind from the obsession that Lessingham must have been the actual thief. Suppose, for a moment, that he had no previous knowledge that the substitution was to take place, that he was not, as the superintendent insists, a professional car thief. In that case, how could Orchard have any knowledge of the means of disposal of Lessingham's car?"

Harold was frankly puzzled, as his expression showed. "I don't quite understand what you're getting at, sir," he confessed.

"Possibly not," replied Dr. Priestley. "Because you persist in regarding the two primary facts as completely isolated from one another. Superintendent Hanslet is, of course, entitled to his own opinion. But I believe that he has yet to discover the real significance of the case upon which he is engaged."

And, without vouchsafing any further explanation, Dr. Priestley took himself upstairs to bed.

CHAPTER IX

DURING the week end, Dr. Priestley made no further reference to the affair of the stolen car. On Monday, Harold lunched out by appointment with Richard Gateman. Bob Weldon, who had come up to London for the day, joined the party.

"That's a most extraordinary yarn!" exclaimed Bob when Harold had recounted the developments which had taken place since Saturday. "With all due deference to Dr. Priestley, I'm inclined to think Lessingham must have been the actual thief — not because there's any evidence that he was, but because I can't imagine how else the substitution can have taken place."

"I agree," said Richard. "It looks very much as though Lessingham was an expert car thief. And it sounds as if the superintendent's suspicions of Orchard were justified. That chap interests me, Harold. What did you make of him?"

"He struck me as being an excellent servant. Apart from that, I don't think I would trust him far. You know the sort of man I mean. Devoted to his master's interest, and all that, and perfectly honest so far as he was concerned. Honest according to his own lights, I mean. For instance, he wouldn't steal anything from him; but I have an idea that he would regard a certain proportion of the things that passed through his hands as his own perquisites."

Richard nodded. "I know what you mean, exactly. How far were his answers to the superintendent's questions reliable?"

"I don't know. But I had no suspicions that he was not telling the truth until that question of the telegram was raised."

"Hanslet's theory is this, I gather," remarked Bob: "Orchard was very possibly the accomplice who took charge of Mr. Lessingham's own car after the theft. The telegram was a code message which really meant 'All well, car in safety.' In that case, Orchard sent the wire himself. That's about it, isn't it?"

"I fancy that's it exactly," replied Harold. "Anyhow, I'll swear that Orchard was taken aback when the superintendent asked him who Lessingham was expecting to meet at Torquay."

"Wait a minute," said Bob. "I've been thinking about that telegram since I saw you last. Lessingham can't have been expecting it. It wasn't part of a prearranged plan, I mean. If it had been, Lessingham would have asked if there was a telegram for him when he reached the Imperial Hotel."

"Oh, I don't know," said Richard. "Remember the circumstances. Personally, I don't remember much about what happened at the Moorchester control. Lessingham must have been as dog-tired as we were. Probably more so, since he and Purvis had driven straight through from Bath, almost without a stop. I can quite understand that he forgot to ask for it when he arrived at the Imperial Hotel. And in the bustle of getting off — he was half an hour later than he meant to be, you told us — he might easily have forgotten it again."

"No, that won't do, Richard!" exclaimed Bob. "There's no doubt that the superintendent is right on that point. Lessingham can't have had any intention of finishing the course. How was he going to explain the fact that there was no stencil mark on the car he was driving? All that bustle and fuss wasn't genuine. It was merely to impress the people at Moorchester. If he had been expecting a telegram of such importance as that, he would have asked for it, all right."

"What's your idea, then, Skipper?" said Richard.

"Why, just this: Orchard knew that Lessingham was going to stay at the Imperial Hotel. There's no reasonable doubt about that, since Lessingham had ordered a room there beforehand. The wire was an afterthought on Orchard's part. Perhaps the same formula, or something like it, had been used on a previous occasion. Orchard naturally supposed that Lessingham had received it and he would assume that he would have destroyed it at once. He was, therefore, taken aback, as Harold puts it, when the superintendent produced it."

"Anyhow, he must be a man of pretty quick wit," remarked Richard. "Faking up that yarn of Purvis being unable to stay at Torquay over Friday was good in itself. But the creation of a mythical George Love to account for the last word in the wire is one of the best things I've heard for some time. I should like to make the acquaintance of friend Orchard."

"He saw that he had made a mistake in sending the telegram," replied Bob. "His natural instinct was to explain it away. I'll admit that he hit on a very ingenious explanation, but I think he would probably have done better to deny all knowledge of it. The only result of his yarn is to convince the superintendent that he's a liar."

"There's just one thing about all this," said Richard. "Nobody seems any nearer knowing why Lessingham ran into the ditch."

"And apparently nobody cares, now that a verdict of accidental death has been given," replied Harold.

Lunch over, Harold executed some commissions for Dr. Priestley and returned home. Nothing further was said about the matter until the evening, when Superintendent Hanslet paid a visit to Westbourne Terrace.

He plunged at once into the subject. "I expect that Mr. Merefield has told you about our adventures on Saturday, Professor?" he asked.

Dr. Priestley nodded. "He gave me a very full account," he replied, non-committally.

"Then you'll have heard what Orchard told us about the telegram. It was quite obvious that he was lying, as Mr. Merefield will tell you. I didn't let him see that I suspected this at the time, but I've been making inquiries. The first thing I did was to call round at the hotel at which Mr. Purvis had been staying. He had told the people there that he was going on the rally. A car, which answers to the description of Lessingham's, called for him on Tuesday at about noon. And he had said that he would be away for a couple of nights, but hoped to be back some time on Thursday."

Harold uttered an exclamation of surprise. "But surely that confirms Orchard's account of the conversation between him and Lessingham!" he exclaimed.

"At first sight it does," replied Hanslet. "But, if you remember that Lessingham never intended to complete the course, Purvis's instructions are explained. He and Lessingham intended to return on Thursday, all along. Orchard only invented the conversation to fit in with the supposition that Lessingham meant to go through the whole rally.

"The next thing I did was to make inquiries at South Kensington about the wire. I got hold of the original form upon which it was written, but nobody in the post office can remember who handed it in. I'd like you to look at the form, if you don't mind, Professor."

He handed it to Dr. Priestley, who scanned it through his spectacles. "This was written with a hard pencil by somebody who seems to have been in a considerable hurry," he said. "The wording is legible enough, but the ends of each word are slurred. There is, however, a full stop inserted between the two last words of the message — 'arranged' and 'love'."

"Which wasn't telegraphed, of course. But that's a detail, Professor. What do you make of the handwriting itself?"

"It is undoubtedly an educated hand," replied Dr. Priestley. "I am not an expert in handwriting, but this appears to display certain feminine characteristics."

"Exactly!" exclaimed the superintendent triumphantly. "What becomes of this mysterious George Love, now?"

"For that matter, Superintendent, what becomes of your theory that Orchard sent the telegram himself?" replied Dr. Priestley mildly. "It seems to me to be quite possible that George Love had a wife or sister who sent the telegram for him."

"That argument works both ways, Professor. Orchard may not have cared to risk sending the telegram himself and got someone else to do it."

"In either case, if the telegram was written out by a woman, a new factor is introduced into the problem."

"Not a very important factor. I expect Lessingham had women among his accomplices. It doesn't affect the main issue. Orchard is lying very low. He hasn't attempted to use the telephone and he's hardly left Cawdor Street at all, and then only to do some shopping. What's even more curious, he's had no visitors. I haven't found anybody yet who can tell me anything of his comings and goings after Lessingham left.

"So much for the telegram. It's not of any great importance, after all, and I'm inclined to put it aside for the present. I had a message from Mr. Farrant this morning. He seems to think the Yard can help him with his troubles, but I don't see how. He seems to be boxed up over the question as to who Lessingham's heir is."

"Harold told me that he intended to advertise," remarked Dr. Priestley.

"He has done so, but so far without receiving any replies. But he has also sent a cable to Purvis's employers out East, asking that a search for a will of his be made. To this he has had a reply that such a will exists and that particulars are being sent by mail."

"Ah I Here we have at last a problem of real interest!" exclaimed Dr. Priestley. "We may assume, I think, that Purvis bequeathed everything of which he might die possessed to some person, or that he made that person his residuary legatee. Now, of what did he, in fact, die possessed? That is the question to be decided."

"Mr. Farrant had that in his mind at the time of the inquest, sir," remarked Harold.

"Exactly. He foresaw the position which might arise, and has now apparently arisen. If Purvis died before Lessingham he never inherited from him, and his estate consists only of what he possessed at the time of the accident. But if Lessingham died first, Purvis succeeded to his estate, though he may have only survived him for a few seconds. In that case, his estate includes Lessingham's."

"Well, Professor, that's a matter for Lessingham's present next-of-kin and Purvis' executors to wrangle over, whoever he or she may turn out to be. It doesn't concern us in any way. I'm afraid we can't help Mr. Farrant's troubles. I only told you about his message because I know you like to hear everything, whether it's really got anything to do with the case or not. And now I'll come to the real point of my call. Can you spare me Mr. Merefield again for an hour or two to-morrow morning?"

"Certainly, if he can be useful to you. May I ask what line your investigations are about to take?"

"Mr Chalk was on the telephone this morning. He told me that he went down to Westernham on Saturday afternoon to see his car. He told me that he had no doubt at all that it was his. He looked in the tool box — in the presence of Sergeant Showerby, by the way. There he found a peculiarly shaped shifting spanner which he is prepared to swear to. It isn't part of the standard equipment of the car — he put it in the box himself. He also pointed out to the sergeant that a brass plate, which he says bore the words 'Supplied by the Supremacy Motor Co., Kingston', had been unscrewed from the dash."

"Doubtless to render the identification of the car more difficult," Dr. Priestley observed.

"Of course. The first thing a car thief would think of. Mr. Chalk went on to tell me that he had made arrangements with his insurance company that the car should be taken to the Comet works for repair. The Comet people have sent a lorry down for it to-day, and it will be in their works by now. I should like to have a look at it myself, and I have arranged with Mr. Chalk for him to meet me there at ten o'clock to-morrow morning. Since Mr. Merefield saw the car directly after the smash, I thought it might be a good thing if he came with me."

Dr. Priestley made no comment for some minutes after Superintendent Hanslet had gone. From his attitude and expression Harold knew that he was plunged in thought. Knowing his employer, he wisely waited for him to speak.

"Any suggestions as to his conduct of the case would be entirely lost upon the superintendent at present," he said. "To me, it becomes every day more and more apparent that the theft of the car was merely a preliminary. However, since I have no theory which would appeal to the superintendent in his present frame of mind we may leave that question in abeyance.

"In order to satisfy my own curiosity, I will give you certain instructions for to-morrow. You should be able to find an opportunity of asking the superintendent whether he possesses copies of the photographs which you say were taken on the spot by Sergeant Showerby. If so, you may tell him that it would interest me to see them. And there are one or two technical points which may escape his observation. If you will make a note of them, I will detail them to you now."

Harold took down the notes and then glanced at his employer, looking for further enlightenment; but Dr. Priestley shook his head. "No, my boy," he said, half humorously. "You have too much in common with the superintendent. If I were to tell you the reasons which prompt me to ask for those particulars, you would, subconsciously, no doubt, cease to be impartial. You would tend to see either more or less than actually exists, as your imagination prompted you. I want the facts themselves, not as observed by a biased witness."

So Harold met the superintendent next morning with the notes which Dr. Priestley had dictated in his pocket. Mr. Chalk had not arrived yet, and he put the question about the photographs at once.

"No, I haven't got them," replied Hanslet. "The accident has nothing to do with me. But there's nothing to prevent the professor having a look at them if he wants to. I'm only too glad that he's taking an interest in the case. I can't quite understand why — it's straightforward enough. If you'll remind me when we leave here, I'll ring up Sergeant Showerby. We may as well go and have a look at the car while we're waiting for Mr. Chalk."

They entered the works, where they were greeted by the engineer who had examined it at Westernham. "Nothing has been touched," he said. "It's exactly as I first saw it. We shan't get to work until we've settled with the insurance company how much it will be necessary to do."

As soon as he saw the car, Harold realised that nothing had indeed been touched. Not even the spots of blood upon the bonnet had been removed. With the professor's instructions in mind, he examined it very carefully. This done, and Mr. Chalk having not yet put in an appearance, he approached the engineer. "You haven't found anything to account for the accident, I suppose?" he asked casually.

"No, I haven't," replied the engineer. "I can't make it out at all. This man Lessingham must have swerved suddenly for some reason and lost control. I can't explain it any other way. There's nothing the matter with the car, except, of course, the damage caused by the crash. Apart from that, she's in as good condition as when we delivered her."

"Nothing about her has been altered? No gadgets fitted, or anything of that kind?"

"Nothing whatever. I examined her pretty carefully at Westernham, and I've been over her again this morning. She has been exceptionally carefully looked after. The oil in the sump has been regularly changed, chassis lubrication attended to, and so forth. The only thing that has been done is that a new pin has been fitted at the front end of the steering rod. I suppose that the original one had worn a trifle, though it's most unusual."

"How can you tell that a new pin has been fitted?" asked Harold.

The engineer smiled. "You can see for yourself if you look closely," he replied. "Do you see that the pin is not quite the same colour as the rest of the chassis? That's one of our pins and it fits perfectly. But what has happened is this. Somebody, probably the agents from whom Mr. Chalk bought the car, thinking the original pin had worn a bit, ordered a new one from our spare parts department. Now, we send out spare parts unpainted. Whoever fitted the pin painted the head as near as they could get to our comet grey, to match the rest of the car, but they didn't exactly hit off the right shade. You can see the difference now I've pointed it out to you? But, of course, a new pin having been fitted wouldn't impair the efficiency of the car in any way."

At this moment Mr. Chalk came in, apologising for being late. He spent some time explaining how he could identify the car as his own. The only things missing from it were a couple of rugs. And then Harold got a chance of a word apart with him. "Do you happen to know what your speedometer was registering when the car was stolen?" he asked,

"Well, not exactly," replied Mr. Chalk. "But, as it happens, I can tell you this: I know I was getting pretty close to the five thousand mark and I meant to make a note in my diary when I reached it. When I came back from the city on Tuesday afternoon I looked at the mileage and saw that I had only four miles to go. The speedometer showed 4996."

"How far do you make it from your house to Mr. Catesby's?" asked Harold.

"Oh, I've measured that often enough on other cars I've had. There are two or three ways of going, but by the road I took last Tuesday it is 26 miles exactly. I must have checked it half a dozen times."

Their conversation was interrupted by Superintendent Hanslet. "Much obliged to you, Mr. Chalk," he said. "I'm glad to have your personal identification of the car. I hope it won't be long before you're on the road again. Next time you go to see Mr. Catesby I wouldn't leave the car in the drive, if I were you. We may as well make a move, Mr. Merefield. There's nothing more we can do here."

Harold followed the superintendent out of the works. "What's the next move?" he asked.

"Get back to our respective jobs," replied Hanslet. "Criminal investigation doesn't always mean dashing about the place. More often than not it pays to sit down and wait, like a cat over a mouse-hole. It's the turn of the other side to play now. Orchard is bound to make a move, sooner or later. And there's Lessingham's own car. That won't stay in hiding indefinitely. It can't have been disposed of already. As soon as it appears on the road, whatever disguise it's in, we'll have it."

Harold smiled. He remembered a certain car that had once eluded Hanslet's search until Dr. Priestley provided him with a clue as to its whereabouts. "You'll be along to see the professor in a day or two, I expect," he remarked.

The superintendent shrugged his shoulders. "Possibly," he replied. "I don't see that he can be much use, though. But as soon as I've found out where Lessingham's car has been hidden, I'll look in. I expect he'll like to hear the end of the story. You might tell him that I'm much obliged to him for letting me take you off like this. I'll have those photographs sent to him, by the way."

They parted and Harold made his way back to Westbourne Terrace, wondering whether even Dr. Priestley could deduce anything from the information which he had collected. That something was at the back of the professor's mind he knew, but as to what it was, he could not even hazard a guess.

CHAPTER X

D R. PRIESTLEY seemed anxiously eager to hear the result of Harold's inquiries. He settled himself at the table in his study and provided himself with pencil and paper. "We will take the question of the speedometer, or, to be more accurate, the mileage recorder, first," he said. "Had Mr. Chalk any idea of the reading when the car was stolen?"

"When he got home from the city on Tuesday the reading was 4996 miles, sir. He says it is twenty-six miles from there to Mr. Catesby's house at Denham."

Dr. Priestley made a note of these figures. "The mileage when the car was stolen was therefore 5022," he said. "Now, were you able to observe the reading now showing on the instrument?"

"It was 5142 miles, sir. And it must have been that at the time of the crash, for it has been impossible to move the car on its own wheels since. The speedometer appeared to be in working order, as far as I could tell."

Dr. Priestley made a second note and then referred to the map, which was spread out on his table. "How far from Moorchester did the accident take place?" he asked.

"Three miles short of Westernham, sir. Westernham is eighteen miles from Moorchester."

"Assuming, then, that the car passed through Moorchester and that the mileage recorder was in order, the reading when it left Moorchester should have been 5127. That seems to me highly significant."

"The car certainly passed through Moorchester, sir. Lessingham reported to the control and he and Purvis signed the route book. Besides, the R.A.C man saw them get into the car and drive off."

"Did the R.A.C man examine the maker's numbers on the car?" asked Dr. Priestley acidly. "If he did not, there is no proof that the car he saw was the one that you found by the roadside. However, for the moment, I will assume that it was the same. How far did you calculate it was from Windsor to Moorchester?"

Harold referred to his schedule. "Eighty-seven miles, sir, by the route we planned to take," he replied.

For a minute or two Dr. Priestley made no reply. He was engaged with a rotary measurer on the map. "I make the distance from Denham to Moorchester ninety-one miles," he said. "That agrees very well with the figure which you have just given me. Now, it is a curious fact that the mileage reading of the car when stolen was 5022, and when it left Moorchester, 5127. The difference is ninety-five miles. Does that suggest anything to you?"

"Why, it is only a few miles more than the distance between Denham and Moorchester, sir!" exclaimed Harold.

"Precisely. But we must not rush to conclusions. It is possible that the car was driven for some distance with the speedometer disconnected. We must not lose sight of that. But, assuming for the moment that the speedometer was connected and in working order all the time, what do the mileage figures suggest to you?"

Harold thought for a moment. "Why, sir, that the substitution did not take place on the night the car was stolen, as the superintendent supposes. If so, Lessingham would have to have driven it through Norwich, Kendal and Droitwich, for his route book shows that he reported at those controls. From Denham to Moorchester by that route is 703 miles, according to our schedule."

"Where, then, did the substitution take place?" asked Dr. Priestley.

"It must have been on the second night, sir, when Lessingham was again close to Denham. And, since we know that the car was stolen on Tuesday night, it must have been hidden close to Denham until then."

Dr. Priestley shook his head. "That does not exhaust the possibilities," he said. "The substitution may have taken place anywhere on the route between Denham and Moorchester. Suppose, for the sake of argument, that Lessingham met the individual who stole the car fifty miles from Denham on that route. The mileage reading would have then been 5072. If the substitution then took place and Lessingham drove the car on to Moorchester, the mileage would have risen to 5127, or thereabouts. The same thing would have happened if the substitution had taken place at Moorchester itself."

Harold considered this for a moment or two. "In any case, it comes to this, sir," he said: "The substitution must have taken place on Wednesday, not Tuesday night. And in that case I cannot see what Lessingham's game was. Why should he hide the stolen car all through Wednesday, with the risk that it would be found during that time?"

"Why, indeed?" replied Dr. Priestley drily. "But remember, there is always the possibility that Lessingham may have put the speedometer out of action, or tampered with it in some way. For instance, he may have stolen the car on the first night and immediately disconnected the speedometer. He may then have driven the car round the rally course and connected the speedometer again when he passed through the neighbourhood of Denham on the second night. But why should he do so? He could not have anticipated the accident and the inquiries that would ensue. No, the balance of probability seems to me that the substitution took place on the second night."

"Well, sir, then this must be the explanation: Lessingham intended to steal Mr. Chalk's car. He could only do so on Tuesday night, since on Wednesday night it would be safely locked up in its own garage. He did so, hid it in some place he had already prepared and picked it up on Wednesday night. But I can't understand why he did not change over at once, unless on Tuesday he had no one to take charge of his own car."

"Then why not leave his own car in this hiding place, thereby lessening the risk of discovery of the stolen car? Your reasoning, my boy, is consistently based upon the preconceived theory that Lessingham stole the car. There is not an atom of proof that he did so. There is no evidence that he was within forty miles of Denham on the first night."

"But even if he didn't steal the car himself, sir, he must have known all about the theft. In fact, it is pretty certain that he must have arranged it. Otherwise, why did he consent to the substitution?"

"That is a question that we cannot yet answer," replied Dr. Priestley, with sudden gravity. "When we can, we shall be considerably nearer a solution of the problem than we are now. Conjecture upon that point is useless at this stage. But I think that the matter of the mileage readings is of the first importance. I should like you to go back to the Comet Motor Company's works and renew your acquaintance with the engineer to whom you spoke this morning. I should like his opinion upon the possibility of the speedometer having been disconnected or tampered with."

Harold went off on his errand and it was not until that evening that he returned. After dinner, Dr. Priestley returned to the subject. "While you were out this afternoon, I received a most interesting collection of photographs," he said. "They were sent to me by Sergeant Showerby, and he must have considered the matter urgent, for he despatched them by passenger train, to save time."

"I expect that he wanted to bring himself to the notice of the Yard, sir," replied Harold. "Superintendent Hanslet's name would mean a lot to him."

"Very possibly. However, we will defer discussion of the photographs until later. Let me hear the result of your investigations at the Comet Motor Company's works."

"I found the engineer, sir, and told him that there was reason to suspect that the speedometer might have been tampered with. He and I examined the car very carefully together. Oddly enough, in spite of the damage to the front of the car, the speedometer and its connections are uninjured.

"We came to the conclusion that the speedometer had never been disconnected. It would have been impossible to do so without leaving marks on the paint. You remember, sir, that the car had been overhauled and repainted just before Mr. Chalk took delivery of it, just a fortnight before the accident. And the paint is still unbroken over the connections. As to tampering with the instrument itself, sir, the engineer assured me that it couldn't be done without leaving still more obvious traces."

"That seems satisfactory. Did you discuss any other method by which the mileage record could be falsified?"

"There was only one other way that was possible, sir, and that not in this case. Some mileage recorders work in the reverse direction when the car is run backwards. Their readings can therefore be set back if the front wheel is jacked up and then revolved counterclockwise. But the particular speedometer fitted to the Comet has a ratchet device, which prevents the mileage recorder functioning when the car runs backwards."

"Then all possibilities of the record having been falsified are eliminated," remarked Dr. Priestley. "We may now say with some certainty that the substitution took place during the night of the 2nd and 3rd, somewhere between Denham and Moorchester, or at either place itself. Now, let us consider these photographs. Will you describe to me again how the bodies of Lessingham and his passenger were lying when you first saw them?"

"They were lying a short distance apart, sir on the farther side of the ditch. Purvis was stretched out on his face; Lessingham was rather more on his left side, with his legs drawn up. Both bodies were directly in front of the radiator of the car, and a few feet from it."

"Suggesting at once that they had been thrown from it, in a forward direction, by the impact?"

"Yes, sir. Purvis had apparently been shot head-first through the windscreen. Lessingham must have cleared it, for he was not cut about at all."

Dr. Priestley had followed Harold's description with the photographs. "Yes, that appears to have been the case," he replied. "We can understand it in the case of Purvis, I think. He was presumably sitting beside the driver, and there was nothing between him and the windscreen.

"The case of Lessingham is slightly different. He was driving, and had the wheel and steering column in front of him. These are damaged, you told me. Did you observe the damage more closely this morning?"

"Yes, sir. The column itself is bent forward at least six inches. The rim of the wheel is flattened, and one spoke of it is broken."

"The medical advice at the inquest was to the effect that Lessingham was suffering from severe abdominal injuries. The natural inference is that he was flung against the steering column by the force of the impact. It seems to me a curious fact that this did not arrest his motion. In spite of the retarding action which it must have had, Lessingham's body continued its progress, and reached a spot approximately the same distance from the seat as that reached by Purvis, who was not retarded."

"But perhaps a fraction of a second later," suggested Harold. "That explains why he was not cut about. Purvis had already broken most of the glass out of the screen."

"A good point, my boy," said Dr. Priestley approvingly. "But still, I should have expected to find Lessingham's body within the car rather than outside it. But that is a matter which concerns the cause of the accident. These photographs taken by Sergeant Showerby show very clearly the tracks of the car before it left the road. There are, I notice, two sets of tracks only — those of the car driven by Lessingham and those of the Armstrong. Since no other tracks are visible, I gather that no great volume of traffic uses the road?"

"Not at that time in the morning, sir. So far as I can remember, we saw nothing on the road after we left Moorchester until we came upon the Comet."

Dr. Priestley took out the map and studied it. "There are two roads westward from Moorchester, I see," he said. "The one followed by you and Lessingham, which passes through Westernham, and a second, running roughly parallel to it, but nearer the coast. By the map, the coast road appears to be the shorter. What made you select the inland road?"

"Because, though it may a trifle longer, it is a good deal faster, sir. The coast road is narrow and very hilly, and, since it is not much used, is not in very good repair."

Dr. Priestley examined the contours on the map. "Yes, it certainly appears to be hilly," he replied. "I see that it follows roughly the crest of a ridge, to the southward of which is the sea. The road you took, on the other hand, lies in the valley. At intervals minor roads connect the two. The lower road should be visible from the crest of the ridge for the greater part of its length. In fact, from the upper road the view would be over the sea to the southward and over the valley to the northward."

"I can't say, sir. I've never been along it. Bob Weldon could tell us; he knows that part of the world."

Dr. Priestley made no reply, but continued staring at the map. Harold wondered why he had strayed away from the subject, but was too wise to ask questions. At last his employer put the map away and turned once more to the photographs, which he studied again intently.

"It appears that Sergeant Showerby took photographs only of the tracks behind the wrecked car," he said. "Were there any tracks visible in front of it — that is to say, on the Westernham side?"

"Not of the Comet, of course, sir. But by the time the light was good enough to take the photographs there were plenty. There were our own tracks, going to and coming from Westernham to fetch the sergeant, the tracks of Doctor Mason's car, coming out, turning and going back, and the tracks of the constable's bicycle."

"So that if any tracks had existed, they would by then have been indistinguishable?"

"I should say completely, sir. I don't think that anybody looked for them in that direction. As you can see from the photographs, sir, nothing had passed the scene of the accident till we came along."

"Passed, no!" replied Dr. Priestley irritably. "However, let us return to the tracks of the wrecked car. You have told me that several explanations have been suggested to account for the curious wobbling visible before the car left the road. Which, in your opinion, is most likely?"

"Well, sir, I'm inclined to hold to my own theory that Lessingham lost control of the car while trying to avoid something that suddenly appeared on the road in front of him. That would account for the wobbling."

"What do you mean exactly by his losing control of the car?"

"Swerving suddenly, sir, and then endeavouring to correct the swerve. If he was travelling at a high speed, he may not have been able to apply the correction quick enough. When the wheel struck the grass edge, it may have wrenched the steering wheel out of his hands — and that would mean disaster."

"The tracks certainly suggest loss of control," agreed Dr. Priestley. "But could this control not be lost through a mechanical failure of the mechanism, rather than through a physical failure on the part of the driver?"

"It could, sir. That was Inspector Harraway's idea. But if such a mechanical failure had occurred, the reason of it would be apparent. And the engineer at the Comet works declares that the car must have been in perfect order when the accident happened."

Dr. Priestley shook his head. "That is going too far," he said. "All that he can state with certainty is that the car, allowing for the damage caused by the accident, was in perfect order when he examined it. And that is an entirely different matter. It is also safe to assume, I think, that the car was in perfect order when it was stolen. But we have no evidence that it was so during the intervening period. The important point seems to be: was it in perfect order at the time of the substitution?"

"Surely, sir, Lessingham would have assured himself of that before he took it over?"

"Lessingham, Lessingham!" exclaimed Dr. Priestley petulantly. "I believe that you and the superintendent have Lessingham on the brain. How do you know that that unfortunate individual knew anything about it?"

"Well, after all, sir, he was killed while he was driving the car!" expostulated Harold.

"Was he? How do you know? Did anyone see him driving a car known to be Mr. Chalk's? Even supposing that he was? Is that any evidence that he stole it? Let me put a parallel case to you. A certain half-crown is marked in such a way that the mark is invisible to the unaided eye. This half-crown is stolen from its owner. Thirty hours later it is found in your possession. Is that proof positive that you stole it?"

"No, sir it isn't," Harold admitted. "But surely —"

Dr. Priestley brushed his protest aside. "Why is it not proof against you?" he persisted.

"Because I might have acquired it perfectly innocently, sir. For instance, the thief might have given it to me, with other coins, in exchange for a pound note. All half-crowns are similar, and I could not be expected to see a mark which was invisible to the naked eye."

"You would, in fact, be an unwitting, and therefore innocent, receiver of stolen goods. Why should not Lessingham have been in exactly the same position? Why should not the cars have been substituted without his knowledge?"

Harold's reply was interrupted by the entrance of Mary, the parlourmaid, with the message that Superintendent Hanslet had called, and would like to see Dr. Priestley. The latter hesitated and a slight frown crossed his face. "Very well, let him come in," he said curtly.

Hanslet entered the room, a triumphant smile upon his face. It was clear that some important piece of news was on his lips. But Dr. Priestley pointed to a chair. "Sit down, Superintendent," he said. "Harold and I were just expounding some possible theories to account for the accident to the car that Lessingham is believed to have been driving when he was killed. Since you have arrived so opportunely, it may interest you to hear them. What was it that you were about to say, Harold?"

But the superintendent, exasperated by Dr. Priestley's manner, could contain himself no longer. "The accident?" he exclaimed. "Why, that's ancient history, Professor. All that's over and done with long ago. I dropped in to tell you something much more important than that. Lessingham's car has been found!"

CHAPTER XI

D R. PRIESTLEY looked gravely at the superintendent over his spectacles. "Indeed?" he replied severely. "That appears to me to be a wholly irrelevant detail, at present. It may, perhaps, become of some importance at a later stage of the problem. No, please do not interrupt me, Superintendent. You are at perfect liberty to remain and listen to our discussion, provided that you do not distract us by introducing extraneous subjects."

Hanslet half rose from his chair, and then, catching Harold's eye, sank down into it again. After all, he knew from past experience that Dr. Priestley never talked at random. His time would probably not be wasted in staying and listening to what he had to say. "All right. I can stop for a few minutes," he said ungraciously.

"I think, Harold, that the superintendent will understand our argument better if we explain to him our theory of the time and place of the substitution," said Dr. Priestley. "Will you do so? Here are the figures I have noted."

Harold explained his employer's deductions from the various mileages recorded, while the superintendent listened impatiently. "That's all very well, Professor!" he exclaimed. "It's an ingenious bit of reasoning, and it may be correct. I shall have to work it out in my own mind. But it doesn't affect the case at all. It merely means that Lessingham or his accomplice stole the car on Tuesday night, but that the change-over wasn't made till Wednesday night. It's really only a matter of detail."

"It may prove to be considerably more than that," replied Dr. Priestley patiently. "Now, just before you came in, Harold and I were discussing a rather interesting possibility. It was that Lessingham had no knowledge whatever of the theft, but was an unwitting and therefore innocent receiver of stolen goods."

Hanslet stared at Dr. Priestley as though he had taken leave of his senses. "You mean that somebody exchanged one car for the other without his knowledge?" he said incredulously. "But, if you'll excuse my saying so, Professor, that's absolutely ridiculous!"

"Rather a strong expression, Superintendent," said Dr. Priestley equably. "Would you mind telling me why you consider it ridiculous?"

"Because there could be no possible point in anybody doing such a thing," replied Hanslet promptly. "You'll admit that the only person who could have substituted one car for another was the man who stole Mr. Chalk's? Very well. What had he to gain? Having stolen a car, his problem was to dispose of it. He would want to get rid of it, to pass it on to someone else, as soon as possible, it's true. But what advantage was it to him to exchange it for an exactly similar car? He had, if you like, disposed of one stolen car, but in doing so he had burdened himself with another. For, in exchanging the cars, he had clearly stolen Lessingham's."

"It is the motive, then, that you consider ridiculous, and not the substitution itself," said Dr. Priestley. "We will consider the motive later. For the moment we will consider the act of substitution. You will not deny that this, in fact, took place?"

"Of course I won't; it's a perfectly obvious fact. But I don't see how it could have been done without Lessingham's knowledge."

"On my part, I consider that it would be a comparatively easy matter. Your investigations have shown that the various cars of this particular model are exactly alike. They are built to standard, are fitted with identical equipments, and are even painted the same distinctive colour.

"Before these two cars, Mr. Chalk's and Lessingham's, left the makers' hands they were indistinguishable, except for the numbers engraved on the engine and the chassis, and these were not readily discernible by the ordinary observer. Subsequently, other dissimilarities began to appear. The cars were allotted different registration numbers, and these were painted on plates attached to the respective cars. Mr. Chalk's car had a brass plate attached to the dash by the Supremacy Motor Company. At the time when Lessingham's car started for the rally, it bore a flag and an official number. All those subsequent distinctive marks were easily recognisable. How were the flag and the official number attached to the competing cars, Harold?"

"In our case, the flag was fixed to the sphinx mascot on the radiator cap with copper wire, sir. The official number was tied with tapes to the front of the car, below the radiator."

"And once fitted, they were readily detachable?"

"It would only take a few seconds to get them off sir."

"Very well, then. Now, let us consider how the substitution might have taken place. We will suppose that Lessingham left his car unattended for a few minutes, during Wednesday night. The individual who stole Mr. Chalk's car, whom we may for the present call the thief, seized his opportunity.

"Remember, he had several hours in which to prepare Mr. Chalk's car to resemble Lessingham's. No doubt he had already removed the brass plate from the dash. He may even have fitted Mr. Chalk's car with registration number plates bearing Mr.

Lessingham's number, ZV96Q4. All he had to do there was to transfer the official number card, and the rally flag, which, as Harold has told us, would be the work of a few seconds.

"He then, one must presume, drove away in Lessingham's car. Lessingham, on returning to the place where he left his car, would have no suspicions of the change that had been made. It was dark, of course, and any distinctive marks, such as scratches on the paint-work and upholstery, would not be noticed. The thief would, of course, have transferred any baggage such as maps from one car to the other. Lessingham drives away without suspecting the trick that has been played upon him. Is there anything impossible in this hypothesis?"

It was Hanslet who replied to this question. In spite of the ill grace with which he had consented to listen to Dr. Priestley's arguments, he had gradually become interested. "There's nothing impossible, Professor. The thing might have been done. I'll admit. But you won't mind if I criticise your theory a bit, will you?"

"Not if you criticise it intelligently," replied Dr. Priestley, still with a trace of severity in his voice.

"I'll try to do so. In the first place, it's almost incredible that the thief should have come by chance upon Lessingham's car standing unattended. The substitution must have been premeditated. You have realised that yourself, since you say that Mr. Chalk's car may have been already fitted with plates bearing Lessingham's registration number. Doesn't that suggest that Lessingham was in the plot? How else could the thief know where his car was to stop, and what his number was?"

"I will reserve my answer to that criticism till later. What is your next objection, Superintendent?"

"Just this, Professor: If neither Lessingham nor Purvis were in league with the thief, the car must have been left unattended in some lonely spot where be could transfer the flag and number unobserved. This seems rather unlikely."

Dr. Priestley turned to Harold. "What have you to say on that point, my boy?" he asked.

"Well, sir, the only time we left the Armstrong unattended was while we were in the controls. And then she wasn't exactly unattended. There were plenty of other cars and people about."

"That is a very vague statement. Who were these people?"

"Other competitors, for the most part, sir. At all the controls there was some enclosed space or park into which competitors drove their cars. There they were left while the driver and passengers signed the route book, snatched a meal, and so forth. Meanwhile, other competitors were busy with their own cars, filling up with petrol, or making adjustments."

"Did any of your party, at any of these controls, notice particularly what other competitors were doing?"

"I don't suppose we did, sir. We were too intent upon our own affairs."

Dr. Priestley nodded. "That is very much what I imagined," he said. "Now, can you describe to us the conditions at the Moorchester control?"

"I'm afraid I can't exactly, sir," replied Harold. "We were so much delayed by the fog that we didn't get there until everybody else had gone. But I can describe the car park there. It was an open space — a sort of courtyard beside the Imperial Hotel. It was a biggish place, with plenty of room, but unlighted. One had to depend on one's own lights to find the way about it. And it must have been very busy earlier in the night, for Moorchester was a control for starters from other places besides Bath."

"Were other than competing cars allowed in this parking place?" asked Dr. Priestley.

"Oh, yes, sir. There were half a dozen or more not carrying flags or official numbers when we were there. I expect that they belonged to the control officials and people like that."

"Now, just one moment. As I understand it, the car that Lessingham was driving and Mr. Weldon's were the last to leave the control. Do you suppose that they all took the road through Westernham?"

"All those which had started from Bath, sir, at all events. Some of the others had another control to reach before they entered on the final stage to Torquay. The road through Westernham is the most direct between Moorchester and the finishing point."

"Then, how do you account for the fact that their tracks were not visible on the photographs taken by Sergeant Showerby?"

"Because the dew only began to fall about the time of the accident, sir. Cars passing over the dry road before then would leave no visible tracks."

"It could be predicted, with some certainty, that Lessingham would take the route through Westernham after leaving Moorchester?"

"I think it could, sir. There are, of course, other roads between Moorchester and Torquay. But the one we took is the most obvious, and I expect that nearly all the competitors followed it."

Dr. Priestley leaned back in his chair. "Well, Superintendent?" he asked, expectantly.

"I see what you're driving at," replied Hanslet. "You're trying to make out that the substitution took place at the Moorchester control. I daresay that it did. What do you think, Mr. Merefield? You've seen the place, and I haven't."

"It could have been done, easily enough," replied Harold, with conviction. "We know that Lessingham got there about half-past ten. Although the control was not open then, I daresay that a good many cars arrived about that time or soon after. The thief, with Mr. Chalk's car, arrived later. The fact that he had not a flag or official number would not be noticed, or, if it was, his car would be supposed to belong to one of the officials.

"He might even be carrying plates with Lessingham's registration numbers. He could feel certain that he ran practically no risk of discovery. Nobody would notice that there were two cars in the park with the same registration number. It was nobody's business to look at the registration number, for one thing. And, for another, everybody concerned had been on the road for over twenty-four hours. I know I shouldn't have noticed anything if all the cars in the park had been carrying the same number, or, for that matter, no number at all.

"The thief could have taken the flag and official number from Lessingham's car and put it on Mr. Chalk's without any difficulty. In the general confusion, nobody would have been a penny the wiser. All he had to do, then, would be to change the cars round, so that Lessingham should find Mr. Chalk's in the place where he had left his own. With cars continually coming in and out, there would be no difficulty about that. And Lessingham, coming out into the dark, not yet thoroughly awake, and in a tearing hurry to get on would notice nothing."

"A most graphic picture of what probably happened," remarked Dr. Priestley approvingly. "By the time that Lessingham came out of the hotel, the thief had already left in Lessingham's car, no doubt. His scheme, so far, had been thoroughly successful."

"But what was his scheme, Professor?" demanded Hanslet. "You're asking me to believe in a car thief who must have known Lessingham's intended movements exactly and yet had no connection with him. This remarkable person exchanges the car he has stolen for Lessingham's. He then drives away, and Lessingham's car is found in a disused quarry in Somersetshire, completely smashed up, I gather. I think I'm entitled to ask what his scheme was!"

"Before I answer that question, Superintendent, how do you reconcile the finding of Lessingham's car with your theory?"

"Easily enough. I've maintained all along that Lessingham had associates — that he was the chief of a gang of car thieves. One of these took Lessingham's own car to a depot established for the purpose. Lessingham was probably on his way there when he crashed. But as soon as they heard of the accident, the gang got the wind up. They would know that the car that Lessingham was driving would sooner or later be identified as Mr. Chalk's.

"They also knew that the discovery of Lessingham's own car would probably lead to their arrest. They would find it impossible to account for their possession of it. So the first thing to do was to get rid of it, and this they have done."

"Have you any details of the finding of the car?" asked Dr. Priestley.

"Not yet. All I have had is a telephone message from the Somersetshire police, saying that a car answering to the description I circulated has been found at the bottom of a disused quarry near a place called Slowford. They are writing me full details, and I should get the letter to-morrow."

"That is very much what I expected," said Dr. Priestley gravely. "The destruction of the car fits in with what I have conjectured as being the scheme of the man we call the thief. Indeed, it is to me an additional proof that this scheme was wholly unknown to Lessingham, who, I believe, had neither associates nor criminal intentions."

"I'm not so sure of that," replied Hanslet. "One thing is quite certain: Whether or not he actually stole Mr. Chalk's car, he was up to some fishy business or other, under cover of the rally. If not, why did Orchard lie to me when I interviewed him? As soon as I tackled him about that telegram, he lied to me like a trooper. You'll hear me out in that, won't you, Mr. Merefield?"

"I certainly got the impression at the time that the story of George Love was an improvisation." replied Harold.

"There you are, Professor. I assure you that there was not a shadow of doubt about it. You'd have spotted it at once if you'd been there with us. If Lessingham's business was perfectly straight and above board, why should Orchard have invented this cock and bull yarn?"

"For some purpose which we have not yet fathomed," replied Dr. Priestley thoughtfully. "For instance — but you are tempting me to conjecture. Besides, we are straying from the subject. You asked me to outline the thief's scheme. But first of all, who was the thief, assuming, as I do, that he and Lessingham were not associated in the theft?

"We know two things about him, of which the first is this: He must have been acquainted with Mr. Chalk, to the extent that he knew his practice of going to Mr. Catesby's on Tuesday evenings. More than this, he must have known that he was the owner of a Comet car similar to Lessingham's, and that he was in the habit of leaving his car in Mr. Catesby's drive. I would point out that it does not follow that he knew Mr. Chalk personally. He may have discovered these data by observation.

"The second thing is that he must have known the details of Lessingham's intended schedule. I am quite satisfied in my own mind that the substitution took place in the courtyard of the Imperial Hotel at Moorchester. The thief must therefore have known the intended time of Lessingham's arrival and departure. I do not press the point of Mr. Chalk's car having been stolen at a time when Lessingham may have been passing near Denham. This, very possibly, was what is termed a coincidence. But I have my own reasons for believing that he knew the route which Lessingham was to follow between Moorchester and Torquay. Finally, he was sufficiently familiar with Lessingham's car to know the registration number."

"In that case, he must be a pretty intimate friend of Lessingham's," remarked Hanslet.

"Probably. Now, what was his scheme? I am convinced that he did not steal Mr. Chalk's car for profit. He stole it because he wanted a car exactly similar to Lessingham's. Anyone of that particular model would have served his purpose. It was probably Mr. Chalk's habit of leaving his car in Mr. Catesby's drive that influenced his selection of this particular car.

"Having stolen it, nearly twenty-four hours must elapse before he could effect the substitution. How he disposed of the car during that period I do not know. He certainly removed the brass plate from the dash and there is reason to believe that he did something else. But I prefer not to discuss that until further evidence is available."

Hanslet smiled. "No guesswork for you, Professor," he said. "It comes to this, then: he wanted for some mysterious purpose of his own to exchange Lessingham's car for one exactly similar to it. In other words, he wanted to obtain possession of Lessingham's car without its owner knowing anything about it. But what did he want it for? Had it any peculiarity that made it of special value to him? In any case, he would not have dared to use it openly for long, for Lessingham would have discovered, by the absence of the stencils, that he was not driving his own car as soon as he reached Torquay."

Dr. Priestley shook his head. "The object of the substitution was not to enable the thief to obtain possession of Lessingham's car." he replied gravely.

"Then what was the object, Professor? According to you, it seems utterly pointless. Was it a joke, or something?"

"Anything but a joke. Has it not occurred to you, Superintendent, that the substitution of the cars was the direct cause of the accident which happened shortly afterwards?"

"It can't have been, Professor. Mr. Chalk's car was in as perfect condition as Lessingham's could have been. We have the word of the experts for that. Inspector Harraway raised the point, and it has been satisfactorily disposed of."

"Did the experts see Mr. Chalk's car before the accident took place?" replied Dr. Priestley swiftly. "You have allowed the comparatively simple matter of the theft to divert your attention from the significance of the so-called accident."

Hanslet shrugged his shoulders. "Well, after all, motor car accidents will happen, as we all know."

Dr. Priestley rapped his desk impatiently. "Yes, yes, of course!" he exclaimed. "And apparently coroners exist who are as ready to take accidents for granted as you are, Superintendent. But in this case there can be no shadow of doubt in the mind of any intelligent person that Lessingham was deliberately murdered!"

CHAPTER XII

I F Dr. Priestley had hurled the ink-pot which stood on his desk at him, Superintendent Hanslet could not have been more amazed. "Murdered!" he exclaimed. "Lessingham murdered! How on earth do you make that out?"

"Not as yet, by logical deduction, I confess," replied Dr. Priestley. "There are many steps to be filled in before the argument is complete. But the overwhelming probability is there for anybody to see."

"But who murdered him, Professor?" asked Hanslet, only half seriously. "The only person with him when he was killed was Purvis. You don't suggest that Purvis snatched the wheel and drove the car into the ditch, do you?"

"I do not suggest anything so ridiculous. But murder can be remote — by which I mean that it is not necessary for the murderer to be present at his victim's death. For instance, I prepare an infernal machine fitted with a time fuse and put it in your pocket. An hour later, when we may be many miles apart, the machine detonates and kills you. Am I none the less a murderer because I am not present at that time?"

"I hope you won't try anything of the kind, Professor. But, seriously, what's that got to do with this Lessingham business?"

"This — that I believe that Mr. Chalk's car had been converted into the equivalent of an infernal machine, and that it was for that reason that it was substituted for Lessingham's."

Hanslet shrugged his shoulders wearily. "We can't go against the evidence of the experts," he said. "Can't you be a little more explicit, Professor?"

"Not at this stage," replied Dr. Priestley decidedly. "To you, as an officer of police, I put the matter like this: You have no proof that Lessingham stole Mr. Chalk's car. I think I have demonstrated that the substitution of one car for another, an admitted fact, could have been carried out without Lessingham's knowledge. Harold has shown us the possibility that such a substitution could have been carried out at the Moorchester control on the Wednesday night.

"Since in any investigation you are bound to consider all the possibilities, you must consider this one. The first question you will then ask yourself is — what was the motive of the substitution? And in seeking the answer to this question, you must bear in mind the fact that shortly after Lessingham began to drive the substituted car he met with a fatal accident, the cause of which has never been satisfactorily explained."

Hanslet nodded, but for some moments he made no reply. Had anybody but Dr. Priestley expounded such a seemingly far-fetched theory, he would have dismissed it at once without giving it serious consideration. But, from long experience, he knew that even the professor's most startling theories had a way of turning out to be correct.

During the conversation that evening his faith in the construction which he had put upon the Lessingham case had been rudely shaken. But he was hardly prepared for it to take the dramatic form which Dr. Priestley had outlined. This was turning the tables with a vengeance Instead of regarding Lessingham as a criminal, he was asked to look upon him as a victim. On the face of it, it seemed absurd. Still...

"You can't give me a hint as to who killed Lessingham, if your theory's right?" he asked suddenly.

Dr. Priestley shook his head. "Not from the facts at present in my possession," he replied. "The discovery of the murderer's identity is surely a matter for the police."

Again Hanslet nodded, and a second pause ensued, longer than the first. "I tell you what I'll do, Professor," he said abruptly. "To-morrow I'm going down to this place Slowford. I want to see the quarry where Lessingham's car was found. And I think I'd better arrange for what remains of the car to be brought up to London for examination. It that doesn't get me any further, I'll see the assistant commissioner and put this murder theory of yours before him. It's for him to decide if any steps are to be taken in that direction. It's a bit awkward, you see. A verdict of accidental death has already been returned."

"It would not be the first instance of an incorrect verdict having been given at an inquest," replied Dr. Priestley. "To cite one instance alone. You know better than I do that it has been found that a victim, whose death was attributed at an inquest to natural causes, has subsequently been found to have been poisoned."

"Yes, I know," said Hanslet, without enthusiasm. He rose heavily from his chair. "I'd better be making a move, I suppose." he continued. "Can I look in again in a day or two, Professor?"

"You had better telephone first," replied Dr. Priestley. "It may save you a journey. I think it is quite likely that I shall be out of London for a day or two."

Harold followed the superintendent to the front door. "Where's the old boy off to?" asked the latter, with a shade of anxiety in his voice. "I don't want to lose touch with him, after what he said just now."

"I haven't the slightest idea," replied Harold. "It's the first I've heard of his going away at all."

But he was soon to be enlightened. When he returned to the study after seeing Hanslet out, he found his employer still sitting at his desk, with a map spread out in front of him. He said nothing for a few minutes and then looked up.

"A change of air would do us both good, my boy," he said benignly. "We might spend a day or two in a bracing atmosphere with advantage. Do you suppose that the Imperial Hotel at Moorchester would be inconveniently crowded?"

Harold with difficulty repressed a smile. So this was the secret of his employer's sudden resolve. "I shouldn't think so, sir, at this time of year," he replied.

"Then you had better telephone in the morning, and reserve rooms for us to-morrow night. Do you think that your friend Mr. Weldon could be persuaded to join us there with his car?"

"I'm sure he'd come, if he knew that you wanted him to, sir!" replied Harold eagerly. "He's never forgotten that business at Clayport. And if there is any chance of repeating the experience, he'll be on to it like a shot."

Dr. Priestley's expression relaxed slightly. He had always looked back upon his elucidation of the murder of Doctor Grinling at the Unicorn Hotel at Clayport with particular satisfaction. "Very well," he said. "You had better telephone to him, too. Put the calls through before breakfast, then, when I hear the replies, I will give you further instructions if necessary."

Next morning, Harold rang up Bob Weldon first. He gave him Dr. Priestley's message and hinted that the summons was connected with Lessingham's death. "Come if you can — there's a good chap," he said. "I think I can promise you that you won't be bored."

"I'll come like a shot," replied Bob. "I'd very much like to know the rights of that affair, and I shall enjoy seeing the professor again. He's the same dry old stick as ever, I suppose? I say, do you think he'd mind if Richard joined us?"

"I think he'd be delighted. I fancy he wants to reconstruct the events of that night last week as nearly as he can. All right, then, I'll reserve rooms for the four of us."

He next rang up the Imperial Hotel and found that there was plenty of accommodation available. He reserved the rooms required and reported to Dr. Priestley when he came down to breakfast.

"That is most satisfactory," was his employer's comment. "I shall be glad if Mr. Gateman comes in addition to Mr. Weldon. We will catch a train which will take us to our destination in time for dinner. Meanwhile, there are certain inquiries which I should like you to make for me."

So it happened that after breakfast Harold set out for Mr. Chalk's office in the city. Mr. Chalk seemed delighted to see him. "Hullo, Mr. Merefield!" he exclaimed.

"Still on the trail, eh? Haven't you brought our friend the superintendent with you this morning?"

"No, he's out of town to-day, I believe," replied Harold. "Look here, I only want to ask you one question. When I was up at the Comet works yesterday, the engineer there pointed out to me that the pin at the end of the steering rod had been renewed. Did you have this done?"

Mr. Chalk shook his head. "Not I," he replied. "I never even noticed that it had been replaced. I've had nothing done to the car since I've had her. She was running perfectly up to the time she was pinched. I only hope she'll be as good when I get her back again. Damn the man who put me to all this trouble, I say!"

"Let's hope the superintendent will run him to earth," remarked Harold.

"I expect he will. He's a blend of the strong silent man and the old British bull-dog, and that always impresses me. But about that pin. The Supremacy people must have put it in. They overhauled the car before they delivered it to me, you know. I tell you what. If you're really interested, you can go and ask them. They'll tell you all about it if you give them my card. They're good people and they know me very well, for I always deal with them. Are you on already? Well, let's go round the corner and have a spot. There's nothing doing in the office this morning."

The consumption of the spot occupied a few minutes, and then Harold, having taken leave of Mr. Chalk, set out for Kingston. He found the premises of the Supremacy Motor Company and asked for the manager, who glanced at Mr. Chalk's card and immediately became communicative.

"Always ready to do anything for a friend of Mr. Chalk's, sir," he said. "He's a very good customer of ours. His car was smashed up in the rally the other day, I hear? Terrible business. Both driver and passenger killed, weren't they? Lucky Mr. Chalk wasn't one of them. That what comes of lending cars to other people."

Harold let this distorted view of the accident pass. Since the manager apparently knew nothing of the theft of the car, there was no point in enlightening him. "I wonder if you could tell me exactly what was done to Mr. Chalk's car before you delivered it to him?" he asked.

"Nothing much — so far as I recollect. We repainted it, I remember, with Comet grey which we got from the Comet people. A demonstration car soon begins to look shabby, you know. I can soon tell you what else we did."

He picked up a file of work sheets and turned them over. "Here we are," he continued. "Comet sport model, 15hp., UQ1754. Purchaser, Mr. Chalk, Byfleet. Repainted. New tyres on back wheels. Set of sparking plugs. Tool kit completed. Cylinders decarbonised. Three new piston rings fitted. Windscreen wiper repaired. Car tested and found correct. That's all."

"You didn't, by any chance, fit a fresh pin to the steering rod, did you?" asked Harold.

The manager shook his head. "We couldn't have done," he replied. "It would have been set down here if we had. Besides, the fitter couldn't have drawn it from the stores without a note. I'll make quite sure, though, if you like. The man who did the job is in the shop now. I'll ask him."

The fitter confirmed the manager's report. He had tested the steering gear at the time of the overhaul, and had found it in perfect order. It had not required a new pin, and he had certainly not fitted one. Harold thanked the manager and returned to Westbourne Terrace, where he informed his employer of the result of his inquiries.

"That is very much what I expected," said Dr. Priestley. "I think that we can take it as definitely proved that the Supremacy Motor Company did not fit a new pin. They painted the car, it appears, and presumably did so after the overhaul. In that case, even had they fitted a new pin, the head would have been the same colour as the rest of the chassis. We must accept Mr. Chalk's statement that he did not fit it subsequently.

"In that case, the new pin must have been fitted between the time when the car was stolen and the time when the Comet Company's engineer examined it. Why was this done if the steering gear was in perfect order when the car passed out of Mr. Chalk's possession? That is the first question. The second is, what is the exact function of this pin? Perhaps you can explain it?"

"I think so, sir. The pin connects the steering rod, which is actuated by the steering wheel, to the front wheels of the car. It is a connecting link between the driver's hands and the pivoting motion of those wheels."

"And if the pin were removed?"

"The driver would be unable to steer the car, sir. He might revolve the steering wheel, but the motion would not be communicated to the front wheels of the car, which would be free to pivot as they pleased."

"That is what I imagined. And yet, the opportunity — Well, well, we shall see."

Dr. Priestley and Harold reached the Imperial Hotel at Moorchester about six o clock that evening. Bob Weldon had already arrived and, after a few words with the professor, he took the opportunity of drawing Harold aside. "Richard's coming down later," he said. "What's on, exactly? I didn't care to ask outright before your old man."

Harold glanced round to see that he could not be overheard before he replied. "What he means to do, I don't know. But he's got some plan of his own on. He wouldn't tell Hanslet where he was going. His latest theory is that Lessingham was murdered, and I think he wants to find out how it was done."

Bob whistled softly. "Murdered, eh!" he exclaimed. "What will our old friend Inspector Harraway say to that, I wonder? Has the professor broken this to Superintendent Hanslet?"

"Yes, last night. Hanslet didn't know what to make of it, quite. He's had news that Lessingham's own car has been found somewhere in Somerset, and he's gone down to have a look-see."

"While we make sensational discoveries down here. I say we, because I gather I'm to be made use of? The professor wouldn't have suggested my joining the party for the sake of my good looks."

"Oh, you'll be made use of, all right, and the Armstrong, too, I expect. Come over here and let's have a cocktail, and I'll tell you what I know of the old boy's theory."

Just before dinner, they were joined by Dr. Priestley, and half-way through that meal Richard arrived. Between them they made a merry party, for Dr. Priestley could get on perfectly well with younger men when he chose. But he steered the conversation away from the object of this meeting, and it was not until after ten o'clock, when the lounge began to empty, that any mention was made of Lessingham or even of the rally.

And then it was Dr. Priestley who introduced the subject. He did so abruptly, after a glance at the clock. "It was about this time that Lessingham drove up to the control," he said. "I should like to inspect the place where competitors' cars were parked. Will one of you show me the way?"

They all rose and Bob led the way. "The room used by the control officials was there," he said, pointing to the farther comer of the lounge. "We came in by a side door, I remember. That must be it."

They passed through the door, and found themselves on a wide gravel sweep, with a high wall round two sides of it. There were no lamp posts within this enclosure, which was illuminated only by the light that filtered through the curtained windows of the hotel on one side and the reflection of the lights of the town on the other. Three or four cars, with their lights extinguished, were ranged against one side, but until Dr. Priestley's eyes had accustomed themselves to the gloom, he did not catch sight of them.

"Looks much the same as when we turned up that morning, doesn't it?" remarked Bob.

"I haven't the least recollection of what the place looked like," replied Richard. "I was walking in my sleep, I believe. But it must have been pretty busy earlier in the night. There's not room for a lot of cars at a time."

"You could get a hundred in, I daresay, if you parked them carefully," said Bob. "But with fellows coming and going every moment, there must have been a bit of confusion. The R.A.C man on duty couldn't possibly look after them all. I expect he had his work cut out to keep the entrance clear, as it was."

Dr. Priestley listened to this conversation with interest. He could well imagine the scene. Cars scattered all over the enclosure, their drivers and passengers, weary with driving and lack of sleep, moving among them like the figures of a dream. Other cars coming and going, their lights dazzling the already bewildered throng. The harassed R.A.C man, hurriedly giving directions, holding up a stream of arriving cars in order to let a competitor out. And over all a confusion of light and darkness, in which nothing could be distinctly discerned.

"This is no doubt where the substitution took place," he said, after a long pause.

Bob, who had heard this theory from Harold, nodded approvingly. But to Richard it came as news. "By jove! I'll bet you're right!" he exclaimed. "It would have been the easiest thing in the world. I don't believe I should have noticed if someone had exchanged Bob's Armstrong for an old Ford. Until I began to drive, of course. But in this case they were exactly similar. Nobody could possibly have noticed the difference."

Dr. Priestley smiled. "We seem to be in agreement on that point," he said. "Suppose we return to the lounge and discuss the various points involved?"

When they had found a quiet corner, the professor gave a detailed explanation of his theory, for the benefit of Bob and Richard. "Mr. Chalk's car was stolen about midnight on the Tuesday," he continued. "There seems to be no doubt about that. If we are correct in our assumption that the substitution took place here, the thief had this car in his possession for twenty-four hours. Where is it likely to have been during that time?"

"He wouldn't have shown himself with it more than he could help in daylight, sir," replied Bob. "He must have known that Mr. Chalk would discover his loss very shortly and notify the police. For the same reason, he wouldn't run it into any public garage."

"From the mileage records, he didn't go far out of the direct road between here and Denham," remarked Richard. "The point is, where did he hide the car during Wednesday? If I had been in his shoes, I should have got as far as possible away from Denham at once."

"There are one or two stretches of wooded country on the road, not far from here," Bob suggested. "I remember passing through them after we had got clear of the fog that night. They looked pretty well deserted. I daresay that there are clearings in them in which a car could be hidden for a day at least."

"An excellent suggestion, Mr. Weldon," said Dr. Priestley approvingly. "I wonder if you would be so good as to drive us along that road to-morrow? If so, we might form ourselves into a party of exploration."

"I'll drive you anywhere you like, sir," replied Bob readily. "It'll be like old days at Clayport."

"Only my deceased uncle no longer figures in the picture," murmured Richard.

Dr. Priestley smiled. "I am much obliged to you, Mr. Weldon," he said. "I will take you at your word. I should like first to explore the road between here and Westernham. Shall we make an early start tomorrow — say at nine o'clock?"

91

CHAPTER XIII

ON the following morning, punctually at nine o'clock, the party left the hotel in Bob's Armstrong-Siddeley. Bob was driving, with Dr, Priestley beside him, map in hand.

As they took the road to Westernham, Bob described the incidents of the morning of the rally. "I was pretty well at the end of my tether, as Harold will tell you, sir. But I do just remember where it was that we first saw the red tail light of the Comet in front of us. I'll show you when we come to it."

They drove on in silence for some miles, Dr. Priestley following the road on his map. "It was just about here, wasn't it, Harold?" he asked.

"Yes, that's right," replied Harold from the back of the car. "I remember that belt of trees on the right."

"Thank you, Mr. Weldon," said Dr. Priestley. "Now, will you do exactly as you did that morning, pulling up exactly in the same place as you did then?"

Bob began to slow up. "That's the place where the Comet was," he said, after a few seconds. "You can still see where the edge of the ditch is broken away. I kept over to my left and pulled up by the side of the road. I believe this is the spot to an inch."

He stopped the car a yard or two in advance of the mark in the ditch. "Then we all got out and ran across to the Comet," he continued. "It was still pitch dark, and we had to use a torch to see what we were doing."

"Did any of you notice if there were marks of tyres on the road, beyond where the two cars were stopped?" asked Dr. Priestley.

Silence followed this question till Bob spoke, half apologetically. "I don't think anybody thought of looking, sir — we were too concerned with what had happened to Lessingham and his passenger to think of anything else. I'll admit that while the other two had gone on to fetch the police, I examined the tracks of the Comet. But, of course, they were behind the two cars. It never occurred to me to look in front of them."

"Perhaps if you had looked, you would have made an interesting discovery," remarked Dr. Priestley. "The road is fairly wide here, it appears. Would it be possible to turn a car in it without much difficulty?"

"Easily enough, sir. We turned this car when we went with the policeman to the White Hart, and Doctor Mason turned his."

Dr. Priestley nodded. He took a pencil from his pocket and made a cross on the map at the point where they stood. "I should like you to look at this map, if you will, Mr. Weldon," he said. "The scale is one inch to a mile. Approximately three miles ahead of us lies Westernham. Half a mile from here, in the Westernham direction, there is a road branching off to the left, which leads to a road running parallel with this, rather over a mile away. Do you know that parallel road?"

"I've driven over it once or twice, sir. You get a magnificent view from it, looking over towards the sea. If you look at the map, you'll see a cross-roads two or three miles out of Moorchester. We passed that as we came along. It was where the R.A.C scout was standing, if you remember. If we had turned to the left there, we should have come out on the parallel road, which runs along the crest of the ridge. I expect we can see it from here, if we get out of the car."

They got out and Dr. Priestley, looking southwards, saw a line of low hills before him. Upon the skyline, clearly outlined against the clouds, was the silhouette of a horse and cart, slowly plodding its way along.

"That cart's on the road you mean, sir. It's not a bad road, but it isn't much used now, except for farm traffic. I believe it was the high road once, before this one was made; but it's abominably steep in places, and the surface is none too good."

"I noticed as we were driving here that the ridge is visible nearly all the way from Moorchester. Does the old road run along the crest of it for the whole of that distance?"

"Practically. It dips here and there, but it always comes up again."

Once more Dr. Priestley studied his map thoughtfully. "Besides the cross roads which you mentioned and the side road which I pointed out, there are two roads, or, rather, lanes, connecting the two roads," he said, apparently to himself. "A better locality for the purpose could not have been chosen. But how could he have foreseen —"

He broke off suddenly and turned to Bob. "Would it be possible for us to return to Moorchester by the old road?" he asked.

"Yes — rather," replied Bob. "We've only got to take that cross road you pointed out, half a mile farther on. Have you seen all you want to here, sir?"

"For the present, yes." Dr. Priestley spoke abruptly, as though his mind was fixed upon something else. He stared for a moment at the mark on the edge of the ditch where the Comet had broken it away. Then he walked to the front of the Armstrong and contemplated it silently.

"What do you suppose your old man has got into his head now?" Richard whispered to Harold, who was sitting beside him in the back of the car.

"If you could tell that by looking at him, you'd be a cleverer man than most," replied Harold, in the same tone. "He'll tell us when he thinks fit, and until then it's no good guessing."

At last Dr. Priestley re-entered the car, and they set off again. Instead of proceeding into Westernham, they took the turning to the left, which proved to be a narrow lane, leading steeply to the high ground. Here they reached the old road, along which they had seen from below the horse and cart making its way. At the junction of the roads Bob turned the bonnet of the Armstrong towards Moorchester.

They were now on the crest of the ridge, with an extensive panorama spread out on either side of them. To their right the downs fell away gradually, fold after fold, with glimpses of the sea beyond them. To the left was the wide and fertile valley, through which the new road ran. The morning, though overcast, was clear of mist, and every landmark stood clearly revealed.

"A magnificent view, indeed!" exclaimed Dr. Priestley. "The more slowly you drive, the more I shall enjoy it, Mr. Weldon."

"It is a picturesque road, sir, isn't it?" agreed Bob. "Far more interesting than the new road, if one merely wants a run round — but not the sort of road to choose if one is in a hurry, especially at night. It's all steep hills and sharp corners, as you'll see presently. But I'm afraid that the best of the view is on my side, over towards the sea."

"I find that the inland view satisfies all my demands." replied Dr. Priestley. And Harold, catching the note of satisfaction in his voice, knew that from his employer's point of view the morning had not been wasted.

They drove slowly back to Moorchester, where they lunched. Afterwards, in the lounge, Dr. Priestley took out his maps and spread them on a table. "You will recall your conversation yesterday evening, Mr. Weldon," he began, in the formal style which never entirely deserted him. "I understood you to say that as you approached this town you noticed certain desolate stretches of country where a car might be hidden. Could you point them out to me on the map?"

Bob leaned over the map and studied it doubtfully. "To tell you the truth, sir, I'm not altogether sure which road we got here by. About a hundred miles from here we ran into fog, as I expect Harold has told you, and lost our way completely. It wasn't until we saw a signpost that we had any idea where we were going, and after that we trusted to them entirely."

"How do you explain the apparent fact that Lessingham was not delayed by this fog?" asked Dr. Priestley.

"Easily enough, sir. He may have reached here before the fog came on. He was three hours and a half ahead of us at Droitwich, the previous control. Or he may have taken a different route — there are at least a dozen possible ones — and so escaped it."

"I see," said Dr. Priestley.

Bob turned once more to the map, exploring the various roads into Moorchester. "I believe I've got it!" he exclaimed after a few moments. "I seem to remember that name, Hedgeworth, don't you, Harold? Didn't you spot it on one of those yellow A.A. signs as we came through?"

"I believe I do, now that you mention it," replied Harold. "About twenty miles out of here, isn't it?"

"That's right," replied Bob, pointing to the map with the stem of his pipe. "This is the road we must have come in by, sir. And it must have been soon after passing Hedgeworth that we struck that patch of wooded country."

Dr. Priestley produced his map measurer. "I make the distance between Denham and Hedgeworth sixty-seven miles," he said. "The thief would have no difficulty in reaching that point before daylight on Wednesday morning. If the theft took place about midnight his journey would have been accomplished during the quietest time of the night. He had probably reconnoitred his route beforehand, with the aid of a map. By the way, were any maps found in the car which Lessingham was driving?"

"By jove, sir, now I come to think of it, there weren't," exclaimed Bob. "I'm quite sure of that. I examined the car pretty carefully twice — first just after the accident when I was waiting for the others to come back from Westernham, and again with Inspector Harraway at the Central Garage. The route book was there, but no maps. Yet Lessingham would never have started on the rally without taking maps with him."

"Looks as if Homer had nodded," remarked Richard. "In other words, the thief forgot to take them from Lessingham's car and put them in Chalk's when he made the substitution."

"That is possible, but not altogether probable," said Dr. Priestley. "A suitcase belonging to Lessingham was, I am told, found in Mr. Chalk's car. It is unlikely that the thief would have overlooked the maps. Their absence might have aroused Lessingham's suspicions. A small point, but one that may prove to be of definite importance."

Dr. Priestley paused and then continued abruptly. "Since you think that you will be able to retrace your route, Mr. Weldon, shall we start? We have not too many hours of daylight before us."

With Bob at the wheel, the Armstrong set out once more on a voyage of exploration. Fifteen miles or so from Moorchester they came to a tract of country, apparently very sparsely inhabited. The road here was un-fenced, and beside it here and there were patches of litter and scattered ashes, probably marking the halting places of gipsy caravans. For the most part, the country was open moorland, heather, bracken and a few scattered birches. But every now and then it was broken by fairly big woods, through several of which the road took its way.

In the centre of the first of these which they entered, Bob, by Dr. Priestley's direction, stopped the car and they all got out. "I do not for a moment anticipate that we shall find actual evidence of a car having been concealed," said the professor. "It is now more than a week since we believe this to have occurred, and all traces are probably by this time obliterated. It will be sufficient if we can demonstrate the possibility of a car remaining unobserved during a whole day."

They scattered and explored the wood. Between the trees ran several rough tracks, most of which a car could have negotiated without much difficulty. These they examined, but without forming any very definite conclusions. It seemed that to hide a car on any of them would be to run risk of its discovery.

They went on to the next wood, which they explored with very similar results. The third looked more promising. The trees were considerably denser and the spaces between them filled with dense undergrowth. And all at once they heard a shout from Richard, who had gone by himself up a more than usually winding track.

Dr. Priestley was the first to join him. About a hundred yards from the road, the track ended in the centre of a dense thicket, with a clearing in it, perhaps twenty feet across. Richard stood on the edge of this clearing, the surface of which was littered with recently severed pine branches.

"This is the place, sure enough, sir!" exclaimed Richard, as Dr. Priestley came up. "There are no tyre-tracks, it's true, but the ground's too springy for them to last all this time. But look at those branches! I'll bet he drove the car in here, then, to make quite sure, camouflaged it, like we did guns in the war."

"I believe you are right, Mr. Gateman," replied Dr. Priestley approvingly. "It might be worth while to search for actual evidence."

The others had by this time joined them. They all set to work to pick up the branches and lay them carefully aside. Then they began a careful search among the grass and dead leaves which thickly carpeted the clearing. This time the credit of discovery fell to Harold. A metal object almost concealed by leaves caught his eye. He stooped and picked it up. It was a double-ended spanner upon which a thin layer of red rust had begun to form. And, stamped upon the flat of the tool were the words, "Comet Cars."

"Well done, my boy!" exclaimed Dr. Priestley. "Though perhaps not actual evidence, the discovery of this spanner is highly significant. It is almost too much to expect further indications, but perhaps we had better continue our search."

But, though they spent another half-hour in the clearing, they found nothing more. Dr. Priestley took charge of the spanner and they drove back to Moorchester.

"That ought to be evidence enough, even for you, sir," remarked Bob, as they sat in the lounge of the hotel before dinner. "It's just as you supposed. The thief drove

Mr. Chalk's car to the wood on Tuesday night, left it there till after dark on Wednesday, and then drove on here. But it was careless of him to leave that spanner behind."

"Careless?" replied Dr. Priestley, with a faint smile. "Perhaps. Yet, after all, from the thief's point of view, the spanner is not a very damaging discovery. It forms no clue to his identity. In fact, can you draw any deductions from it?"

"Only that he left the car in that particular spot, sir," replied Bob. "But surely that is something?"

"Not very much, I am afraid," said Dr. Priestley. "It is most unlikely that he was seen and recognised. But perhaps the spanner may suggest something to us, after all. How did it come to be where we found it? Did it drop from the car accidentally?"

Harold was the first to reply to this question. "Hardly, I should think, sir. When I was at the Comet works I noticed that the tool kit was carried in a special recess behind the driver's seat. The cushion has to be removed to get at it."

"Then the bold bandit who pinched the car must have had it out for something. He probably wanted to make some adjustment or other."

"It would be interesting to know what that adjustment was," said Dr. Priestley quietly. "Shall we go in to dinner?"

Rather to Bob's surprise, he discovered during dinner that the investigations were not over for the day. "I hope that you will not think that I am imposing on your kindness, Mr. Weldon," said Dr. Priestley, during a pause in the conversation. "You have shown me the neighbourhood of the accident by day, but I should like to see it again under conditions resembling those which obtained when the accident occurred. By the time that we have finished dinner it will be quite dark. Would it be troubling you too much to drive to the spot again, then?"

Bob agreed to this readily enough. Though he had no idea what was in the professor's mind, he knew very well that he would not have made the request without some definite object in view. So, shortly after nine o'clock they set out once more in the faithful Armstrong. But, when they reached the cross-roads where, during the daytime, the R.A.C scout was stationed. Bob received another surprise.

"I think that we will go by the old road, if you have no objection," said Dr Priestley. "I presume that it is possible to negotiate it by night?"

"Oh, yes, rather," replied Bob. "It'll take us a bit longer — that's all. But we'll go that way if you prefer it, sir."

They followed the old road, with its curves and sudden gradients, until they reached a point which Dr. Priestley judged to be roughly level with the spot on the new road where the accident had taken place. Here he stopped the car. "Now, Mr. Weldon, I am going to ask you to help me with an experiment. I want you and Mr. Gateman to drive back towards Moorchester, leaving Harold here with me. Take the first convenient turning, leading on the new road, which you come to. When you reach the new road, turn towards Westernham. Drive as rapidly as possible in that direction, and when you come to the scene of the accident stop the car, at the same time switching off your headlights. Wait there till Harold joins you, and when he reaches the car, switch on your headlights again for a moment."

Bob and Richard set off without asking unnecessary questions. Dr. Priestley and Harold, waiting by the roadside, saw the tail light of the Armstrong recede into the distance and disappear. Beneath them, on the new road all was darkness. There seemed to be little traffic upon it after nightfall. Then, as they watched, a glare appeared in the distance towards Moorchester.

"That is probably Mr. Weldon's car," remarked Dr. Priestley. "When I give the word, I want you to make your way to it as fast as you can. It is all open downland between here and the new road. But you had better take this torch with you in case you fall."

The glare rapidly increased and resolved itself into the beam from a pair of powerful headlights. They saw the trees beside the lower road light up one by one as the car advanced, to plunge into sudden obscurity again as it passed. The twin cones of light swept on until, as they watched, their speed decreased. Then, suddenly, they vanished.

Dr. Priestley was standing with his watch in his hand, and a second torch directed upon the dial. "Off you go, my boy," he said.

Harold set off across country For a while the professor could hear his footsteps and see the wavering beam of the torch on the ground in front of him. Then he lost them both. He paced up and down restlessly to keep himself warm. The minutes passed, the hands of the watch crept on. Ten minutes, quarter of an hour. And then at last the beam of light in the valley below reappeared for an instant. It had taken Harold seventeen minutes to reach the car.

Dr. Priestley waited where he was until the Armstrong reached the spot. As it stopped, Bob opened the door for him to get in. "All right, sir?" he asked.

"Excellent!" replied Dr. Priestley as he climbed into his seat. "We can now return to Moorchester by any route you please, Mr. Weldon."

Once back in the hotel, Dr. Priestley condescended to explain his experiment to his puzzled audience. "We have, I believe, reconstructed the events of the morning of the accident," he said. "I have reasons for believing that the thief, or the murderer, as I now feel justified in calling him, knew that the accident would take place shortly after Lessingham left Moorchester. I also believe that it was part of his plan to be on the spot as soon as possible after it had taken place.

"But, until this morning, I was faced with a difficulty. He did not know when the accident would take place, since he could not tell exactly when Lessingham would start from the control. Nor, I think, could he forecast the exact spot on the road where Lessingham's car would come to a stop. How, then, could he arrange to be present?

"The topography of the neighbourhood gave me the clue. I saw this morning that, from the old road, practically the whole of the new road from Moorchester to Westernham was visible. I verified this evening that the headlights of a car travelling along the new road would be plainly visible from a car following a parallel route on the old road. The murderer, I have no doubt, actually followed this parallel route in Lessingham's own car."

"But how could he tell that the headlights were those of the car Lessingham was driving, sir?" asked Richard. "They might have been those of any of the competing cars."

"An interesting point, Mr. Gateman," replied Dr. Priestley. "Under normal circumstances, the car that Lessingham was driving would have been the last to leave the Moorchester control. It was only the accident of the fog that caused you to be behind him. I feel sure that the murderer was intimately acquainted with Lessingham's schedule and intentions. Had you been only a few minutes earlier, I think that by now we should be aware of his methods and possibly his identity."

"By his methods, I suppose you mean the way he brought the accident about, sir?" remarked Bob. "That beats me, I must confess, especially if be was on the old road all the time."

"I am not yet prepared to explain his methods in detail," replied Dr. Priestley. "But I am becoming more and more convinced that they involved the necessity of his being on the spot as soon as possible after the accident occurred. If he had been where Harold and I stood this evening, he would have seen the sudden extinguishing of the lights of the car which Lessingham was driving and possibly heard the crash.

"It took Harold, who is at least of average activity, seventeen minutes to reach you. Now Lessingham cannot have been much more than half an hour ahead of you, as we know from his route-book. If the murderer had proceeded on foot to the wrecked car, he had only a quarter of an hour to do what he had to do before you arrived on the scene. I do not think that he could have accomplished it in the time.

"It seems more probable that he reached the spot by way of the connecting lane which we used this morning in Lessingham's own car. In that case, he would have approached the scene of the accident from the Westernham direction and would have reached it in considerably less time than seventeen minutes. In this case, the tracks of his car must have been visible on the Westernham side of the accident when you arrived."

"Dash it, I wish I'd thought of looking in that direction!" exclaimed Bob regretfully.

"And I must have driven clean over those tracks when I went to rouse up Sergeant Showerby!" chorussed Richard. "You must think that we've none of us got any eyes in our heads, sir. The only possible excuse is that we were all more than half asleep at the time."

"You may comfort yourselves with the reflection that Sergeant Showerby, whose business it was, did not think of looking for tracks in the Westernham direction," replied Dr. Priestley cheerfully. "Besides, but for such oversights, the task of the investigator would become so ridiculously easy as to lose all interest."

CHAPTER XIV

ON the day of Dr. Priestley's departure for Moorchester, Superintendent Hanslet took a morning train from Paddington. He alighted at the nearest station to Slowford, where he was met by the local superintendent, who introduced himself at once.

"My name is Drake," he said. "I'm very glad to have the honour of making your acquaintance, Mr. Hanslet. I've got a car outside. Shall we drive over to Slowford straight away?"

Hanslet agreed and they set off. On the way, Drake described the finding of the car. "It was a party of gipsies who came upon it," he said. "As you'll see when we get there, the quarry is disused, and has been for years. The only people who go near it now are these gipsies, who camp there for a night sometimes. Didicais, the country people call them about here, and they're fairly honest if they think there's any chance of being found out.

"On Monday afternoon one of the gipsies came to the constable stationed at Slowford and told him that he had found a wrecked car in the quarry. He was certain it wasn't there on the previous Thursday morning, for he had been camping in the quarry on the Wednesday night and had left next morning. The constable went along and looked at the car, then reported the make and registration number to me. I saw that these agreed with the particulars you had circulated, and communicated with you at once. The car has been left just as it was found, except that I've had a few loose bits lying around put in a place of safety."

"I'm very much obliged to you, Mr. Drake. No signs of the driver, I suppose?"

"Not a trace. I fancy he made himself scarce. It's my idea that the car was deliberately wrecked, but you'll be able to judge for yourself."

They reached the quarry, which had at one time been cut out of the side of a steep hill. All that could be seen from the road was a sheer wall of rock, with a few stunted shrubs growing in the crevices, rising to about a hundred feet or more. The track that had once led to the quarry was now overgrown. The brambles had encroached upon it and it was obviously too narrow for the passage of the car. Hanslet and Drake dismounted and pursued their way on foot.

"The car you're taking me to see didn't come in this way, I suppose?" asked Hanslet.

"No, nothing comes along here now but gipsy vans," replied the other. "The car came a much shorter way than this. You'll see in a moment. There it is!"

They had come to an end of the pathway and the floor of the quarry, or so much of it as was free from undergrowth, lay open before them. At the farther side, close to the old working face, lay a car, so battered as to be hardly recognisable. But at the first glance Hanslet noticed the now familiar Comet grey.

It required no explanation from Drake to show him what had happened. The car had fallen from the top of the face and had been utterly wrecked on reaching the hard ground below. The body had been wrenched clean off the chassis and lay torn and bent a few yards from it. The chassis was buckled, the front axle with the wheels had been torn off and the back axle was fractured.

"I don't profess to know a lot about cars," said Hanslet thoughtfully, as he gazed at the wreck. "But I should say that lot's only fit for the scrap-heap. Driven over the edge, eh?"

"That's about it," replied Drake. "There's a lane runs along the top, about fifty yards back from the edge. There's no fence to the lane, and between it and the quarry there's a strip of rough grass. You can still see the marks of the wheels where the car was driven over this grass. We'll go and have a look, later."

"Driven — not pushed?" Hanslet inquired.

"Yes, driven, I think. When you come to examine the chassis, you'll see that the car is still in second gear. That's what makes me pretty certain that it was deliberately wrecked. It looks to me as if the driver had got her into second, then jumped out and ran beside her, holding the steering wheel. He could have guided her to the edge that way easily enough."

"I expect you're right. He wanted to get rid of her pretty badly, and thought this was a nice secluded spot to dump her in, I suppose. I'd better verify the numbers, so as to make sure."

Very gingerly he made his way among the nettles into which the car had fallen, swearing beneath his breath as he did so. The number-plates, though crumpled up, could still be deciphered. They bore the registration number allotted to Lessingham — ZV9003. During his visit to the Comet works, Hanslet had learned where to look for the engine and chassis numbers. These he found to be 63208 and 431722 respectively.

"That's the car I was looking for, all right," he said, as he made his way back to where Drake was standing. "It ought to be sent up to London for expert examination, I suppose, but it's going to be a devil of a job to get it out of here. What do you say, Mr. Drake?"

"There's a firm of engineers not far from here," replied Drake, "They would be able to tackle the job, I expect. I'll get them to come and have a look at it, if you like."

"I wish you would. You can ring me up when you've had their report. Now then, what about going round and looking at the top? I'd like to see where the car went over."

They made their way out of the quarry and back to Drake's car. A circuit of half a mile or so brought them to the lane above the quarry. Here Drake stopped the car and they got out. "There you are," he said. "The tracks are still quite plain."

"They couldn't be plainer," Hanslet agreed. The marks of two pairs of wheels curved off the lane and ran over the grass beside it towards the edge of the quarry. Hanslet followed them to the spot where they ended abruptly. Peering over the edge, he could see the wreck of the car directly beneath him.

"No doubt about that," he said. Then he stood up and looked about him. From the slope of the hill on which he stood, he could see field after field stretching into the distance. The only sign of human habitation was a grey stone farmhouse, about a mile distance. Rows of sheds, lines of wire netting and a quantity of various-coloured fowls, suggested the use to which it was put.

"Not exactly over-populated round about here, is it?" remarked Hanslet. "Not a bad place to choose to smash up a car — especially after dark — if one didn't want to be seen. Did you think of asking the folk in the poultry farm over there if they'd seen or heard anything?"

"Yes, I went and questioned them, but they knew nothing about it. Hadn't seen or heard anything, they told me."

"What sort of people are they? Some of these country folk wouldn't notice anything if a thunderbolt was to fall at their feet."

"They aren't the ordinary type of country folk. They're a youngish couple who have gone in for poultry farming as a living. I believe he was a naval officer; you may have noticed that naval officers have a passion for that sort of thing."

"I shan't go in for poultry when I retire," said Hanslet. "I hate the things — they haven't as much intelligence as the average bench of magistrates — and that's saying a good deal. Do these folks over there make a good thing out of it?"

"They're not doing as well as they expected when they came here, I fancy. In fact, I believe that they have been pretty hard put to it lately. The place is mortgaged, I believe, and they've been trying to raise money for some time. At least that's what the local constable told me. Talking about the local constable, would you care to run over to his place? That's where the loose stuff I told you about has been put."

They drove to the little village of Slowford, a couple of miles or so distant, and stopped at the policeman's cottage. Here, in an outhouse, Hanslet was shown a miscellaneous collection of debris, broken lamps, the cushions from the seats, a jack, part of a tool kit, and various other accessories from the car. He looked them over and arranged for them to be sent up to London with the wreckage of the car. Then Drake drove him back to the station, where he caught a train to Paddington.

It was after six o'clock when he reached Scotland Yard, to find a message on his desk that Mr. Farrant had rung him up and would like to see him at his convenience. Hanslet glanced at the clock. "Too late this evening," he muttered. "Farrant will have left his office by now. I'll look round and see him in the morning. It can't be very urgent."

About eleven o'clock on the following morning he called on the solicitor. Mr. Farrant received him with his habitual old-fashioned courtesy. "I am sorry that you have had the trouble of coming all this way. Superintendent," he said; "but perhaps you will be interested to hear that I have had an answer to my advertisement."

"Your advertisement?" replied Hanslet, rather blankly. "Oh, yes, I know — about Lessingham's next of kin. Have you found him?"

"I had a visit yesterday from a lady who claims to be a distant relation of my late client. I am verifying the particulars which she gave me and, if they prove to be correct, I shall advise her to apply for letters of administration of Mr. Lessingham's estate."

"Which means, I suppose, that she'll become his heir. But what about that will of Mr. Purvis's which you mentioned to me?"

"It will be for the executors under that will to oppose this lady's application. The courts will then have to decide the question of priority of death. It will prove, I imagine, a very puzzling and intricate case."

The professional relish with which the solicitor spoke was not lost upon Hanslet. There would be some pretty fat pickings for Mr. Farrant, he thought. "It seems a difficult point to decide," he said. "Who is the lady, by the way?"

"Her name is Mrs. Ellingwood. She was Miss Joan Singer, and her mother and Mr. Lessingham's were cousins. Some years ago she married a naval officer, Lieutenant Ellingwood, who has since retired."

Hanslet felt a faint quickening of his interest. Somebody had been talking to him about retired naval officers quite recently. Who was it? Why, Drake, of course, as they were standing above the quarry. "Where do they live?" he asked.

The solicitor turned to a pad which lay on his desk. "The address that Mrs. Ellingwood gave me was, Highcroft Poultry Farm, Slowford, Somerset," he replied.

Fortunately for Hanslet, the solicitor was somewhat short-sighted and did not notice his visitor's sudden start. "There is no reason to doubt Mrs. Ellingwood's statement," he continued. "She told me that although she had herself not seen Mr.

Lessingham for many years — since they were both children, in fact — her husband had met him comparatively recently, not more than three weeks ago," he said.

This was getting more and more interesting. But Hanslet guessed that any display of inquisitiveness on his part would probably arouse the solicitor's suspicions. "Indeed," he said politely. "Mr. Ellingwood would naturally call upon his wife's relations if he happened to be in London."

"From what Mrs. Ellingwood let drop, I gather that her husband's visit to Mr. Lessingham was with a definite object," the solicitor replied confidentially. "It seems that Mr and Mrs. Ellingwood own this poultry farm in Somersetshire, and that they require capital for extensions. Mr. Ellingwood put a proposition before Mr. Lessingham, but apparently nothing was settled then. A further meeting was to take place. I think that Mrs. Ellingwood intended to see Mr. Lessingham herself.

"Mrs. Ellingwood told me that they knew nothing of Mr. Lessingham's death until they saw my advertisement. Her husband had been away for a few days, and she said she had not had time to read the papers. In fact, it was her husband who saw the advertisement, the day after his return home, and they decided that Mrs. Ellingwood, as the claimant, had better come and see me at once."

Hanslet carefully refrained from asking questions. He had heard enough to give him ample food for thought for the present. "I'm glad that you have found the next of kin, Mr. Farrant." he said carelessly, as he took his leave of the solicitor. "You'll keep me in touch with the developments, won't you?"

From Bedford Row he went straight to Cawdor Street. Orchard opened the door to him and greeted him respectfully. Hanslet stared hard at him for a moment, but could detect no signs of uneasiness in his manner. "Look here, Orchard," he said abruptly. "Do you know a gentleman by the name of Mr. Ellingwood?"

The name seemed to produce no particular impression on Orchard. "I can't say that I know the gentleman, sir," he replied. "So far as I am aware, he has called here once. That was about three weeks ago."

"He was a friend of Mr. Lessingham's, then?"

"Well, hardly that, sir. When I took his name into Mr. Lessingham, he said he had never heard of it, but he said he would see him, sir, just the same. Mr. Ellingwood stayed quite a long time — a couple of hours at least. Mr. Lessingham told me afterwards that Mrs. Ellingwood was a distant connection of his whom he hadn't seen for years, sir."

"I see. Do you know what their conversation was about?"

"Mr. Lessingham did not tell me, sir. But, shortly before Mr. Ellingwood left, Mr. Lessingham rang for me to get them drinks. While I was in the room, sir, they were looking at maps and talking about the rally. I heard Mr. Lessingham tell Mr. Ellingwood that he had entered for it, and that if he liked, Mr. Ellingwood could go with him as his passenger and second driver. Mr. Purvis had not come home to England then, sir."

"And Mr. Lessingham hadn't thought of George Love then, eh?" asked Hanslet swiftly.

"Evidently not, sir," replied Orchard, without a trace of embarrassment.

The superintendent left Cawdor Street and returned to Scotland Yard, where he retired to his own room to think. The information which he had picked up that morning inclined him to the opinion that Dr. Priestley's theory that Lessingham had been murdered was not so far-fetched after all. Putting aside the improbability of such a thing, Hanslet's difficulty had been to assign a motive for the crime. And now, most unexpectedly, a motive was beginning to emerge.

Here were the Ellingwoods, in need of money — more desperately in need, probably, than had yet transpired. They had approached Lessingham, perhaps as a last resort, in the hope that the ties of blood, however remote, would prove an inducement to him to help them. According to Mr. Farrant, a meeting between Lessingham and Mrs. Ellingwood had been arranged.

And here the superintendent's mind went off at a tangent. Was it possible that that meeting was to have taken place at Torquay? Was Mrs. Ellingwood the sender of that mysterious telegram? If so, how had it come to be handed in at South Kensington, and why had Orchard so obviously lied about it? These were matters that would bear looking into

But to return to this matter of motive. The result of Ellingwood's interview may not have been very promising, or it may have occurred to him that the surest way out of his difficulties would be for his wife to inherit Lessingham's money. But this would involve Lessingham dying intestate. Even so, Purvis, not Mrs. Ellingwood, would be his heir.

Had Ellingwood discovered that Lessingham had not made a will and that Purvis was to accompany him on the rally? Not at that single interview at Cawdor Street, surely. But the two men might have met subsequently, at one of the night clubs frequented by Lessingham, for instance. Probably Ellingwood had made it his business to find out everything he could.

And from the first, according to Orchard, who, on this occasion at least, seemed to have been telling the truth, Ellingwood had known all about the rally. Probably Lessingham had discussed with him the route he should take. In that case, Ellingwood would have known of his intention of stopping for a few hours at Moorchester. So would Mrs. Ellingwood, for that matter. But was she a party to her husband's schemes? The telegram, if indeed she had sent it, would seem to suggest not.

The more Hanslet considered the theory of Ellingwood having been the murderer, not only of Lessingham, but of Purvis as well, the more plausible it seemed to him.

How should anybody else have known of that particular quarry? On the other hand, how convenient it was for Ellingwood's purpose. But for the gipsies, the chances were that the car would never have been found. Perhaps Ellingwood had intended in the course of time to dissect it, as a surgeon dissects a body, and to bury the pieces.

There were objections, of course, as there always must be to any theory. For the present the superintendent was not worrying about the way in which the apparent accident had been engineered. He felt pretty certain that Dr. Priestley would be able to explain this, sooner or later. But it was rather difficult to understand how Ellingwood knew exactly where to lay his hands upon Mr. Chalk's car. No doubt that would be discovered by careful investigation.

Investigation — that was the thing. But there was precious little to go upon as yet. The first thing to do was clearly to find out full particulars of the Ellingwoods' movements during the past three weeks. That was more or less in the nature of routine work, which would be delegated to subordinates. Drake seemed a good fellow; he would lend a hand without asking too many questions.

But there was one thing that Hanslet determined to see to himself. He put a call through to an office in Fleet Street, and in a very short time, an alert-looking young man was seated in the superintendent's room, note-book in hand. The result of this interview was that the newspapers on the following day contained an inconspicuous paragraph.

"In connection with the motor car accident on March 3rd near Westernham, resulting in the loss of two lives, the police are anxious to get into touch with the sender of a telegram to Mr. Aubrey Lessingham, the driver of the car involved. The telegram was addressed "Lessingham, Imperial Hotel, Moorchester", and was handed in at South Kensington Post Office at 6.12 pm on March 2nd. Information should be given to Superintendent Hanslet, New Scotland Yard, London, or to any police station."

"That ought to do the trick," said the superintendent to himself, as he read the paragraph. "There's nothing to alarm Mrs. Ellingwood in that, even if she is in the know, which I don't somehow expect she is. Much better than confronting her with the wire and asking her outright if she sent it. That would look as though we had suspicions. If she admits sending it, it will give us an excuse to ask questions about Lessingham, and so of finding out how intimate her husband was with him."

From which it will be seen that Hanslet was beginning to be sure of his line of action. The word 'love' at the end of the telegram had surprised him at first. Would Mrs. Ellingwood who, by her own account, had not seen Lessingham for years, have added this endearment? But perhaps the two had corresponded since her husband's visit! Perhaps they had been fond of one another as children, and she had added the word in memory of old times. The ways of women were incalculable, in the superintendent's experience.

His thoughts reverted to Dr. Priestley. It was a confounded nuisance that he had taken it into his head to disappear at this particular juncture. It was now three days since he had first propounded that astonishing theory of murder, and nothing had been heard of him since. Hanslet had rung up his house every day, to receive the unpromising answer that Dr. Priestley had not yet returned to London.

It was all the more irritating because the superintendent felt that he had been left in the air. The professor had stated definitely that Lessingham had been murdered, but had declined to say how. Hanslet, for his part, had discovered a person who had a clear motive for desiring Lessingham's death. Not only that, but the locality in which Lessingham's car had been discovered pointed unmistakably to that person.

The obvious thing was to correlate these two points of view. The professor could hardly fail to agree that Ellingwood must be his hypothetical murderer. And he might be able to suggest some means of proving it, for so far as the superintendent could see, that was going to prove the difficulty.

Unless Orchard knew and could be frightened into giving the game away. Why had Orchard, who seemed to be as truthful as the average, lied about that telegram? Had he been in league with Ellingwood to murder his master?

So, in a maddening circle, Hanslet's thoughts revolved. He rose angrily from his desk, with the intention of going out to lunch and putting the problem out of his mind for an hour or so.

Just as he was leaving the room, his telephone bell rang. With a muttered oath he turned back and picked up the receiver. "Superintendent Hanslet speaking," he said curtly.

"Hallo, Superintendent!" was the reply. "This is Merefield speaking from Westbourne Terrace. Dr. Priestley would like to know if you can come along at once and have lunch with him?"

An expression of intense relief came over Hanslet's face. "Rather!" he exclaimed. "I'll be with you as soon as a taxi can get me there."

CHAPTER XV

SUPERINTENDENT could not conceal his delight at finding himself once more in the presence of Dr. Priestley. "I'm awfully glad you've got back, Professor!" he exclaimed, as soon as he was well inside the door. "I've got some news for you. I believe I know who it was that was responsible for Lessingham's death."

Dr. Priestley's eyes twinkled. "Indeed?" he replied. "Then my theory has proved to be not so ridiculous as it appeared to you at first sight?"

"I'm sorry if I seemed a bit incredulous that evening. But you must admit, Professor, that you sprang it on me a bit suddenly. As I told you I meant to, I went down to Slowford next day, and there —"

"You will pardon my interrupting you, Superintendent," Dr. Priestley put in quietly. "Lunch is waiting for us. You can give your news in the dining-room."

Dr. Priestley was something of an epicure in his way, and meals at his house in Westbourne Terrace were always excellent and leisurely. Hanslet set to work upon the hors d'oeuvres with gusto. "Had a good time while you were away, Professor?" he asked, as he selected an olive.

"Harold and I have enjoyed a most instructive visit to Moorchester." replied Dr. Priestley. "In the course of it we inspected the spot where Lessingham met with the accident."

Hanslet stared at him, the olive poised upon the point of his fork. "You've been investigating the case for yourself?" he exclaimed. "And all the time I thought you were busy with something else!"

"Hardly investigating the case," replied Dr. Priestley mildly. "Merely testing the possibility of certain theories which I have formed. I will outline the results of my experiments later. I believe that I interrupted you just now. You were going to tell me about your journey to Slowford, I think?"

Thus encouraged, Hanslet launched into a long account of his adventures at Slowford. He followed this up by describing his visit to Mr. Farrant, and the startling information he had obtained there. "Ellingwood's our man, Professor!" he exclaimed in conclusion. "There isn't a doubt of it. The fact that Lessingham's car was found within a mile of that poultry farm of his is enough to damn him without anything else."

"A jury would hardly take that view of the case, I am afraid," Dr. Priestley remarked. "In preparing a case against this Mr. Ellingwood, you would have to explain how he contrived the death of Lessingham and his friend. From the confidence you display in his guilt, I assume that you are prepared to do this?"

Hanslet's face fell perceptibly. "Well, not yet, exactly, Professor," he replied. "As a matter of fact, I don't mind telling you that I was rather counting upon you to help me out there."

Dr. Priestley paused as though choosing his words before he spoke. "I will not disguise from you the object of my visit to Moorchester," he said at last. "I wished to ascertain whether a theory I had formed as to the cause of the accident, as we must continue to term it for the present, could stand the test of actual fact. In the light of the experiments which I carried out, I am now satisfied, up to a point. There remain certain considerations of a technical nature. An actual demonstration would probably throw light upon them."

"This sounds promising, Professor. How can the demonstration be arranged?"

"I was about to suggest that, when we have finished lunch, Harold and I should accompany you to Scotland Yard. If a car and an expert dnver could there be placed at our disposal for a short time, the results would probably be most instructive."

"There won't be any difficulty about that," the superintendent replied readily. "I suppose you won't tell me what you want to do with them? A bit of reconstruction work, eh?"

"I have found by experience that the most certain way to prejudice the success of an experiment is to describe beforehand the results that may be expected from it," replied Dr. Priestley urbanely.

Hanslet did not venture to refer to the matter again until lunch was over and Dr. Priestley had finished his usual cup of coffee. Then, at the latter's suggestion, the three of them entered a taxi and drove to Scotland Yard.

Once there, the superintendent felt rather more in his element. "Now, then, Professor," he said, "I'll have a car and driver ready in a couple of shakes. Will you stay here or come up to my room?"

They were standing in the courtyard, a considerable open space, with a smooth and level surface. Dr. Priestley looked closely at this and then at the sky. "There does not appear to be any likelihood of a shower," he replied. "Is there, by any chance, a quantity of sand, or some similar substance, available?"

Hanslet frowned slightly. If such a thing had been within the bounds of possibility, he would have thought that the professor was pulling his leg. "Sand?" he replied. "I don't know, I'm sure. I'll find out. If you don't mind, Professor, it would help things along a bit if I knew what you wanted it for."

"The success of the experiment depends upon the wheel tracks made by the car being visible," said Dr. Priestley curtly.

"Oh, I see. Well, we'll soon fix that up for you," replied the superintendent. He gave an order to an attendant officer, and in a short time a gang of men were busily engaged in scattering sand over the surface of the courtyard.

"A patch thirty yards long by ten wide should be ample," remarked Dr. Priestley. "Meanwhile, this is the car, I suppose?"

He turned to where an open four-seater was waiting, and surveyed the uniformed driver over the rim of his spectacles. The man saluted nervously and looked at the superintendent for guidance.

"That's the car, Professor," replied Hanslet. "What is it that you want the driver to do?"

"I want him to place his car facing the sanded patch, and about forty yards from it," said the professor.

The driver manoeuvred his car into the required position. When he had done so, Dr. Priestley beckoned to Harold. "I want you to look at the steering connections of this car," he said. "Point out to the superintendent and myself the pin corresponding to the one which has been replaced on Mr. Chalk's car."

Harold bent down and examined the rods and pins. "The arrangement here isn't quite the same as that on the Comet," he said. "But the pin on the front end of the rod between the steering arm and the tie rod corresponds as nearly as possible."

"Very well. Now, can you remove that pin for us?"

"I could do it in a moment, sir, if I had the tools." replied Harold, looking inquiringly at the superintendent.

"What tools do you want?" asked Hanslet. "I'll send for them, if you'll describe them."

"No, no, surely that should not be necessary," interposed Dr. Priestley. "Is there not a tool kit carried on the car?"

The driver jumped out, produced a tool kit and offered it to Harold, who unrolled it. He selected a spanner and a pair of pliers and set to work on the pin. In a couple of minutes or so he had extracted it.

"Let me see it, my boy," said Dr. Priestley. He took the pin and turned it over in his hand. His inspection seemed to satisfy him, for he nodded encouragingly. Then he took a sheet of stiff paper from his pocket and rolled it up into a cylinder of the same diameter as the pin.

"That should serve our purpose, I think," he said. "Now, my boy, will you insert this paper in such a way that it will replace the pin which you have just extracted?"

When Harold had done so, Dr. Priestley turned to the driver. "Now, I want you to listen carefully to my instructions," he said. "When I give the word, drive straight towards the sanded patch in front of you, accelerating to as high a speed as possible in the space at your disposal. When your front wheels reach the sand, give your steering wheel a sharp wrench to the right. You win then find, in all probability, that you have lost control of the steering. When you feel that you have done so, apply your brakes, but not too violently."

The driver saluted. "Very good, sir," he replied phlegmatically. Dr. Priestley, followed by the superintendent and Harold took up his position at a safe distance from the sanded patch. "Go!" he exclaimed.

The driver raced his engine, let in his clutch, and had attained quite a respectable speed by the time he reached the sand. Then he turned the steering wheel sharply, thus wrenching the paper pin from its hold. The front wheels of the car wobbled alarmingly, and by the time the driver could pull up, the car had swerved clean off the prepared patch.

"Excellent!" exclaimed Dr. Priestley. "A most successful demonstration! Now, Superintendent, let me show you something else."

He produced an envelope, from which he extracted a set of photographs. They were those taken by Sergeant Showerby of the tracks after the accident. "Compare these tracks with those which have just been made on the sand," he continued.

There was no denying that they were almost exactly similar. The car which Lessingham had been driving had proceeded rather farther before taking the final swerve, probably owing to the greater speed at which it had been travelling. But in other respects the photographs showed tracks almost exactly similar to those made by the police car.

They repeated the experiment half a dozen times always with much the same result. In every case there was the same characteristic wobble and the final swerve. And at last, when Dr. Priestley was completely satisfied, the pin was replaced and the car and driver dismissed.

"Well, Professor, I see what you were driving at," said the superintendent. "The accident to Lessingham took place owing to the steering pin, or whatever you call it, breaking or falling out. That's it, isn't it?"

"Breaking, I expect," replied Dr. Priestley. "It would be an easier matter to contrive. Now, if you are still interested, I suggest that we pay a visit to the works of the Comet Motor Company and examine Mr. Chalk's car in the light of the information which we have just acquired."

Once more they took a taxi and drove out to the Comet works in London. There they found that work had already begun on Mr. Chalk's car. The body had already been removed and the chassis was in process of being stripped. The engineer in charge placed himself at their disposal, and informed them that the steering gear had not yet been touched.

"You discovered that a steering pin has been replaced at some time, I believe," said Hanslet. "Would you mind taking it out for us?"

The engineer agreed and set to work. As he did so, Dr. Priestley spread a sheet of paper on the ground under the joint. As the pin was extracted, a few particles of mud fell upon this. The professor wrapped them up carefully in the paper and put it in his pocket. Then he turned to the engineer, who had watched him in puzzled astonishment. "Is that pin one of your standard spare parts?" he asked.

"Yes, sir, there's no doubt about that," replied the engineer. "It's got our mark on it."

Dr. Priestley then proceeded to examine the socket from which the pin had been taken. He spread a second sheet of paper, scraped round the socket with a sharp pocket-knife, and collected the particles thus dislodged. Finally, he wrapped the pin itself in a third sheet of paper.

"That is all, I think," he said at last. "There is nothing to detain us any longer. You will want to return to Scotland Yard, I expect, Superintendent. You can drop Harold and me at Westbourne Terrace on your way."

During the drive back Dr. Priestley refused to discuss the case any further. It was not until they reached his door that he suggested, almost casually, that Hanslet should visit him after dinner that evening. "Unless, of course, you have other calls on your time," he added.

"I'll come along, right enough, Professor!" exclaimed Hanslet eagerly. "I'm not clear yet how that accident was managed."

"Is that so?" replied Dr. Priestley. "I hope to be able to explain it in detail by the time we next meet."

The rest of the afternoon the professor spent in his study with a microscope. It was not until shortly before dinner that he summoned Harold to put his apparatus away. By that time he had prepared a number of slides, each carefully labelled.

The superintendent turned up almost indecently early, an expectant look in his eyes. But Dr. Priestley seemed in no hurry to begin his explanation. As he sipped his coffee he talked at length of the beauty of the country round Moorchester, and so, by slow and irritating degrees, he came to the object of his visit to the town.

"You may be interested in a full account of the observations which I was enabled to make there, Superintendent," he said. "Harold, will you spread out the map on that table, so that the superintendent can follow my descriptions."

Hanslet listened, while Harold pointed out on the map the various places mentioned by his employer. "By jove, Professor," he said at last. "You seem to have had a pretty good idea what you were looking for. But I wish you'd tell me what all this means, for I am bound to say I don't understand exactly what happened, even yet."

"I think that the results of the investigations which we have made establish the cause of Lessingham's death, almost conclusively," replied the professor. "Perhaps, however, I had better explain the chain of my reasoning, link by link.

"I started with the following assumption: Mr. Chalk's car had been stolen and substituted for Lessingham's in order that Lessingham should be killed while driving it. It followed, therefore, that Mr. Chalk's car had in some way been rendered dangerous to its driver. But expert examination of the car after it had been found wrecked by Mr. Weldon and his friends, revealed no defect which would account for the accident.

"If my assumption was correct, this meant that the defect which had been the cause of the accident had been remedied since then, and before Mr. Weldon's car arrived on the scene. And since the time available had been extremely short — not more than half-an-hour — the work must have been capable of being performed very rapidly.

"Now, unlikely though it seemed that anybody had been on the scene of the accident before Mr. Weldon, I was inclined to favour this theory from the first. You have not studied the excellent photographs taken by Sergeant Showerby, I believe, Superintendent?"

"Only the ones of the tracks which you showed me this afternoon, Professor," replied Hanslet.

"Here are some others, showing the wrecked car and the position of the bodies. Now, they show a state of things which is confirmed by Harold's description. Both bodies have apparently been thrown forward out of the car by the force of the impact. They are lying at approximately equal distances from where they were sitting.

"This struck me as curious as soon as Harold described it to me. The motion of Purvis's body was impeded only by the glass of the windscreen. Lessingham struck the steering wheel with sufficient force to break it and bend the column. The medical evidence confirms the force of this blow. Yet, in spite of the retarding effect which this must have had, his body, as I have said, travelled approximately the same distance as Purvis!"

"You mean that somebody altered the position of his body after the accident?" exclaimed Hanslet. "I say, this is getting interesting, Professor. What was the idea?"

"That we may be able to suggest later. For the moment, my point is that if somebody had moved the body, that same person might have remedied the defect on the car. What that defect had been, I could not guess. It had escaped the minute examination of the experts. It was not until I heard that a steering pin, the head of which was painted a slightly different colour from the rest of the chassis, had been found on Mr. Chalk's car, that I formed a theory how the accident might have been caused.

"We saw this afternoon that the failure of this pin would cause a car to behave as these photographs show the car driven by Lessingham to have behaved. But how could such a failure be controlled? This was the question I set out to investigate and I believe now that I have found the answer.

"Having stolen Mr. Chalk's car, the criminal drove it down the same night to the wood near Hedgeworth, where the spanner was found. It is established that at that time the original steering pin was in position. The criminal proceeded to extract this and to replace it with one of his own manufacture. He used the tool kit kept on the car and, while doing so, the spanner we found fell from it. You saw for yourself this afternoon that the removal of the pin was a rapid and simple process.

"Now, without the pin, the car could not be steered at all. The criminal had therefore to replace it with something which would fulfil his requirements. This substituted pin must be strong enough to allow him to drive the car to Moorchester, also Lessingham must be able to drive some distance out of the town. In fact, the pin must not fail until Lessingham was travelling at a high speed.

"Before stealing Mr. Chalk's car, the criminal provided himself with a spare pin. This is a standard component, and could, I suppose, be obtained from any agent for Comet cars. With this pin as a model, he made an imitation and then painted the heads of both a colour as near as he could mix to Comet grey.

"But of what did he make his imitation? It was in order to answer that question that I visited the Comet works this afternoon. As you saw, I collected the debris that remained when the pin had been extracted. This I examined under the microscope. I found it to consist mainly of particles of grit. But among these were traces of short woody fibre and of a substance akin to putty.

"It seemed to me that a wooden pin would have been too strong. It might not have failed for a considerable distance. On the other hand, a putty pin would not have resisted the slightest strain. I was puzzled until I remembered the substance known as plastic wood. This is sold in tins and in its original condition can be moulded like clay. On exposure to air it hardens rapidly and assumes the appearance of wood. It can be worked like wood, but does not possess the same resistance to fracture.

"This, as the slides which I have prepared show, was the material of which the imitation was made. It was ideal for the criminal's purpose. It can be procured at any ironmongers, and it can be worked into any shape with the simplest tools. Further, when set, it possesses sufficient strength, but not too much.

"Having inserted the imitation pin, the criminal drove Mr. Chalk's car to the Moorchester control during Wednesday night. Here he substituted it for Lessingham's and drove the latter away. At the time of the substitution, of course, he transferred the articles which he found in Lessingham's car to Mr. Chalk's. He then took the old road along the crest of the ridge and took up a position from which he could overlook the new road as it came out of Moorchester. Harold will explain this to you on the map, Superintendent."

When Hanslet had grasped the lie of the land, Dr. Priestley continued. "I think we must assume that the criminal was aware of Lessingham's schedule. Lessingham left the control later than he intended, as we know, but at last the criminal saw the glare of his headlights. He then proceeded on a parallel course along the old road. The sudden extinction of Lessingham's lights told him when the accident happened. He drove on and reached the scene by a route which Harold will point out to you.

"His first care was to ascertain that Lessingham and Purvis were dead. Purvis almost certainly was, but Lessingham may not have been. I imagine Lessingham's body, dead or dying, to have been still in the car, sprawled over the bent steering column.

"Whether, if Lessingham was not actually dead, the criminal accelerated his death, I cannot say. But I think it is almost certain that he dragged him from the car and laid his body beside that of Purvis. There are two possible reasons for his having done this. He may have found it difficult to examine Lessingham in his original position, or he may have wished to have unimpeded access to the interior of the car.

"The criminal then removed what remained of the plastic wood pin and inserted the spare pin which he had procured. He must have had some reason for not using the pin which he had removed previously. Perhaps he had damaged it in some way in removing it and was afraid that this would attract attention subsequently.

"At this stage a point arises, which may or may not prove to be significant. No maps of any kind were found in the car. We believe that Lessingham possessed maps, for Orchard says that he saw him show them to Mr. Ellingwood. If so, it is highly probable that he took them with him on the rally. Did the criminal remove them from the car after the accident, and if so, what was his object in doing so?"

"That doesn't strike me as being particularly important," remarked Hanslet, as Dr. Priestley paused. "But I'm bound to admit that I can't find a hole in your theory. That's what happened right enough. We can prove it, almost step by step. I can't say how much I'm obliged to you, Professor. I've got a cast-iron case against the fellow, now."

"I am very glad that you regard the matter in that light," replied Dr. Priestley. "It only remains to identify the criminal."

"And I don't think there'll be a lot of difficulty about that," said Hanslet, with a satisfied smile.

The superintendent took the cigarette which Harold offered him and lighted it deliberately.

"I'll see the chief first thing in the morning," he said. "I haven't said anything to him yet, because I wanted to be able to explain how those poor fellows were murdered before I raised the hare. It's not at all a bad thing that that fool coroner returned a verdict of accidental death. It will have put the fellow off his guard."

"You are hardly yet in a position to apply for a warrant, are you?" asked Dr. Priestley, with a ghost of a smile.

"I'm not far off it, Professor. This is how I look at it: The only imaginable motive was Lessingham's money. He had made no will, and his estate would go to his next of kin. Now, this was Purvis. But since Purvis was with Lessingham all the time, he can't have been the criminal — that's logical enough, isn't it?"

"I am afraid that I cannot conscientiously answer that question in the affirmative," replied Dr. Priestley.

"Well, anyhow, Professor, it's common sense. Now, the fact that Purvis was with Lessingham was very convenient for the criminal. It was no use his killing Lessingham and leaving Purvis alive to snap up his money. Purvis had to be killed too. If the car could be successfully wrecked, the two would be polished off at once. Two birds with one stone.

"Of course, all that lawyers' stuff about which died first complicates things a bit. I don't suppose the criminal thought of that. As he saw it, Mrs. Ellingwood was the next heir."

"Therefore her husband must irrefutably have been the criminal," remarked Dr. Priestley, with almost superhuman gravity.

Hanslet glanced at him sharply. Even after the years he had known him, he was never quite sure of the professor's meaning.

"It's a good enough assumption to start off with, anyhow. But there's another thing, Professor. You said just now that the criminal must have known all about Lessingham's schedule, and what his plans were. And Orchard told me that he overheard Lessingham discussing the rally with Ellingwood."

But Dr. Priestley made no comment, and Hanslet continued triumphantly. "Lessingham told Ellingwood that he was going to spend a few hours at Moorchester. I haven't a doubt that he showed him his car as well — took him for a run in it, perhaps. We know from Mrs. Ellingwood that her husband was away from home about that time. I'll bet he spent as much time with Lessingham as he could, watching his preparations for the rally."

"When did he discover Mr. Chalk's habit of leaving his car in his friend's drive on Tuesday nights?" asked Dr. Priestley.

"You can't expect me to have an answer for everything at once, Professor," replied Hanslet sharply. "When I asked you the other evening how the murder had been arranged, you couldn't tell me, could you? Ellingwood's movements are being investigated, and very soon I'll be able to tell you all you want to know,

"We've got a good deal of information about the criminal already. He must be able to drive a car and he must have some knowledge of car mechanism — enough to remove and replace a steering pin, anyhow. And we know his movements pretty well. He was at Denham on the night of the first, when the car was stolen. He was at Moorchester on the night of the second, when he substituted one car for another. He probably spent the intervening day skulking in the wood near Hedgeworth. He was on the spot directly after the smash, round about five o'clock on the morning of the third. Have you got a small scale map of England handy, Professor?"

"Harold will find you one." replied Dr. Priestley. "The one on a scale of eight miles to an inch will be the best."

Harold found the map and spread it out. The superintendent took a foot rule from his pocket and laid it on the map.

"It's thirteen inches from Westernham to Slowford." he said. "That's 104 miles as the crow flies. If we say 130 or 140 by road, we shan't be far out. It's a rough and ready method, but it's near enough for the purpose. Say four hours' drive at the most in a fast car.

"Now it's pretty clear to me what the criminal did. He drove straight from the scene of the smash to Slowford. Why shouldn't he? He was all right. Even if the description of Mr. Chalk's car had been circulated by then, which was most unlikely, he ran no risk. Supposing he had been held up and questioned? He was driving Lessingham's car and could prove it, and, of course, the news of Lessingham's death did not spread until some time later.

"By nine o'clock he would have reached Slowford. It's a pretty desolate spot, but even allowing for that, I don't believe that anyone would hare crashed the car in the quarry in broad daylight. Too much chance of someone being about and seeing or hearing something. But if the criminal was Ellingwood, everything was easy enough. He merely ran the car into one of his own sheds and disposed of it in perfect safety that night."

"Very ably reasoned, Superintendent," said Dr. Priestley encouragingly. "I take it that if Mr. Ellingwood cannot produce a satisfactory alibi covering the period you have mentioned you will feel justified in arresting him."

At that moment the telephone bell in the hall rang and Harold got up to answer it. In a moment he came back. "It's a call for you from the Yard, Mr. Hanslet," he said.

Hanslet in his rum went out, leaving the door open. "Superintendent Hanslet speaking." A pause. Then — "Right. I'll be along in a few minutes. Keep her till I get there, at all costs." He banged down the receiver and put his head through the study door. "Sorry, Professor, I've got to go; urgent call. I'll explain when I see you again. Good-night."

CHAPTER XVI

ALTHOUGH by now Hanslet was pretty well convinced that Dr. Priestley was correct, and that Lessingham had been a victim rather than a criminal, he had never relaxed the watch that had been set upon his rooms in Cawdor Street. For one thing, he was not at all satisfied about Orchard. That Orchard was withholding information of some kind, he felt pretty certain. It was quite likely that he knew more about the affair than he had chosen to disclose. In any case Hanslet considered that nothing would be lost and something might be gained by keeping an eye on him."

So the rooms were watched day and night, and the telephone in particular was kept under observation. But since Hanslet's first visit to Cawdor Street, Orchard had shown no disposition to communicate with anybody. He had received no visitors except Mr. Farrant, who had called once or twice, presumably in connection with his client's affairs. Apart from this single visitor, Orchard had lived the life of a recluse. He had emerged regularly every morning, made a few necessary purchases in Shepherd Market and retired once more to his fastness. The officers detailed for the task of watching him were getting heartily sick of their job.

And then at last, on the evening of Hanslet's visit to Westbourne Terrace, something had happened to relieve the monotony of their vigil. A woman tightly wrapped in a heavy fur coat, so that her features were quite indistinguishable, had appeared at the end of Cawdor Street at half-past eleven. Seeing nobody about, for the watcher was hidden in the shadows some little distance away, she had hurried to the door of Number 14 and rang the bell.

The watcher on duty, an intelligent young man of the name of Bradder, had crept up as close as he dared. The woman had huddled into the doorway, as though to escape observation. So, for three or four seconds, the two stood motionless, forty yards or more of quiet street separating them.

Then a window at the top of the building opened and Orchard's head appeared. He said nothing, but craned his neck out of the window. The woman, hearing the sound, stepped back, so that Orchard could see her.

Not a word was spoken, but Orchard's head disappeared instantly, and the woman swiftly resumed her former position. A minute passed and then the door opened furtively. Bradder could see Orchard's outline, clad in an overcoat. It was probably his substitute for a dressing-gown, thought Bradder. It looked very much as though he had not expected his visitor. A whispered colloquy took place which Bradder could not hear. But it seemed as though Orchard was trying to persuade the woman to go away, while she insisted upon entering the house.

Apparently her arguments prevailed, for she slipped into the house and the door closed behind her. Bradder waited no longer. He raced to the nearest telephone box and rang up the Yard. His call was transferred to Dr. Priestley's number. It was Bradder's hurried report which had been the cause of the superintendent's unceremonious departure from Westbourne Terrace.

Hanslet hailed a passing taxi. "The end of Cawdor Street, and drive like hell," he said to the driver, as be jumped in. There was not much traffic about, and the taxi-man made excellent time. At the corner of Cawdor Street he pulled up behind another taxi which was standing there. Hanslet glanced at it curiously and noticed that the flag was down. "What are you doing here?" he asked brusquely.

The driver of the second taxi turned slowly in his seat and looked at him. "And what business might that be of yours, guv'nor?" he asked.

"It'll be bad business for you if you talk like that to me," retorted Hanslet savagely. "I'm an officer of Scotland Yard. Now, then, out with it."

"Beg pardon, sir, I'm sure," said the taxi-man. "I'm not doing no harm. I'm just waiting for a lady what's paying a call up the street. She told me to wait here, and that she wouldn't be more than a few minutes."

"Where did you pick her up?"

"She called me off the rank outside South Kensington Station, sir."

"Right. Now listen to me. Wait for her till she comes back. She'll probably be more than a few minutes, but I can't help that. Drive her back to wherever she tell you, and see that you don't breathe a word to her that I've spoken to you. And then come to the Yard and report where you dropped her. Ask for Superintendent Hanslet. If he's not there, they'll take a message. Understand?"

Having noted the man's number, in case he should not carry out these instructions, Hanslet walked up the street towards the number 14. As he did so, a shadow detached itself from the gloom and glided up to him. "Woman's still there, sir," it whispered.

"Good man, Bradder," said the Superintendent. "I'll have a word with her. What's she like?"

"Couldn't see her face, sir. She was all muffled up. But I should say she was a youngish woman, by the way she moved along, sir."

"Well, we'll soon find out. You stay here outside the door. If either of them tries to make a bolt for it, arrest them. I'm going in."

The superintendent walked up to the door, placed his finger on the bell and kept it there. For a few seconds the house remained silent. Then a window, this time on the first floor, was raised softly.

"Is that you, Orchard?" said the superintendent sternly. "Come down and open this door, and look sharp about it."

"Why, it's Superintendent Hanslet!" exclaimed Orchard. "Very good, sir, I'll be down in a couple of shakes."

But it was fully a minute before the door opened and Orchard appeared, in an overcoat and a pair of bedroom slippers. His expression was one of pained surprise, but it seemed to Hanslet that his eyes looked craftier than ever. "Beg pardon, sir, for keeping you waiting," he said. "But you see I was just going to bed when you rang."

"I always knew you were a liar. Orchard," replied Hanslet equably. "I want a little chat with you in Mr. Lessingham's sitting-room. No, I'd rather you went up first, if you don't mind. That's right."

Very reluctantly Orchard went upstairs. Hanslet close on his heels. The lights were on in the sitting-room and Hanslet fancied that he detected a faint aroma of scent. But of Orchard's visitor there was no trace.

Hanslet left the door wide open and sat down in a chair close beside it. "Well, Orchard, and who's the lady?" he asked.

Orchard's eyes narrowed. Clearly it was useless to deny the presence of his mysterious visitor. Yet, for a moment he hesitated, while the superintendent watched him with a scornful smile.

Then Orchard's eyes fell. "I'm very sorry about it, sir," he said. "I shouldn't like it to come to Mr. Farrant's ears, sir. I don't know that he would understand it exactly, if you know what I mean, sir. But it's only my cousin, sir, that's just dropped in to see me for a moment. And I'm sure I don't know how you came to know she was here, sir."

"Your cousin, eh?" replied Hanslet, raising his voice slightly. "And she comes to see you at this time of night? But perhaps she can't get away in the daytime. Where does she live, this cousin of yours?"

"She's a dressmaker's assistant, sir, and she lives in Walworth," replied Orchard.

Hanslet shook his head disapprovingly. "Well, if I were you, I should talk pretty seriously to this cousin of yours," he said. "She seems to me to have very expensive tastes for a woman in her position. Fur coats are all very well, but they cost a lot of money, you know. And fancy taking a taxi from South Kensington when there's a tube almost to the door! I'm afraid I shall have to make inquiries about all this, Orchard."

There was a moment's pause, and then, as Hanslet had half expected, the door leading into the dining-room opened and a woman appeared on the threshold.

The superintendent rose from his chair and bowed gravely. The woman had thrown the folds of her fur coat back and stood revealed in an evening frock of pearl grey. To Hanslet she seemed about thirty, and of a rather disconcerting loveliness. In the shaded light of the lamps, her eyes shone green, and golden gleams came and went in her hair as she moved. A beautiful woman, beyond a doubt. But there was a hard, unscrupulous look in her set face that seemed in strange contrast to her beauty.

For a moment she stood there, looking not at the superintendent, but at Orchard, who stood staring at her with wide open, frightened eyes. Then she came forward and sank with a graceful gesture into a chair. "Thank you. Orchard," she said in a curiously low and husky voice. "You did your best, I know. Now you can leave me to talk to the superintendent."

Without a word, Orchard turned and left the room, shutting the door behind him. His footsteps died slowly away up the stairs, leaving the room in tense silence.

She was the first to break it. "This is an unexpected meeting, Superintendent," she said lightly. "But, as it happens, it is merely an anticipation of a few hours. When you came in I had just made up my mind to come and see you to-morrow morning."

Hanslet had resumed his chair by the door. He felt awkward and ill at ease. Women of this type were rather outside his experience. He felt half inclined to open the window and call to Bradder to join him. But in that case Orchard might slip out and disappear. He would have to go through with it alone. "What did you wish to see me about?" he asked abruptly.

She opened her bag and produced a newspaper cutting. "I expect you recognise this," she said, holding it up. "I was the person who sent the telegram to Aubrey Lessingham at the Imperial Hotel, Moorchester."

Somehow Hanslet had not expected this. She had spoken casually, as, though it were a matter of no moment. And when she had done so, she took out a cigarette and lighted it with studied unconcern.

"Would you mind telling me the contents of the telegram?" asked Hanslet.

"I forget the exact wording," she replied. "It was merely to tell Aubrey that I should not be able to meet him at Torquay as we had arranged."

"You had arranged to meet Mr. Lessingham, then?" Hanslet asked in a slightly embarrassed tone.

She glanced at him swiftly. "Yes, why not?" she replied. "I had known Aubrey for years."

"Indeed?" said Hanslet. "Then no doubt you will be able to tell me several things about him which I am anxious to know. In the first place, I must ask you for your name and address."

An unmistakable look of alarm came into her eyes at this. But still her voice betrayed no token of emotion. "Is that absolutely necessary?" she asked. "Won't it do if I answer your questions as well as I can?"

"I'm afraid that is absolutely necessary," replied Hanslet. "And it is only fair to warn you that I shall have to verify what you tell me."

She inhaled a deep breath from her cigarette and the hand holding it shook slightly as she did so. "I suppose you would find out from Orchard anyhow," she said, after a long pause. "I am Mrs. Burford, of 8B Shetland Mansions, South Kensington. And if you show that telegram to my husband, you will ruin his life as well as mine, if that is any consolation to you."

She spoke without a touch of melodrama and Hanslet had an instinctive feeling that the statement, startling as it was, was true. He produced his note-book and wrote down the name and address which she had given him, hoping that thus he would be spared the necessity for comment.

"I wonder if a man can rise to your position and still retain any trace of human feelings?" she continued, in a detached voice, as though the question were wholly impersonal. "I'm going to chance it, anyhow. It doesn't seem as if I'd much option now. As I told you, I had known Aubrey for a long time. And then — well, my husband got jealous and made a scene about it. And if he knew that I had arranged to meet Aubrey at Torquay, he would make things very unpleasant for both himself and me. You see, he's still in love with me, is my husband."

Hanslet was beginning to understand the situation now. From his point of view the telegram had ceased to be of importance. Merely an incident in a clandestine love affair. But still, there were matters in connection with it which required explanation.

"There is one question I must ask you, Mrs. Burford," he said gravely. "When I showed Orchard the telegram, he first of all said that he did not know who had sent it, and then made up a ridiculous story to account for it. Why did he do this?"

"It was perfectly true that he knew nothing of the telegram, for I did not tell him I had sent it," she replied. "And then, when you showed it him, he guessed at once who had sent it. Poor Orchard! He did his best on the spur of the moment, but the mythical George Love must have sounded a bit thin. You see, I had begged him to keep my name out of it, at all costs."

"You had seen him since the accident?" inquired Hanslet sharply.

"As soon as I heard that Aubrey had been killed I came straight round here. That was on the Thursday evening. I saw the news in the evening papers. Orchard knew me well enough and when I had shown him the paper, he agreed to help me at once."

"Help you with what, Mrs. Burford?"

She looked at him with a faint smile, as though amused at his simplicity. "Why, don't you see, there might have been letters and a photograph or two. I knew that somebody would go through Aubrey's things, and I didn't want anything of mine to be found. I certainly didn't imagine that the police would search these rooms. I thought it would be Mr. Farrant or somebody like that."

So Hanslet's original suspicions had been correct. He had been pretty sure, on his first visit, that somebody had been through the rooms before he arrived on the scene. This remarkably self-possessed woman, looking for compromising letters? But was that all she had taken? "Did you find any letters?" he asked.

"I found a dozen or two and some photographs, which I took home and burned. And I was careful to see that they were completely destroyed."

"And you removed nothing whatever from these rooms except those letters and photographs?"

"Nothing, whatever. Why should I? All I wanted was to make sure that nobody would find anything of mine here."

"You mentioned Mr. Farrant just now, Mrs. Burford. Do you know him?"

"I have never met him, but Aubrey often spoke of him, and I knew he was his solicitor."

"Did you know that Mr. Lessingham had never made a will, though Mr. Farrant had frequently urged him to do so?"

She threw away the end of her cigarette and lighted another. Her hand no longer trembled, and it seemed to Hanslet that she was gaining confidence as time went on. "Surely, Superintendent, it is hardly necessary for us to discuss Aubrey's private affairs, is it?" she replied.

"I am afraid that I must insist upon an answer to my question," replied Hanslet firmly.

She shrugged her shoulders slightly, as though complying with a foolish whim. "Yes, I knew it. I rather gathered that Aubrey had his own reasons for not making a will yet. I can't be expected to guess what those reasons were, can I?"

Hanslet tried a slightly different tack. "Do you know who inherits his estate, since he died intestate?" he asked.

"He always told me that so far as he knew the only relation he had was Tom Purvis. But a week or so before he went off on the rally he told me that he had had a visit from the husband of a distant relation of his, whom he had forgotten all about. I forget the name, but he told me the man was trying to raise money on a farm, or something. I suppose, since Tom Purvis was killed at the same time as Aubrey, these people will get the money."

Hanslet paused, as though considering her reply. And then abruptly he asked, "When did you last see Mr. Lessingham?"

She looked at him steadily. "I dined with him here on the Friday before the rally," she replied. "It was then that we arranged to meet on the following Friday at Torquay."

"How was it that you were unable to keep the appointment, Mrs. Burford?"

She flicked off her cigarette ash with an impatient gesture. "Surely it's enough that I found myself unable to go," she replied.

"It is my duty to investigate the facts," said Hanslet quietly. "If you refuse to give them to me, I must seek them elsewhere."

Her eyes flickered at this, and Hanslet knew that he had scored his point. "Well, if you must know." she said, with studied carelessness. "I thought my husband would be away from home when I made the arrangement. He was to have been abroad all that week. There's nothing unusual in that; he often has to go abroad on business. He went on Monday, but on Wednesday I got a wire from him, from Boulogne, saying that he would be home on Thursday. I wired Aubrey at once — I knew where to catch him — and that was that."

"And did your husband actually come home on Thursday?"

"Oh, yes. He's a most punctual person. He came home to lunch and then went back to his office. He told me that he had some arrears of work to make up, that he would dine at his club and would not be home till late. It was lucky for me, for otherwise I should never have dared to come here when I read of Aubrey's death."

"May I ask what brought you here to-night, Mrs. Burford?"

Hanslet fancied that she smiled faintly. "You are the cause of that, Superintendent. When I came here on the night of Aubrey's death, Orchard promised to keep in touch with me and let me know that everything was all right. I was terrified that I might have overlooked something, and that my name might crop up. I never thought that my telegram to Aubrey could have been found, or I should have been worried to death.

"I couldn't think how it was that I heard nothing from Orchard, He never wrote to me or rang me up. I didn't like to ring him up, for fear that Mr. Farrant or somebody might be here at the time, and I didn't want to come round again myself, in case somebody should see me. It wasn't until I risked it and came round this evening that he told me he hadn't dared to communicate with me, as the police had been here next day and the house had been watched ever since."

So Orchard had been cunning enough to find that out, thought Hanslet. "These rooms have been watched because I considered Orchard's manner highly suspicious when I questioned him," he said severely. "You came here to consult him as to the notice in the newspapers about your telegram, I suppose?"

"Yes, partly. I was terribly upset when I saw it. I didn't know what to do. If I went to you and told you that I had sent it, I was putting myself entirely in your hands.

And if I kept quiet and said nothing, I thought you might find out somehow and then my husband would be bound to hear of it.

"So I came here to ask Orchard what he thought. He was terribly upset when he saw me, for he knew I had run my head into the trap. However, I made him let me in, and he told me about your visit, and what be had said to you about the telegram. You know the rest. Now, Superintendent, what are you going to do about it?"

There was no concealing the anxiety which underlay this last question. She had lost the careless, self-confident expression which she bad maintained hitherto, and sat watching Hanslet expectantly, with eyes from which the tears were not far distant.

Hanslet paused before he replied. He knew well enough what she meant. Was there, after all, any necessity to drag her intrigue into the light of day? She clearly had no suspicion that Lessingham had been murdered. The telegram had been merely incidental, and had played no part in the tragedy.

"So long as you can convince me of the truth of what you have told me, I see no reason to trouble your husband in the matter," he said at last.

Her relief expressed itself in a hysterical laugh, which she repressed immediately. "You don't know how grateful I am for that!" she exclaimed unsteadily. "You don't know what it would mean to me if my husband found out, now that Aubrey's dead. I swear I've told you nothing that isn't true. I'll do anything, anything, to prove it."

Hanslet tore a leaf from his note-book. Then he handed her this and a pencil. "Thank you, Mrs. Burford." he said. "Now will you please write this? 'I declare that I am the sender of the telegram addressed Lessingham, Imperial Hotel, Moorchester, which was handed in at South Kensington at 6 pm on March 2nd and was worded: "Cannot meet you at Torquay as we arranged, love."'"

Without hesitation she picked up the pencil and wrote the required words. "Now will you sign it, please?" continued Hanslet. "It is for official use only and will be treated in the strictest confidence. Thank you."

He took the signed sheet of paper and put it in his note-book. "Just one more question, and then I need not detain you any longer, Mrs. Burford. Do you know anybody of the name of Ellingwood?"

Hanslet was watching her carefully as he put the question. She shook her head, and then a light of memory came into her eyes. "That's the married name of that distant connection of Aubrey's that I was telling you about!" she exclaimed. "No, I have never met either her or her husband. Didn't I tell you that Aubrey told me that he hadn't seen her himself since he was a child?"

"I thought perhaps that you might have come across Mr or Mrs. Ellingwood," said Hanslet casually. "Now, Mrs. Burford, perhaps you will allow me to escort you to the taxi which you have waiting?"

She smiled and held out her hands towards him.

"You've been more generous towards me than I deserve, Mr. Hanslet," she said. "Believe me, I shall never forget it. I should feel it an honour if you would give me your arm as far as the taxi."

So, with her fingers resting lightly on his arm, Hanslet escorted her to the end of the street. He waited until she had given the address of Shetland Mansions, and driven off. Then he beckoned to Bradder, who had again materialised something in the manner of the Cheshire cat.

"You can go home to bed, Bradder," he said. "There's no point in watching this place any longer."

"Very good, sir. What about Orchard? He hasn't left the house since you've been in it."

"Orchard can go to hell, for all I care," replied Superintendent Hanslet shortly.

CHAPTER XVII

AFTER the Superintendent's abrupt departure, Dr. Priestley sat for some time in silence. To Harold, who knew his moods, it was clear that he was revolving the conversation in his mind. And when thus engaged, his employer was better not interrupted.

As Harold had expected, his thoughts were suddenly expressed in words. "The superintendent's conjecture as to the identity of Lessingham's murderer may very possibly be correct," he said abruptly. "I say conjecture, for at present he can produce no evidence whatever that Mr. Ellingwood was the criminal. He may be able to verify the fact by the means he suggests of tracing Mr. Ellingwood's movements. But, for my own part, I should be inclined to approach the problem from a different direction."

He paused and looked severely at Harold, as though he was responsible for Hanslet's methods. Harold, recognising the symptoms, ventured to reply. "How would you set about it, sir?" he asked diffidently.

"I should, while bearing Mr. Ellingwood in mind, not restrict my field of inquiry to any single individual," replied Dr. Priestley. "For instance, there are certain clues available, the importance of which the superintendent appears to underestimate. It would not be unprofitable to consider them. Suppose, as the superintendent believed at first, that the object of his inquiries was merely to identify the thief of Mr. Chalk's car. If you were engaged upon that, how would you begin?"

Harold thought a little before he spoke. "It seems to me, sir, that the thief wanted a car exactly similar to Mr. Lessingham's. Any car of that particular model would do, since they are all built to standard. As the Comet sales manager told us, there are a good many of them about, especially in the home counties. How did the thief happen to choose this particular car for his purpose?"

Harold paused and glanced at his employer rather timorously. But Dr. Priestley nodded encouragingly. "A question you might well ask yourself, my boy," he said. "And how would you proceed to answer it?"

"I should say, sir, because he knew when and how it could conveniently be stolen. This means that he knew that Mr. Chalk had bought a Comet similar to Lessingham's. He hadn't much time to find that out, for Mr. Chalk only took delivery of his car on February 17th. Therefore, it seems likely that the thief was somebody who had means of keeping Mr. Chalk under observation. In fact, it is possible that he knew Mr. Chalk, in some capacity or other."

"Excellent, my boy!" exclaimed Dr. Priestley. "That, I think, is one of the conditions which the thief must fulfil. But there are others. The procuring of the spare steering pin, for instance. I do not know whether it would be possible to trace all those who have been issued with these from the Comet company's stores. In any case it would be a very lengthy process. There is, however, another question which I have asked myself, without being able to suggest a satisfactory answer."

"What is that, sir?" asked Harold.

"It concerns a point which we have already touched upon. We cannot say definitely that Lessingham carried a map or maps with him on the rally. But we have reason to believe that he possessed a set, and that none have been found in his rooms. It is not too much to say that it is highly probable that they were in the car when he started from Bath.

"Now, what became of them? It is quite possible that the criminal left them in Lessingham's own car when he substituted Mr. Chalk's for it. But I think it highly improbable that he did so. He took care to transfer everything else, and it is most unlikely that he neglected an item of such importance as the maps. I believe that he removed them when he visited the car after the accident."

"But what could have been his object, sir? He left the route book and everything else that Lessingham was carrying."

"That is just the question that I have been asking myself. But we cannot say that he left everything else, since we do not know what Lessingham had with him when he started from Bath. However, we may put that speculation aside for the moment. The only reason that I can suggest for his taking the maps is this: Lessingham may have marked upon them the route which he actually followed.

"It is possible to imagine that the criminal had his own reason for not wishing that route to be known. With both Lessingham and Purvis dead, the maps would furnish the only evidence. If, for instance, it could be shown that Lessingham had taken a route between Bath and Norwich which passed at a considerable distance from Denham, the superintendent's original theory that he had stolen Mr. Chalk's car himself would have fallen to the ground at once. This should be borne in mind in connection with the undoubted fact that the criminal had an intimate knowledge of Lessingham's plans for the rally. Of that, there is no doubt whatever, as his actions fully prove. And with regard to this, there is another point which must not be lost sight of. The criminal could not have put his plan into operation had Lessingham's schedule been other than it was. Show me the time-table once more, my boy."

Dr. Priestley glanced at the paper which Harold gave him and made a few rapid notes in pencil. "This will explain my point," he said. "Suppose that Lessingham had elected to start from Bath at any other time but nine o'clock. If, for instance, he had started at seven o'clock, his times, other things being equal, would have been two hours earlier throughout. He would have reached Moorchester at about half-past eight on Wednesday evening, and would have been obliged to leave again between two and three of Thursday morning.

"Now, while the criminal would still have had the same opportunities for substituting the cars, the accident would have taken place at a most inconvenient time for him. The car driven by Lessingham would have been in the centre of the stream of competing cars running from Moorchester to Torquay. The wrecked car would almost certainly have been found within a few minutes. In any case, the criminal would not have ventured to interfere with it. As it was, but for the fact that your car was delayed by fog, the accident would probably not have been discovered for a considerable time, which might have extended into an hour or more."

"That's true, sir," replied Harold. "Nothing came along the road while we were there, and we didn't leave till after daylight."

"Just so. No doubt we shall learn how far this Mr. Ellingwood conforms with the necessary conditions. I should not be surprised if the superintendent were to visit us to-morrow night, in order to resume our interrupted conversation."

Dr. Priestley was right. Hanslet turned up on the following evening, at the same time as before.

"Sorry I had to run away like that yesterday, Professor," he said. "However, since then, I have got a lot of reports in about the Ellingwoods. Perhaps you would like to hear them?"

"I would rather that you gave me the facts as briefly as possible," replied Dr. Priestley.

"Very well. We'll take Ellingwood first. He retired from the navy three years ago, with the rank of lieutenant-commander. Married Joan Singer a few weeks later. Bought Highcroft Farm about the same time, went in for poultry keeping on a large scale and apparently expended most of his capital. Kept on increasing his stock and took up a mortgage on the farm for the purpose. Interest on that mortgage now in arrears.

"Now for Mrs. Ellingwood. Left a small income by her parents. Spent her time in small hotels or staying in friends' houses. Believed at one time to have been engaged to a distant connection, Thomas Purvis — rather queer, that, isn't it, Professor? Engagement broken off shortly before Purvis went abroad for the first time. Later, married Reginald Ellingwood. I think those are the principal facts, Professor."

"The skeleton of them, certainly," agreed Dr. Priestley. "You have more recent particulars, of course?"

"I'm coming to those. The Ellingwoods started off with a bit of a flourish. Kept a big car, a couple of men and two or three maids. Their establishment has gradually dwindled. The car had to be sold, which was a bitter blow to them, I'm told, as they were both keen drivers. They only employ a boy to clean out the fowl-houses, and one woman in the house, both of whom come in by the day. Nobody sleeps on the place but themselves.

"Now we come to the last few weeks. Ellingwood left the farm on February 16th. That was the day before Mr. Chalk took delivery of his car — nearly a fortnight after Lessingham took delivery of his, and a fortnight before the rally. These dates are worth remembering, I think. He left Mrs. Ellingwood to look after the place, and it was believed that he went up to London. He was not seen again at Slowford until the afternoon of Thursday March 3rd."

Hanslet paused significantly. He was delighted to see that he had aroused Dr. Priestley's interest, for the latter had signed to Harold to take notes of what he was saying.

"I won't press the importance of these dates for the moment," he continued, rather pompously, "but they are amply confirmed. The man I put on the job traced Ellingwood to a place called the Copdock Hotel. You've probably never heard of it. It's one of those cheap places near Earl's Court. He stopped there from February 16th till March 1st. And that was the day the rally started. While he was staying there, he seems to have been out all day and most of the night."

"You have no clue as to his business in London?" asked Dr. Priestley.

"Not yet. I don't want to press my inquiries too far, for fear of alarming him. Naturally, he thinks he's safe enough after the verdict at the inquest. But I've seen my chief and told him the whole story. I've his instructions to carry on as though the verdict had been one of wilful murder.

"So far, we have not traced Ellingwood's movements after he left the Copdock Hotel, on the morning of the 1st, until he was seen in Slowford on the afternoon of the 3rd. And from what you've told me, we're not likely to. But it is quite dear that he had plenty of opportunity for seeing Lessingham between his first visit to him and the time the rally started. But even if he didn't, he could have secured the information he required in another way."

"Indeed! How do you suggest that he could have done so?" added Dr. Priestley.

"Well, I had a bit of a brain wave this morning. I was looking over the reports, and I was struck by that reference to Mrs. Ellingwood having once been engaged to Purvis. Now Purvis was a connection of hers as well as Lessingham. It's pretty clear that Ellingwood's original reason for coming to London was to try to raise money. He tried Lessingham, without apparently any decisive result. But, in the course of their conversation, Lessingham probably mentioned to him that Purvis was coming back from abroad. Now it occurred to me that since Ellingwood had called on Lessingham, he might have called on Purvis, too. Purvis might, perhaps, be persuaded to put money into this concern of his. Whatever Lessingham had said to him, he might have thought it as well to have two strings to his bow. So I went round myself to the Hotel Purvis was staying at and made inquiries.

"I hit the nail right on the head that time, Professor. On February 27th the Saturday before the rally started, Ellingwood had called and asked for Purvis. That was in the morning, soon after breakfast. They spent a long time together talking, and apparently the best of friends. And that evening Ellingwood called for Purvis, and they went out to dinner together. Purvis did not come back till very late."

Dr. Priestley nodded approvingly. "A most successful piece of deduction. Superintendent," he said. "You believe that, in the event of Ellingwood not having obtained details of Lessingham's plans from that individual himself, he may have done so from Purvis. It certainly seems quite possible."

"I'm glad you think that, Professor. Now, just let's see how we stand for a moment. Ellingwood had a motive, and a very pressing one, apparently, for desiring the death of Lessingham and Purvis. If he could bring that about, his wife would come into Lessingham's money, and money was badly wanted. He must have known that Lessingham and Purvis were going to the rally together. He is described as having been an enthusiastic motorist, and was therefore technically capable of carrying out the crime. He had ample opportunity of discovering Lessingham's plans. His movements from the 1st to the 3rd are not accounted for. Lessingham's car was found abandoned in a quarry, barely a mile from his house. Honestly, now, isn't that a good enough case?"

Hanslet lay back in his chair and nibbed his hands together briskly. But Dr. Priestley's caution would not allow him to share his friend's enthusiasm. "Superficially, it appears to be a very good case, indeed," he replied. "But, as no doubt you realise, many details remain to be fitted in before you can frame a definite charge of murder against Ellingwood."

"I guessed that was pretty much about what you would say, Professor!" exclaimed Hanslet. "The details are beginning to fill themselves in already. I haven't told you everything yet.

"You remember that I said I had arranged to have Lessingham's car and everything found with it sent up to London? Well, I thought it best to have them sent straight up to the Yard, and not to the Comet works. I wanted to have a good look over them myself. They arrived this afternoon and I spent an hour or two with them. Everything was pretty well smashed up. But the body of the car, although it had been torn off the chassis, was still fairly whole.

"I went over the body pretty carefully and found there was a pocket on the near side door. I looked inside this without much hope of finding anything interesting, I must confess. But, as it happened, I had a stroke of luck. It's a wonderful thing, but I've always found that the most careful criminal overlooks something. And this is what I found in the pocket, Professor."

With an air of triumph, Hanslet took an official envelope from his pocket and took out the contents. These he laid on Dr. Priestley's desk. "What do you make of those?" he asked confidently.

Dr. Priestley examined the objects with particular care. "This is an envelope addressed to 'R. Ellingwood, Esq., Highcroft Poultry Farm, Slowford, Somerset'," he said. "It bears a penny-halfpenny stamp, but does not appear to have been posted, since there is no post mark. The envelope has been gummed down and subsequently torn open."

"The address is in Lessingham's writing." said Hanslet, "and the envelope is exactly similar to those in his desk at Cawdor Street. I've verified both those points beyond the possibility of doubt."

Dr. Priestley nodded and laid the envelope aside. The second object was a folded map. Dr. Priestley opened it and as he did so a card fell out of it. He picked up the card and read the printed inscription upon it. 'Highcroft Poultry Farm, Slowford, Somerset. Sittings of prize strains a speciality. Prices on application.' He glanced at the map. "This is a sheet of the ordnance survey, on a scale of four miles to the inch," he remarked.

"Yes, and it includes the road between Denham and Moorchester," replied Hanslet significantly. "The card was folded up in it exactly as you found it."

Dr. Priestley said nothing. It was obvious that this discovery impressed him more than anything that the superintendent had yet said. He examined the envelope, the card and the map minutely. Finally he handed them back to Hanslet, almost, it seemed, with regret. "This is most extraordinary," he said at last. "How do you account for the presence of these things in the pocket of Lessingham's car?"

"I don't see much difficulty about that," replied Hanslet. "Take that envelope first; I think that tells its own story. Lessingham wrote a letter to Ellingwood before he started on the rally. If Mrs. Ellingwood spoke the truth and there was to be a further meeting, it was probably about that. By the way, the fact that the envelope is addressed to Slowford is interesting. Ellingwood must have given Lessingham to understand that he had gone back home, whereas we know that he didn't do so till the following Thursday.

"Lessingham put the letter in his pocket, intending to post it and forgot it. There's nothing out of the way in that — I've done it myself. It was still in his pocket when he was killed. Now, when the criminal came along after the accident, no doubt he went through Lessingham's pockets to make sure that no clues were to be found there. He came across the letter and took it. Anybody but Ellingwood would have left it there. But Ellingwood naturally did not want his name to appear. Besides, he probably wanted to find out what was in the letter. Later on, when he had got clear away, he opened the letter and put the envelope in the pocket of the car."

"Ingenious and not improbable," Dr. Priestley commented. "And this map with the card folded inside it?"

"The map is quite new. If you look at it you will see that it is perfectly clean, and has not even begun to fray at the folds, as maps always do when they have been used a bit. Ellingwood bought it in London; he'd want that particular map to mark out his scheme with. He had it in his pocket when he stole Mr. Chalk's car. I have no doubt that he had one or two of those cards in his pocket as well. This one evidently got in between the folds of the map.

"After it was all over, he put the map, with the card still in it, in the pocket of Lessingham's car, perhaps at the same time as he put the envelope there. And then in his excitement he forgot all about them and pushed the car over the edge of the quarry without giving them another thought."

"Surely this displays a carelessness strangely at variance with his carefully thought-out scheme?" remarked Dr. Priestley.

"It wasn't his only piece of carelessness," retorted Hanslet. "Look at that spanner which you people found. By the way, there's no doubt where that came from. I rang up the Comet works and asked them to check the tool kit on Mr. Chalk's car. They told me that it should contain three double-ended spanners. One was missing — five-sixteenths at one end and three-eighths at the other. And that's just the size of the spanner picked up by you."

"You appear to have a convincing answer to every possible objection, Superintendent," said Dr. Priestley. "What further steps do you propose to take?"

"What I should like to do is to go down to Slowford and have a heart-to-heart talk with Mr and Mrs. Ellingwood," replied Hanslet. "But I simply daren't do it. You know how it is, Professor. The public seems to regard the detection of crime as a sort of game of skill, to be controlled by carefully framed rules. It doesn't seem to have occurred to anybody that, though you may impose rules on the police, which they are bound to observe, you can't impose corresponding rules on the criminal."

Dr. Priestley smiled. He knew that this was a very sore point, not only with the superintendent, but with the whole of Scotland Yard. "You mean, I suppose, that you dare not question Ellingwood without previously warning him, I take it?"

"Exactly. It is all so damn silly that it makes one laugh. But for that absurd rule, I could go down and have a chat with Ellingwood without arousing his suspicions in the least. I would say, for instance, that I was making inquiries as to how Lessingham came to be driving Mr. Chalk's car. Since I had heard that Mrs. Ellingwood was his nearest surviving relation and that Ellingwood had been in touch with him recently, it would be quite natural for me to ask them, in a perfectly friendly way, if they knew anything about it. And once I got started, I could lead the conversation in any direction I liked."

"And now you would have to divulge the fact that you suspected Ellingwood of having murdered Lessingham?"

"That's what our instructions are. And Ellingwood, if he had any sense, would tell me to go to hell, until he had sent for his solicitor."

"The rule would certainly seem to impose a severe handicap upon the police," replied Dr. Priestley. "But failing what we may call the direct method, how do you propose to obtain further evidence in confirmation of Ellingwood's guilt?"

"I'm dashed if I know, Professor. If you can suggest any line of inquiry, I shall be grateful. Of course, there are more reports to come in yet, and I may find a hint among them. Failing that, there is just one thing I've thought of."

"And what is that?" inquired Dr. Priestley.

"Well, I've been thinking about what Mr. Farrant said the other day. Ellingwood has got to prove that Purvis died first, before his wife gets Lessingham's money. And how is he going to do that, I'd like to know?"

"There would certainly seem to be difficulties in the way," replied Dr. Priestley. "But does waiting for that event exhaust all the possibilities? There would seem to be other clues remaining unexplored. Have you, for instance, discovered who sent the telegram to Lessingham?"

Hanslet laughed shortly. "Yes, I have," he replied. "That clue's a dead end, I'm afraid. The telegram was genuine enough, and it was sent by one of Lessingham's lady loves. A policeman finds himself in queer situations sometimes, Professor. Would you like to hear about an adventure that happened to me last night?"

Dr. Priestley nodded, and Hanslet described his interview with Mrs. Burford. "She was telling the truth all right; I could see that at the time. She had to, for she was fairly cornered, in spite of Orchard's desperate attempt to save her. And that's the secret of the George Love yarn he told us, Mr. Merefield."

"I don't altogether blame him," replied Harold. "He did his best to keep the woman's name out of it."

"I suppose he was justified, to a certain extent. Anyway, there's no great harm done. Orchard knows nothing about his master's murder, of that I'm pretty certain. Nor does this Mrs. Burford. She gave the right name and address to me. By the way, I verified that, and I got our handwriting expert on to the statement I made her write out. Pretty neat that, I thought, making her write the telegram over again, I mean. I was able to compare it with the same wording on the telegram form. The expert says that there isn't a shadow of doubt that they were written by the same hand."

"So that disposes of the telegram," remarked Dr. Priestley. "I fear that you have a difficult task before you, Superintendent. There is a vast difference between suspecting a criminal and being able to bring him to justice, as we have learned by experience. I can only assure you of my heartiest wishes for your success."

"What do you think would be the best way for me to get to work, Professor?" asked Hanslet hopefully.

Dr. Priestley glanced at the clock as he shook his head. "At the moment I can offer no suggestions that would be likely to be helpful," he replied. "But if you happen to see Mrs. Burford again, I should ask her if she or Lessingham were acquainted with Mr. Chalk."

Hanslet correctly interpreted Dr. Priestley's manner as a sign of dismissal. "I'll do that," he said, as he got up to go. "But you'll remember that Chalk said definitely that he had never heard of Lessingham. Still, there's no harm in asking. I'll let you know the result."

CHAPTER XVIII

SUPERINTENDENT, always discreet, called at Shetland Mansions next day, at a time when he guessed that Mrs. Burford's husband would be at his office. The ostensible reason for his visit was to make inquiries about a suspicious individual alleged to have been seen hanging about the place. But as soon as he found himself alone with Mrs. Burford, he put the question which the professor had suggested.

"Chalk?" she replied thoughtfully. "No, I know nobody of that name. He may have been a friend of Aubrey's. That I cannot say, but I do not remember that he ever mentioned him to me. And I think he must have mentioned the names of most of his friends to me at one time or another."

"Mr. Chalk owns a car exactly similar to Mr. Lessingham's," suggested Hanslet.

"Then I am pretty sure that they did not know one another," she replied. "When Aubrey first thought of going in for the rally, he talked to me about the difficulty of finding some one suitable to go with him. He said that he would like to take somebody who owned a sports Comet himself, so that they would know all about driving the car. And he said definitely that he didn't know any other Comet owners."

Hanslet rang up Dr. Priestley's number and reported this conversation. Harold took the message and repeated it to his employer, who frowned slightly as he heard it. "It was merely a bow drawn at a venture," he said. "But a possibility occurred to me, which I thought it worth while inquiring into. This possibility was that Mr. Chalk's car was not stolen."

"Not stolen, sir!" exclaimed Harold. "But we know it was stolen. The car Lessingham was driving has been identified as Mr. Chalk's, beyond any possibility of doubt."

"Certainly, my boy. But you do not grasp my meaning. A car can only be said to be stolen when it has been appropriated by some person other than the owner."

"I'm sorry, sir, but I still don't quite follow what you mean," said Harold doubtfully.

"Has it not occurred to you that we have only Mr Chalk's word for what happened on the night he lost his car? It is at least possible that when he went out to fetch it he found it where he had left it. He was familiar with the neighbourhood and could have concealed it elsewhere. Then when the search for it was in progress he could have hidden it more safely. The theory that Mr. Chalk, if not the actual criminal, was in league with him, cannot be dismissed as impossible."

"But what possible motive could he have for wanting to murder Lessingham, sir? The two were complete strangers."

"So far as we know, they were. But perhaps we have been too ready to assume that Lessingham was the intended victim. It is equally possible that it was Purvis whose life was sought. How do we know that Purvis and Mr. Chalk were not acquainted?"

Harold repressed an inclination to smile. He flattered himself that he could read his employer's mind like a book. It was Dr. Priestley's way, if any one propounded a theory, to set up an alternative, apparently in a pure spirit of contradiction.

"All that's possible, I'll admit, sir," he replied. "But, after all, there's not much doubt that Hanslet's got his finger on the spot he's found an uncommonly plausible motive. And from what he tells us, everything points to this chap Ellingwood being the criminal."

"You are probably right, my boy," said Dr. Priestley, with unexpected mildness. "I was only trying to emphasise the fact that it is unwise to follow one line of reasoning to the exclusion of all others. It is always advisable to keep as open a mind as possible in these matters. But it is the business of the police and not ours to bring the murderer to justice."

Meanwhile, Hanslet, finding himself in that direction, resolved to pay a visit in person to the Copdock Hotel. It was an unpretentious sort of place, evidently run on the cheapest possible lines. Even the entrance had an unkempt appearance, and once inside, he detected a heavy penetrating smell, compounded of fried onions and stale tobacco smoke.

In reply to his inquiries he learned that Ellingwood had stayed in room number 36 on the top floor. That room was at present unoccupied and at the superintendent's request, he was taken up there and left alone. It was a particularly uninviting apartment. Its single window with grime-obscured panes and dingy lace curtains looked out upon a depressing vista of roofs and chimneys. The only furniture was an iron bedstead, covered with a quilt of questionable cleanliness, a painted deal chest of drawers and a ricketty washing-stand. On the floor were the tattered remnants of what had once been a cheap carpet. And at one side of the room was a rusty iron fireplace, empty but for a piece of newspaper placed behind the bars.

"By jove, Ellingwood must be pretty hard pressed to stop at a place like this!" exclaimed Hanslet. "The point is, did he leave any traces of his visit behind him?"

He set to work methodically. The chest of drawers was empty, save for a few torn scraps of newspaper, a year old, which had served as lining for the drawers. The washing-stand and bed were equally bare. Then Hanslet approached the fireplace and peeped in. As he had expected, the paper in front concealed an extensive collection of unsavoury looking litter.

This he removed and laid upon the floor. It was pretty clear that the grate had not been cleaned out for months. The litter consisted for the most part of discarded shaving papers and haircombings, intermingled with cigarette ends and fragments of torn up letters. Even Hanslet, accustomed to such things, had to summon up all his resolution before he could bring himself to handle it.

He began by sorting out the torn letters as best he could. But none of them seemed to bear any reference to Ellingwood, and from such dates as he could decipher, they seemed to have been discarded by previous occupants of the room. And then, as he raked over the debris, he came upon a rolled-up ball, which, from its colour, he recognised as a telegram.

As he unrolled it he caught sight of the address and knew that his labour had not been wasted. It was with a growing feeling of triumph that he read the message. The telegram had been handed in at Slough at 12.47 pm on March 1st, and the wording was as follows: "Ellingwood, Copdock Hotel, Earl's Court. Meet me at the Feathers Inn, Hedgeworth, 9.30 to-morrow evening — most urgent." And the telegram was signed "Lessingham."

"Well, if that isn't the finishing touch that will put the rope round Ellingwood's neck, I'm a Dutchman!" muttered Hanslet. He raked over the debris once or twice again, without finding anything further. Then he went downstairs and interviewed the melancholy-looking individual who appeared to combine the duties of porter and reception clerk.

This man remembered the incident of Ellingwood's departure. He had given notice of his intention of leaving at breakfast that morning. Then he had gone out and did not return till some time between one and two. "He'd been very poor-spirited all the time he was here, sir. A nice enough gentleman, as you might say, but you could see he had something on his mind. And when he came in that time he looked terribly downcast.

"I gave him a telegram that had just come for him and he tore it open and read it. He seemed puzzled at first, and then he brightened up. He said something about his luck having turned, or something like that. I don't exactly recollect his very words now. Then he went up to his room to pack, and soon after he came down carrying his suitcase and left. And that's the last I saw of him."

"You've no idea where he went to, I suppose?"

"No, that I haven't, sir. He just said good-bye to me and walked out of the door."

Hanslet asked for a Bradshaw, and rather to his astonishment the man produced one. It was some months old, but that was to be expected in such a place. He turned over the pages until he found the table referring to Hedgeworth. There was a train leaving London at 12.55. It was now just after half-past. There was no time to be wasted if he was to catch it.

A taxi from the Copdock Hotel took him to the terminus with five minutes to spare. By the time he had bought his ticket and a couple of sandwiches these had dwindled to one. However, he was lucky enough to find a corner seat, into which he subsided as the train moved out.

Hedgeworth station, which he reached soon after three, proved to be a busier place than he had expected. Apparently it served a fairly extensive residential area. The village, he was told, was half a mile or so away, and, having learned that there was a train back to London shortly after five, he set out to walk it.

He found Hedgeworth a straggling sort of place, as though it had grown up haphazard. Places of refreshment seemed fairly plentiful, ranging from the pretentiousness of "Ye Olde Redde Lyon" — a modern redbrick structure displaying the usual lures for the unsuspecting motorist — to the more modest comfort of such ale houses as "The Waggon and Horses." But of the "Feathers" there was no sign. It was not until he reached the farther end of the village that he found it — a retiring little house standing by itself. But he noticed that the main road from London to Moorchester passed the door.

It being during those hours in which licensed premises are compelled by law to suspend business, the place was shut. But after repeated knockings the door was unbolted and an elderly man peered out. Seeing the stranger before him his expression became slightly more affable. "Sorry, master," he said, "but we don't open till six in these parts."

"That's all right," replied Hanslet. "Here's my card. I want a few words with you." Then, seeing the look of apprehension on the man's face, he added, "I only want to make inquiries about a man who called here a few days ago."

The landlord, somewhat reassured, let him in. He informed him that his name was John Trumper, and that he'd never had any complaints — no, not in the thirty years or more he'd held his licence.

"Well, that's a very good record, Mr. Trumper," replied Hanslet. "Now, look here, I'm a bona fide traveller if ever there was one, and though the asses who made the laws say I mustn't have a drink, what about it?"

But Mr. Trumper smiled cunningly. "No, sir, you don't catch an old bird like me that way," he replied firmly.

Hanslet laughed heartily. "Lord, man, I wasn't trying to catch you!" he replied. "The law says that police officers may enter licensed premises at any time — and if that doesn't mean that they can have a drink when they're there, what does it mean,

I should like to know? Now, you draw me a pint of beer and one for yourself, like a good chap, and let's get to business."

The superintendent's manner prevailed over the worthy publican's scruples. He asked his visitor into the bar parlour and drew the beer. "There you are, sir, and here's my respects," he said, as they raised their tankards simultaneously.

"Ah, that's the stuff to keep a man alive!" exclaimed Hanslet, after a long and earnest pull. "Now, Mr. Trumper, I'd like to take up a few minutes of your time, if you don't mind. Do you remember the evening of Wednesday the 2nd?"

Mr. Trumper rubbed his nose thoughtfully. "Wednesday," he remarked slowly. "That's early closing day. Tuesday was the first I recollect. Why, yes, sir, I remember that evening well enough. It was when all they cars were driving through here with flags and numbers on them. Kept it up best part of the night, they did. 'Twere a competition, or something, the chaps were saying."

"That's right," replied Hanslet encouragingly. "Now, did you have any strangers in that evening?"

"Why, yes, we did, sir. A gentleman that said he was looking out for somebody in one of them cars with flags."

Hanslet heaved a sigh of relief. His journey had not been wasted. "What was the gentleman's name?" he asked.

But this question proved too much for Mr. Trumper. "Ah, now you're asking, sir," he replied. "He did tell me, but it's slipped my memory. Maybe the missis will mind; she's got a wonderful head for names." He put his head out of the door of the bar. "Mother!" he bawled. "Can you recollect the name of the gentleman what was here that evening all them cars went by? Him as said he was waiting for one of them to stop."

A woman's voice answered him from somewhere in the upper part of the house. "Lor, now, I've got it on the tip of my tongue. Something to do with cutting down trees, it was. I recollect it at the time I thought it was a queer sort of name. I know — Fellingwood. That was it!"

"Aye, so it was!" exclaimed Mr. Trumper. "That's the name, sir — Fellingwood. I knew the missis would be sure to mind it."

This was eminently satisfactory. The addition of an initial letter did not alter the identity of the individual. "That was the man, I expect. I want to get into touch with him if I can. You don't know where he came from or went to, I suppose?"

"No, that I don't, sir. He came in about half-past seven that evening, shortly before the first of them cars began to go past. He asked me if I could give him a bite of bread and cheese, and when he'd had that and a drop of beer, we got chatting. He told me that a gentleman in a car had asked him to meet him here at half-past nine."

"He didn't happen to mention the name of the gentleman in the car, I suppose?"

"Not that I can recollect, sir. It struck me as queer at first that the gentleman should want to meet him here. That sort of folk generally stops at the Red Lion, or one of them posh places up the street. But when he said that the gentleman would be in a hurry and would probably only be stopping for a minute or two, I saw how it was. If he was coming from London way, he'd have to pass my door. That was it, you may be sure, sir."

"Yes, that was it, I expect. Did Mr. Fellingwood bring a suitcase with him, or anything like that?"

"No, sir, he wasn't carrying anything. As I say, we was chatting in here. There weren't more than one or two of the regular chaps in-there never is on early closing nights. Most of them goes into Moorchester to the pictures. And every time he hears a car go past, he goes to the window and looks out. It seemed to me he was all of a fidget, as though he was terribly anxious to meet this other gentleman."

Hanslet walked across to the window and looked out. Just outside at the edge of the pavement was a lamp post. It was evident that this would throw enough light upon the passing cars to enable the rally flag to be seen and the R.A.C official number to be read easily.

"I expect he was a bit anxious." remarked the Superintendent grimly. "What happened when his friend turned up?"

Mr. Trumper shook his head. "That I can't say, sir," he replied. "You see, 'twas like this: Half-past nine came and nothing happened. They cars was going past all the time, but none of them stops. And this Mr. Fellingwood was getting more and more fidgety every moment. At last he asks me what time we closed and I tells him ten o'clock. He asks me if he could have a bed here, so as he could stop on after then. I told him I was sorry, but he couldn't. You see, sir, though we've got a couple of rooms where we sometimes put folk up, the missis doesn't care to be bothered unless she knows them."

"I don't blame her. It's a nuisance having people in the house, and there are plenty of other places in the village they can go to."

"That's just what I said myself, sir. But he said he couldn't go anywhere else, for fear of missing his friend. 'I'll just have to stand outside the door then.' he says. 'My friend can't be long now,' he says, just like that."

The superintendent nodded. "And what was the last you saw of him?" he asked.

"Why, sir, when I closed the house at ten o'clock he says 'good-night', and walks out. Whether or not he met his friend I can't say. The missis and I sits down to supper and then goes to bed. I expect he did, though, for them cars wasn't finished yet by a long way. It must have been nigh on four o'clock in the morning before the last of them went through."

Hanslet thanked Mr. Trumper for his information, and, after consuming another pint, strolled back to the station. He reached London soon after seven, went straight to Scotland Yard and immediately became busy on the telephone. Supper was brought up to him while he was thus engaged. He did ample justice to it, to make up for the loss of his lunch. Finally, when he had secured the information he required, he left the Yard and took a taxi to Dr. Priestley's house in Westbourne Terrace.

He was later than his usual hour, and when he sent in his name, Harold came out to meet him in the hall. "The professor says he'll see you for a few minutes if it's really urgent," he said. "But, between ourselves, he's in one of his bad moods to-day. I don't know what's come over him. He's irritable and restless and snaps at me if I say anything to him. He gets like that sometimes, as you know."

Hanslet made a grimace. "I know, right enough," he replied. "Still, I think I'll risk seeing him, now that I'm here. I think what I've got to tell him is urgent enough for him to listen to."

Harold had not exaggerated his employer's mood. He barely looked up as Hanslet entered the room. "Well, Superintendent?" he asked curtly.

"I have some information that I think will interest you, Professor," Hanslet replied quietly. "It concerns Ellingwood. I have definite evidence of his presence at Hedgeworth on the evening of March 2nd."

It seemed to the superintendent that a slightly puzzled expression came into Dr. Priestley's eyes. "Indeed!" he replied more genially. "That is certainly interesting. Perhaps you will give me the details as briefly as possible."

Hanslet recounted his discovery of the telegram in the room which Ellingwood had occupied at the Copdock Hotel. He produced the crumpled message and gave it to the professor. Then he described his journey to Hedgeworth and his conversation with Mr. Trumper.

Dr. Priestley listened until he had come to an end. "And what deductions do you draw from this, Superintendent?" he asked.

"It seems to me that it completely proves your theory, Professor," replied Hanslet diplomatically. "But there are two more points I would like to mention. After I came back from Hedgeworth I got the police at Slough to make inquiries about the telegram. They got hold of the original and are sending it up to me. I haven't seen it yet, of course, but they say that it is written in a small, neat hand, whereas Lessingham's writing, as you saw by that envelope I showed you, is fairly large and straggling.

"That's the first point. The second is this: Ellingwood was carrying a suitcase when he left the Copdock Hotel. What had he done with it? Had he dragged it about with him during the night of the first and second? It seemed most unlikely, and then I had an idea. He might have deposited it in the cloak-room at Paddington.

"I knew that at Great Western cloak-rooms they always ask the name of the depositor. So I rang up and made inquiries. It was a long shot, I'll admit, but it came off, A suitcase had been deposited at Number One cloak-room in the name of

Ellingwood at about half-past two on Tuesday 1st, and removed in the course of the afternoon of the 3rd."

"This appears to introduce a complication with which I had not reckoned," muttered Dr. Priestley, as though speaking to himself. Then, in his normal voice, he continued. "And what is your explanation of these facts?"

"Take the telegram first, Professor," replied Hanslet. "Slough is on the main road from London to Bath. If Lessingham left London when Orchard says he did he could easily have been in Slough at the time the telegram was sent off. But it seems pretty certain, from what they tell me of the handwriting, that Lessingham didn't send it.

"Well, then, who did? I think I can make a pretty good guess. Ellingwood sent it himself. Slough is only half-an-hour from London by train. Ellingwood could have gone down to Slough on Tuesday morning, sent the telegram at 12.47 and been back at the Copdock Hotel, as the chap there told me, some time between one and two."

"That would certainly be possible," said Dr. Priestley. "But what was Ellingwood's object in thus sending a telegram to himself, and signing it Lessingham?"

"Why, don't you see, Professor, he was taking precautions in advance!" exclaimed Hanslet. "Why did he throw the telegram into the grate in his room? So that it should be found. There was always the risk that somebody might suspect Lessingham had been murdered. There was also the risk that Ellingwood might be seen hanging about Hedgeworth after he had stolen Mr. Chalk's car; so he decided to provide a reason for being there. The apparent rendezvous with Lessingham supplied that."

"Ingenious, Superintendent, but, if I may say so purely conjectural," was Dr. Priestley's comment. "Have you a specimen of Purvis's handwriting?"

"Purvis!" exclaimed Hanslet in a puzzled tone. "No, I haven't. Why? What had Purvis got to do with it?"

"Possibly nothing at all. But I suggest an alternative theory, not necessarily the correct one, but to show you that your own is not the only one which will fit in with the facts at present known. Purvis, we believe, drove from London to Bath with Lessingham. Is it not possible that Lessingham stayed in the car while Purvis despatched the telegram for him?"

"But Lessingham can't have sent that telegram," objected Hanslet. "He had already written a letter to Ellingwood, which he put in his pocket and meant to post. You've seen the envelope yourself, Professor. And that letter was addressed to Slowford. If he had wired Ellingwood he would have addressed the telegram there as well."

Dr. Priestley shook his head. "I do not think that our knowledge of the relations between Lessingham and Ellingwood is yet complete," he replied. "However, let us pass on to Ellingwood's visit to Hedgeworth."

"Showing himself at the Feathers was all part of his plan," said Hanslet positively. "To make quite sure, he told the landlord his name, which he certainly needn't have done. No doubt your reconstruction is right, Professor. He had driven Mr. Chalk's car down to the wood near the village the previous night. The Feathers was just the observation post he wanted. He could watch the cars go past, as in fact he did. Lessingham must have passed somewhere round about ten o'clock.

"As soon as he had seen him go through, Ellingwood knew that everything was all right. He walked back to the wood, uncovered Mr. Chalk's car, in which he had already changed the steering pin and drove carefully to the Moorchester control, and after that everything went exactly as you explained it."

"But, according to your theory, Superintendent, Ellingwood took pains to ensure that his visit to Hedgeworth should become known. What, then, have you gained by the discovery?"

"The discovery in itself is nothing, since we knew already that he must have been there. It's just an example of the common tendency for the criminal to be too clever or not clever enough. He was cocksure that we should never find out how Lessingham was murdered, or he wouldn't have been so anxious to show up at Hedgeworth. As it is, it shows how carefully he had premeditated the whole thing."

"What you have told me certainly furnishes a proof of premeditated action," replied Dr. Priestley. "But it is by no means so certain that the premeditation was on Ellingwood's part."

CHAPTER XIX

HAD Dr. Priestley's attitude been more sympathetic, it is pretty certain that Hanslet would have applied for a warrant for Ellingwood's arrest without further delay. He felt that his case was as complete as it was ever likely to be, and that no reasonable person could harbour any doubt as to where the guilt of Lessingham's murder lay. But Dr. Priestley had been scarcely encouraging, and Hanslet had a deep respect for his opinion. Dr. Priestley never made a move until he was certain that the move was justified. And he was obviously disposed not to make a move as yet. One remark of his possibly explained this — "I do not think that our knowledge of the relations between Ellingwood and Lessingham is yet complete." There was something in that, certainly. Hanslet decided to stay his hand for a few days, meanwhile keeping Ellingwood under the closest observation. Thus, perhaps, the missing link would be supplied.

During this period, Dr. Priestley never referred to the Lessingham case in Harold's presence. In fact, so far as his secretary was concerned, he seemed definitely to have put it out of his mind. Nevertheless, his proceedings were in the highest degree mysterious. He sent Harold out upon errands which took him the whole day, or employed him in looking up obscure references in remote libraries. On one of these occasions, Harold, returning earlier than could have been suspected, could hardly believe his eyes. He almost ran into a young woman of rather startling and distinctly foreign appearance, who was leaving the house.

It was on the evening of this most unexpected encounter that Dr. Priestley returned again to the subject of the Lessingham case. Harold was describing his lack of success in a certain research which had been allotted to him and rather expected some acid comments upon his stupidity. But, rather to his astonishment, Dr. Priestley waved his excuses aside. "It does not matter, my boy," he said. "You may be more fortunate on a subsequent occasion. Instant success comes to very few of us. There is Superintendent Hanslet, for example. Since we have heard nothing further from him, it is to be supposed that he has not yet secured definite and positive proof of Ellingwood's guilt."

"I expect he is gathering all the details he can before he arrests the fellow, sir," replied Harold.

"Possibly, possibly. Undue haste in such matters is always to be deprecated. But I hope very shortly to be in a position to help him to make his decision. I did not tell you that I had an interview with a friend of yours, yesterday afternoon."

Harold wondered who this could be. Not another of those strange females, surely!" Who was that sir?" he asked.

"Mr. Gateman," replied Dr. Priestley. "A most entertaining conversationalist. And, I may say, a young man of exceptional talent. We spent a very entertaining hour together."

"Richard!" exclaimed Harold. "Did he come here, sir? I suppose he wanted to see me."

"Oh, dear, no," replied Dr. Priestley urbanely. "He came here upon my invitation. He was sorry to find that you were out, of course. But it is probable that you and he will meet in a day or so."

Harold might have ventured upon another question, but at that moment the telephone bell rang and he ran to answer it. "Hold on, please, Clayport wants you," said the voice at the exchange, and a moment later Bob Weldon's voice: "Hallo, is that you, Harold? Richard tells me that the professor is going away for a few days and that you'll be at a loose end. Why don't you come down here? We shall be delighted to have you."

"Richard told you what?" replied Harold. "Dash it all, I am getting a bit out of my depth. Hold on a minute — there's a good chap."

He went back to the study and reported Bob's message. "He must have got hold of the wrong end of the stick, somehow, sir," he added.

The shadow of a smile passed across Dr. Priestley's face. "Oh no," he replied. "I should have mentioned the matter to you before, but I have scarcely seen you during the past few days. I told Mr. Gateman that I should find it necessary to be away from home for a few days, and he must have passed the information on to Mr. Weldon. It is very kind of him to ask you to stay with him at Clayport. You must, of course, accept his invitation. To-morrow would be a suitable day for you to go. There is, if I remember rightly, an excellent train from Waterloo at ten-thirty."

Harold went back to the telephone. "I say, it's awfully good of you," he said. "Dr. Priestley says that I had better come to-morrow by the ten-thirty. Will that suit you?"

"Perfectly. I'll meet you at the station in the car. So long till then."

Harold returned to the study in a state of considerable mystification. It was perfectly clear to him that his employer was preparing some scheme, but the nature of it he could not guess. Why had he sent for Richard, and through him prompted Bob to issue his invitation? It looked very much as though his employer was about to undertake something in which he was not to participate. This was a most uncomfortable thought. "When will you want me back, sir?" he asked sulkily.

It seemed that Dr. Priestley had read his mind like a book. "It will be of material assistance to me if you will join Mr. Weldon at Clayport to-morrow, my boy," he replied gently. "You need not be afraid that you will miss anything of interest by so doing. Within a short time of your arrival you will receive further instructions. When you get them, I shall want you to use your influence with Mr. Weldon to induce him to assist me a second time."

And with that, Dr. Priestley turned to other matters having no bearing whatever upon his projected absence.

So Harold went down to Clayport without any clear idea of what was expected of him. Nor was Bob particularly helpful. He had received a letter from Richard in which he had mentioned that he had seen Dr. Priestley. The latter had told him that he was going away for a few days, and that it would be a good opportunity for Harold to take a holiday. He had suggested that Bob might put him up for a few days. He had also expressed a hope that Bob would make no appointments for the coming week-end.

"I got that letter yesterday morning," said Bob. "Of course, I was only too glad of the hint, so I rang you up yesterday evening, when I knew you'd be in. I also rang up Richard, to see if he could come down, too, but he's got something on — a fancy dress ball, I think he said. Just the sort of thing he revels in."

"I never heard a word of all this till you rang up," replied Harold. "My old man never breathed a word that he was going away and he hasn't told me even now when he's going or where he's going to. And what the dickens does he mean by hoping that you will keep yourself free over the week-end? He's got some game on, you may depend upon it."

"Well, to-day's Thursday, so we ought to know pretty soon what it's all about. I've purposely made no plans and I'm entirely at his disposal. I enjoyed our time at Moorchester the other day, and I hope he's got something similar in his mind."

That evening Harold acquainted Bob with the latest developments of the Lessingham case. "I don't think there can be any doubt that Hanslet is on the right track," he said. "The professor didn't seem very enthusiastic about it at first, but now that he's had time to think about it, I fancy that he sees there's no alternative. He hinted to me as much last night. He said that he hoped to be able to help Hanslet to come to a decision."

"Well, from what you tell me, it sounds as though Ellingwood must be the man." replied Bob. "Pretty ingenious bloke he must be, too. If it hadn't been for Dr. Priestley, he'd never have been found out. And even now it seems to me that friend

Hanslet will have a bit of a job to prove his case. If you ask me, it looks as though the professor had hit upon some dodge to make it quite certain that Ellingwood did it. Certain in the eyes of a jury, I mean."

Next morning Harold received a letter from Dr. Priestley, enclosing another for Bob. His own was brief and to the point, merely a request that he would hand on the enclosure and endeavour to persuade Bob to comply with the request contained in it. Harold passed both on to his host.

"Now we're getting a move on," he remarked. Bob opened his letter and read it aloud.

"DEAR MR. WELDON, I retain very pleasant memories of our recent meeting at the Imperial Hotel at Moorchester. I shall be staying there again to-morrow night (Friday) and it would afford me the greatest pleasure if you and Harold could join me as my guests. If you can do so, perhaps you would drive over in your Armstrong-Siddeley, which has already performed such excellent service, arriving before dinner on Friday evening.

"I am very greatly looking forward to this second meeting, and I hope most sincerely that you will not disappoint me. Yours sincerely, LAUNCELOT PRIESTLEY."

"So that's it, is it?" was Harold's comment. "Why couldn't the old boy have told me before I came down here? He's thought of something that hasn't struck anybody else, I'll be bound. What about it? Is it putting you out at all?"

"Not in the least." replied Bob heartily. "We'll go along and see what his game is. I shouldn't wonder if we had a most interesting evening of it. Moorchester is about a hundred and twenty miles from here. We'll start after lunch, take things easy, and have plenty of time for a cocktail before dinner. But I'm a bit surprised that it's Moorchester again. I should have thought that the professor had seen everything there was to be seen there last time."

"But he didn't know then that Ellingwood had been to the Feathers at Hedgeworth," replied Harold. "I shouldn't be surprised if that had given him an idea. But what beats me is the roundabout way he's gone about it. What made him send for Richard like that while I was out? It would have been much easier to tell me that he wanted you to meet him at Moorchester, like he did before."

Bob chuckled. "Perhaps he doesn't want you to know everything he's up to," he said. "But I admit that I don't quite see where Richard comes in. It struck me that he was a bit mysterious when I rang him up the other night. Still, as your old man would say, conjecture is unprofitable. We shall know all about it when we get to Moorchester."

The weather was remarkably fine for the middle of March, and they had a very enjoyable drive. Their way lay through Westernham, and as they approached the little town Bob smiled. "It isn't opening time yet," he said. "If it was I'd stop at the

White Hart and have a drink for old times' sake. Failing that, how would you like to pay a call on Sergeant Showerby?"

"I wouldn't mind, but I don't think that the Sergeant would be particularly thrilled," replied Harold. "He's forgotten all about the affair by now. An unfortunate accident, like dozens of others you read about. If we were to tell him that we had proof positive that those two poor chaps had been murdered, he'd make a note of it and get rid of us as soon as he could."

"He'd probably want to take our photographs first. That hobby of his turned out pretty useful, after all. I must confess I thought it rather ridiculous at the time."

"It wasn't until the professor asked for the photographs that any real use was made of them, all the same." said Harold.

They reached the Imperial Hotel soon after 6 o'clock. Dr. Priestley had not yet arrived, but they found upon inquiry that four rooms had been reserved in his name. "And who's the fourth?" asked Bob, as they took up a position in the corner of the lounge.

Harold shrugged his shoulders. "Heaven alone knows," he replied. "I'm out of this. Perhaps he has persuaded Richard to give up his fancy-dress ball, though it seems unlikely. We'll know pretty soon, now, if the professor comes down by the same train as we did before."

"I have an idea that things are going to happen this evening," said Bob. "I think I'll slip up and see that the car's full up with petrol."

He had barely returned from his inspection of the car when Dr. Priestley entered the lounge. He was not alone. By his side was the burly form of Superintendent Hanslet.

Harold and Bob exchanged inquiring glances as they rose and joined the newcomers. But Dr. Priestley offered no explanation. He introduced Hanslet to Bob, led the way to a group of chairs and ordered cocktails. "I am so glad that you were able to join us, Mr. Weldon," he said. "We shall be a very happy little party, I am sure. You will find that they serve a most excellent dinner here, Superintendent. I feel sure that you will enjoy it, after your journey from London."

Hanslet muttered something unintelligible in reply. It was clear that he was not yet in the professor's confidence, and that he was wondering why he had been brought to Moorchester. He swallowed his cocktail hastily. "Since I'm here, I'd like to see the place where you say the cars were substituted for one another, Professor," he remarked.

"There will be plenty of time for that later," replied Dr. Priestley. "You could not form an adequate idea of the conditions unless you saw it when it was really dark. Besides, dinner will be ready very shortly now."

And with this, Hanslet had to be content. But his feelings, whatever they may have been, did not interfere with his enjoyment of dinner, to which he did full justice. During the meal Dr. Priestley guided the conversation into other channels, and it was not until dessert and a bottle of port had been placed on the table that he referred to the reason of the meeting.

"On the occasion of my last visit to Moorchester, Mr. Weldon was kind enough to assist me in a series of experiments," he said. "You have been informed of the result of these, Superintendent. I am going to ask him to repeat his kindness, and to take part in another experiment which we shall all witness. Would you be so kind as to drive us to Hedgeworth, Mr. Weldon?"

"Certainly, sir; any time you like," replied Bob promptly.

"Thank you very much. You remember the place where the spanner was found, and where we decided that Mr. Chalk's car must have been concealed? I should like, if possible, to reach that spot exactly at ten o'clock."

"I remember it perfectly," replied Bob. "It's about nine now. If we start at half-past or soon after, we shall do it comfortably."

It was twenty-five minutes to ten when they left the hotel. Bob was at the wheel, with Dr. Priestley sitting beside him. In the back of the car were Harold and the superintendent. The latter took the opportunity of whispering to his companion: "What's this stunt we're on?"

"I haven't the slightest idea," replied Harold. "He said nothing to me. What did he say to you?"

"Told me that if I'd come down here and stay a couple of nights with him he'd show me something. But it strikes me that ten o'clock on a dark night is a queer time to choose to show anybody anything."

The night was certainly dark — there was no doubt about that. And a slight ground mist did not improve matters. It was not opaque, but it restricted the field of the lights and made fast driving difficult.

"I don't care about this mist, sir," remarked Bob. "This is how that fog began that we ran into on the second night of the rally. Fortunately, it's a pretty straight road to Hedgeworth, and we're not likely to lose our way."

"A slight fog may assist as to carry out our experiment," replied Dr. Priestley enigmatically. "As long as it does not prevent us from reaching the vicinity of the wood by ten o'clock, there will be no harm done."

But it seemed that evening as though they were fated to be delayed. Scarcely more than five miles out of Moorchester a row of red lights stretched across the road before them, and the beam of their headlights revealed the ominous notice — "Road Closed. Fork left for London." This meant a long detour through winding byways before the main road was regained. When the dock on the dash showed ten o'clock they were still five miles from their destination.

However, the mist had become no thicker, and Bob pushed the Armstrong along as fast as he dared. They shot through the trees of the first wood and the second, and were approaching the third, when Bob uttered a sudden exclamation and clapped on his brakes. Close in front of them a man had leaped out from the shadows into the road. He was followed by a female figure apparently in full pursuit. The man ran a short distance and jumped into a small car, drawn up by the roadside and hitherto invisible. The tail light of this car showed suddenly red, and from the Armstrong they could hear the roar of a violently accelerated engine. Then the car drew in to the gleam of their headlights, and set off at high speed in the direction of London. The woman reached it as it was on the move and jumped for the footboard. But the driver leaned out and pushed her off and she fell back staggering on to the roadway.

This sudden drama took no more than a few seconds. Dr. Priestley opened the window and thrust out his head. "Is that you, Mr. Gateman?" he called anxiously.

The female figure spun round. The headlights revealed a seemingly young and pretty girl. But the voice was Richard's. "Oh, there you are, sir," he replied. "He's your man all right. Sorry I couldn't keep him longer."

Dr. Priestley made no reply, but resumed his seat and gripped Bob's arm. "You must overtake that car in front of us!" he exclaimed insistently.

Bob wasted no time in unnecessary questions. The Armstrong leaped forward as he replied, "I'll do my best, sir."

But the superintendent was not so easily satisfied. He had opened the rear door and was half out of the car to the rescue of the damsel in distress when Bob let his clutch in. It was with the greatest difficulty that Harold managed to drag him back. "Dash it all, Professor, what does all this fooling mean?" he demanded angrily. "Is this part of your precious experiment?"

"Certainly," replied Dr. Priestley over his shoulder. "You will understand it when I explain that the driver of the car ahead is undoubtedly the murderer of Lessingham and Purvis."

"Ellingwood, eh?" exclaimed Hanslet. "Well, if that doesn't beat the band! How the dickens do you know that?"

But Dr. Priestley made no reply. His attention was directed to the road in front of him. The car they were pursuing had gained a start of several hundred yards, and all they could see of it was the red eye of its tail lamp on the straighter stretches of the road. The Armstrong had got into her stride now, under Bob's steady hands. But it was impossible to tell whether they were gaining or losing.

The scattered lights of Hedgeworth appeared in front of them, but the speed of the red light did not slacken. It kept straight along the main road, scattering the few pedestrians who were abroad at that hour. They were still swearing as the Armstrong in turn flashed through the village. When they reached open country once more, it seemed as though the red light had gained a little upon them.

"Can you catch him?" asked Dr. Priestley anxiously.

"I can keep him in sight at all events," replied Bob. "Thank heaven we seem to have run out of that confounded mist."

"We can only see him by his tail light. What if he turns that off?"

"Unless he's got a very unusual set of switches, he can't do that without turning off his headlights at the same time. He daren't do that, and he'd have to stop to disconnect the tail lamp, so we're safe enough as far as that goes."

They relapsed into silence, absorbed in the excitement of the chase. The relative distance between the two cars seemed to change very little. Now, the Armstrong seemed to gain slightly, now the red light seemed to be outdistancing them. Dr. Priestley glanced at the speedometer needle and then, alarmed at the reading it showed, averted his eyes quickly.

When the road curved ahead of them, they lost the red light, to pick it up again when the road straightened. But, after this had happened several times, upon emerging upon a straight stretch the red light was nowhere to be seen. The ribbon of road stretched into darkness ahead of them, bare and deserted.

"Hallo, where the devil's he got to?" exclaimed Bob. And then he nodded towards the left of the road, where a faint reflection could be seen above the hedges. "He's turned off somewhere," he continued. "That's the glare of his headlights. Yes, that's right. I can see a turning ahead of us."

The Armstrong rocked as Bob took the corner at high speed. And then the four occupants uttered a simultaneous exclamation. Ahead of them, breasting a long, straight slope was the familiar red light.

"Confound the fellow!" exclaimed Bob. "He probably knows this road and I don't. He'll give us the slip if we're not careful. Let's see if we can't get another ounce out of the bus."

He succeeded, for as both cars roared up the hill, the Armstrong seemed to gain slightly. But, by the time they reached the crest, the red light was still half a mile away and showed no signs of slackening its speed.

"He's got something pretty hot there," remarked Bob grimly. "Still, we're holding him, and this can't go on for ever. Something's bound to hold him up sooner or later, and then we've got him."

But the roads seemed phenomenally clear that night. Now and then pursued and pursuer flashed past a solitary vehicle, or sped with undiminished speed through a village. Once a policeman, startled from the usual peacefulness of his nightly round, held out a warning hand, but retreated hastily as both cars in turn charged at him. "He can't read our numbers while we're going at this pace," said Bob cheerfully. "And if he could, I expect the presence of Scotland Yard would be an excuse in the eyes of the beak. But I'd like to know how much longer this is going to last. It's lucky that I thought of filling up the tank before we started."

It seemed, as he spoke, that the chase might continue indefinitely. It had already lasted nearly an hour, and, try as he would, Bob could not diminish the distance between the two cars, which were still about half a mile apart. They had entered a tract of rolling country, through which the road wound, a succession of long and not very steep ascents and descents. And then at last, as they reached the summit of one of the ridges, they saw the dim glow of a second red light perhaps a mile or more away and stationary, in the valley below them.

"By jove, I believe we've got him at last!" exclaimed Bob. "That's the light of a level crossing and the gates are closed. See some way above it, there's a green light? That's a railway signal down, which means there's a train coming. He'll have to slacken down now, or crash through the gate!"

For a moment it seemed as though Bob's prediction was correct. The man in the flying car ahead of them had evidently seen the warning and his speed slackened appreciably. Then all at once his tail-light swerved off the road to the right.

Bob swore viciously. "He's got all the luck!" he exclaimed. "I wonder where that turning leads to? It must avoid the level crossing, anyhow. Hullo, what in thunder is he playing at?"

For the red glow of the tail-light appeared once more, backing on to the road again. Then it swung out of sight, and in its place appeared a pair of dazzling suns, blinding them. The car had turned and was now coming back towards them with undiminished speed.

Bob slowed up, helpless in the glare. And then with a thrill of horror he realised the meaning of this manoeuvre. "By God!" he shouted. "He's going to run us down! Hold on, all!"

There was no time to stop the Armstrong and leap out. The two cars were approaching one another at fully a hundred miles an hour. Bob, in a frantic endeavour to avoid collision swerved from side to side. But his opponent followed his every movement. It was clear that his intention was that the cars should meet head on in an all-destroying crash.

And then, in the fraction of a second left to him, Bob took an instant decision. He wrenched the steering wheel sharply round, trusting to providence for what might be beside the road. The driver of the on-rushing car followed his example, but just too late. He struck the Armstrong, but not as he had intended. There was a crash, and the tearing sound of rending metal. The occupants of the Armstrong, hurled from their off seats, felt the car heel over as she bumped over the rough ground beside the road. She swayed ominously on two wheels, then recovered her balance with a shuddering shock. And then at last she came to rest, in silence and total darkness.

CHAPTER XX

BOB, who had managed to cling to the wheel, was the first to recover his scattered senses. He groped for the electric torch which he always carried and found it fortunately unbroken. He turned its rays first on Dr. Priestley, to find him sitting dazed, but apparently unhurt. His spectacles had fallen off, however, and lay at his feet.

The superintendent and Harold were picking themselves up from the bottom of the car into which they had been thrown. The former's nose was bleeding, and he was muttering objurgations beneath his breath. Harold had a nasty bruise on his cheek and seemed badly shaken, but mutual inquiries established the fact that nobody had sustained serious injury.

"We all owe our lives to you, Mr. Weldon," said Dr. Priestley gravely. "But what about the other car? The driver has not escaped, has he?"

"If he's still alive, I shall arrest him on the spot," growled Hanslet. "I don't know whether he murdered Lessingham, but he very nearly succeeded in murdering us. Confound it, I can't get this door open!"

They all managed to scramble out at last and, led by Bob with his torch, began their search for the other car. They were not long in finding it. After the crash its impetus had carried it for a few yards. Then it had left the road and overturned. The driver had been flung clear, and lay motionless on a bed of soft bracken beside the road.

The superintendent and Harold knelt down and examined him. "He'll be all right," said Hanslet after a while. "There doesn't seem to be much the matter with him. Just knocked out, that's all. It's Ellingwood, I suppose?"

"None of us have ever seen Mr. Ellingwood," replied Dr. Priestley.

"Well, he must have something in his pockets which will tell us who he is. Could you hold the light a little closer, Mr. Weldon? Thanks very much." Hanslet put his hand in the inner coat pocket of the unconscious man and produced a bundle of papers. Among them was a driving licence. Hanslet opened it, and by the light of

Bob's torch read the name and address inscribed upon it. A puzzled frown spread over his face as he did so. "I don't understand this at all, Professor," he said, "unless Ellingwood is an expert in stealing licences as well as cars. This licence was issued to Henry Burford and the address is 5B Shetland Mansions, S.W. Why, damn it all! That must be the husband of Mrs. Burford who sent the wire to Lessingham."

"Very possibly," replied Dr. Priestley. "But surely the man's identity can be verified when he recovers consciousness. The immediate problem appears to me to concern the disposal of him, and incidentally, of ourselves. I never for a moment contemplated such an unpleasant termination to my experiment. Have you any idea where we are, Mr. Weldon?"

"Not the foggiest, sir," replied Bob cheerfully. "I was too busy following the other fellow to think of where we were going."

"It seems to me, sir, that the best thing will be for me to walk along the road to the level crossing," remarked Harold. "There's bound to be somebody there."

Dr. Priestley agreed to this, and Harold set off, leaving the other three to guard the prisoner. Bob turned his attention to the Armstrong, to find that although she was pretty badly knocked about, she was still capable of being towed. The other car was lying by the roadside with all four wheels in the air, and it was obvious that a breakdown gang would be needed to shift it.

While they were waiting for Harold's return, the superintendent made several attempts to induce Dr. Priestley to explain the nature of his experiment, but without result. "There will be time enough for that when we have disposed of our prisoner safely," said the professor, who had recovered his spectacles, miraculously unbroken. "You have retained the objects which you found in his pockets, I hope?"

"I've got them safe enough," replied Hanslet. "He'll have to answer a very serious charge when he wakes up. Why, it was a deliberate attempt to kill the lot of us."

The prisoner was still unconscious when Harold returned, though he was beginning to show signs of recovery. Harold's news was distinctly reassuring. "I found the watchman at the level crossing," he said. "He had heard the crash and seen the lights of the cars go out, so he promptly telephoned to the police at the nearest town, which isn't more than half a dozen miles away, and they're on their way out now."

So it happened that within an hour the prisoner was lodged in hospital with a policeman sitting by his bedside and Dr. Priestley and his party were installed in the local hotel But the Professor refused to give any explanation that night. He pleaded that they all required rest after the ordeal which they had been through. "Besides, the explanation would be incomplete without Mr. Gateman's statement. I suggest that we return to Moorchester as early as possible, and telephone to Mr. Gateman, who should be at the Red Lion at Hedgeworth, to meet us there."

It was not until they were all assembled next day in a private room at the Imperial Hotel that Dr. Priestley consented to speak. "First of all, Superintendent, have you established the identity of the prisoner?"

"I can't make it out, Professor," replied Hanslet. "Apart from the driving licence, the man was carrying visiting cards and a lot of letters, all belonging to Burford. Yet, if you say he's the murderer of Lessingham, he must be Ellingwood."

"You shall judge that for yourself," said Dr. Priestley. "Among the letters you found was there one in a female handwriting, and signed, 'A friend of Mr. Lessingham?'"

"How on earth did you guess that, Professor?" replied Hanslet, in astonishment. "Yes there was, and —"

Dr. Priestley checked him with a gesture. "Let us begin at the beginning," he said; " or rather, at the point where the method of Lessingham's murder had been established. You quite correctly sought for a motive and found it in Ellingwood's circumstances. He was undoubtedly pressed for money, and his wife, after Purvis, was Lessingham's next of kin.

"You were perfectly justified in regarding Ellingwood with suspicion. Clearly he was the first person about whom inquiries should be made. But, if you will forgive my saying so, you made the mistake of concentrating entirely upon him and making no inquiries elsewhere."

"But, hang it all, Professor, look at the evidence I've collected against Ellingwood," Hanslet protested. "The envelope addressed to him, the map with his card in it, the telegram from Slough and the fact that he was at Hedgeworth that night, to say nothing of the fact that Lessingham's car was found in the quarry near his house. You must admit that there's no need to look any further."

Dr. Priestley shook his head. "I'm afraid that I cannot admit it," he replied gravely. "Upon reflection, I came to the conclusion that not a single one of the facts you have mentioned is necessarily an indication of Ellingwood's guilt."

"I don't see that!" exclaimed Hanslet obstinately. "All I can say is that a jury wouldn't think so."

"Very possibly not. The verdict of a jury is not always dictated by logic. I regarded the matter from a slightly different viewpoint from yours. I was prepared to admit that the facts tended to prove that Ellingwood was the criminal. But I could not disguise from myself the possibility of his innocence. This possibility involved the existence of an unknown person, X, who had planned and carried out the murder.

"My first problem was this: How could the guilt of X be made to conform with the facts in your possession? It was clear that X had endeavoured to throw the responsibility of his crime upon Ellingwood. Therefore he must have been aware of his existence, his address and his relations with Lessingham. Again, from the circumstances, X and Lessingham must have been comparatively intimate.

"Given these postulates, I thought that I could account for the facts. Consider first the envelope addressed to Ellingwood, which you found in Lessingham's car. Your explanation of that was extremely plausible, but it was not exclusive. I found myself able to suggest another.

"Suppose that Lessingham, after Ellingwood's visit, had discussed him with X. X might have displayed interest in the matter. Learning of Mrs. Ellingwood's relationship with Lessingham, he might have seen a way of diverting suspicion from himself. I assume that the crime was by then already projected. X may have gone so far as to tell Lessingham that he would consider investing money in this poultry farm. He would like to investigate the matter for himself. Would Lessingham give him Ellingwood's address?

"With such a request, Lessingham would comply readily enough. He would take an envelope, write the name and address upon it and give it to X. At the same time he would give him one of Ellingwood's business cards, which Ellingwood himself had left on the occasion of his visit. X retained these; he stuck up the envelope, then tore it open again and affixed a stamp, to produce the impression that it had contained a letter. He procured a map and inserted the card between the folds. These he put in the pocket of Lessingham's car at the time when he effected the substitution.

"This supposition was, I admit, purely conjectural; but it supplied a possible explanation, which did not involve Ellingwood's guilt. In dealing with the telegram from Slough I felt that I was on surer ground. Your explanation that Ellingwood sent it to himself in order to account for his presence at Hedgeworth seemed to me to imply an undue degree of cunning. To my mind, there was a simpler one. If X wished to throw the responsibility for his crime upon Ellingwood it would be greatly to his advantage if it transpired that Ellingwood was at Hedgeworth on the night of the 2nd. He could assure his presence there by making an appointment in Lessingham's name. However strange Ellingwood might think it that Lessingham should stop to discuss business in the middle of the rally, he probably knew that Lessingham would be passing through Hedgeworth about that time. And his financial straits would not permit him to refuse such an invitation.

"As for Lessingham's car being found in the quarry near Ellingwood's house, that had never greatly impressed me. If it indicated anything, it was Ellingwood's innocence. Had he been guilty he would have chosen almost any other place in which to dispose of the car. But if someone else was trying to fix the guilt upon him, the quarry was a very convenient place.

"Having thus shown the possibility of the existence of X, I wondered whether it would be possible to resolve this unknown quantity. And at this point, Superintendent, I must mention how greatly struck I was with the account you gave me of your interview with Mrs. Burford. Her story, if it was true, seemed to me to suggest a number of the most interesting possibilities. It explained the telegram addressed to Lessingham here, and also Orchard's reluctance to give information when you first interviewed him."

"You can take it from me, Professor, that her story was true enough!" put in Hanslet. "After all the experience I've had I know pretty well now whether anybody is speaking the truth or not."

"I have no doubt that, to the best of her knowledge, it was true." replied Dr. Priestley. "You were perfectly right in accepting it as the truth. To you it explained the incident of the telegram and Orchard's evasiveness. These matters, having been thus accounted for, lost their importance in your eyes. They had no further bearing on the case upon which you were engaged.

"But I was so impressed with this sidelight upon Lessingham's life that I resolved to carry the matter further. You see, we know little or nothing about Lessingham, and this was a possible opportunity for gaining information."

"I had already tried all the people whose names were in that address book of his," remarked Hanslet. "I had picked up a good deal, one way or another, but nothing worth bothering you about, since it had nothing to do with the case."

Dr. Priestley nodded. "I quite appreciate that," he replied. "My first step was to call at Shetland Mansions, at a time when I felt certain that Mr. Burford would not be at home. There I got into conversation with the hall porter, who told me that I should almost certainly find Mr. Burford at his office, the address of which was 222 Paternoster Square. I immediately proceeded to Paternoster Square and walked past the door of No. 222. The name written up there was 'W. Burford & Son, Publishers'. Displayed in a window of the premises were a series of guide-books and several sheets of maps of England on various scales.

"I recognised the firm at once. Burford's guide books and maps are known all over the world, and have a deservedly high reputation. I learned by inquiries in publishing circles that Henry Burford was the sole surviving partner, and this Henry Burford was undoubtedly Mrs. Burford's husband."

Hanslet smiled rather patronisingly. "I could have saved you all that trouble, Professor," he said. "I put the usual routine inquiry through to verify Mrs. Burford's story as far as I could. I learned who her husband was that way. But I can't see how that could get us any further."

"To my mind it opened a train of thought. I had never been able to account satisfactorily for the fact that no maps were found after the accident in the car which Lessingham was driving. I could only conclude that the criminal had removed them, fearing that they would afford a clue to his own identity. How they could have done so, I was at a loss to understand. But now the discovery that Mrs. Burford's husband was a map publisher suggested a reason.

"I said just now that I believed Mrs. Burford's story to have been true, to the best of her knowledge. Her fear, and we have the superintendent's evidence that it was a very genuine one, was lest her husband should discover her intrigue with Lessingham. But suppose that, unknown to her, he had already discovered it, and had determined to kill Lessingham? Suppose, in fact, that he was the hitherto unknown quantity, X?"

"No, no, Professor, that won't do," Hanslet interrupted. "That is, if Mrs. Burford told me the truth. He was abroad when Lessingham was murdered. She told me that she had a telegram from him from Boulogne on Wednesday. That's why she sent the wire to Lessingham."

"We can deal with that objection later," replied Dr. Priestley equably. "Let us return to my train of thought. Suppose that Burford had deliberately cultivated Lessingham's acquaintance, seeking his opportunity. Lessingham would have mentioned to him his intention of competing in the rally. What more suitable person than Burford, in his capacity as a map publisher, could be found to draw up the route? If Burford did this, he probably advised Lessingham as to his starting time, and lent him the necessary maps.

"At this stage I telephoned to Orchard, and learned from him that Burford had been to Cawdor Street on at least two occasions since Ellingwood's visit. If my conjecture as to the proceedings of X with the envelope and card were correct, Burford could have carried these out at either of these visits. Further, if Burford had lent Lessingham a series of maps, these would almost certainly bear the imprint of his firm. The reason for his removal of them after the accident thus becomes dear.

"Up to the present, Burford fulfilled the necessary functions of X. But this was not sufficient. Others yet remained to be fulfilled. And among these were the circumstances surrounding the theft of Mr. Chalk's car. X must have undoubtedly been familiar with Mr. Chalk's habits. Had Burford the necessary knowledge?

"You will remember, Superintendent, that I suggested you should ask Mrs. Burford if she knew Mr. Chalk. Here, I am bound to admit, my suggestion was not wide enough. I should have added Mr. Catesby's name to the scope of your inquiry."

"Catesby!" exclaimed Hanslet. "I've never so much as set eyes on him. How does he come into all this?"

"Only indirectly, as I shall show. Mrs. Burford's denial that she knew Mr. Chalk puzzled me. I decided to check her statement and got into communication with Mr. Chalk. He told me at once that he knew no Mrs. Burford, but that he had met a Mr. Henry Burford, since he occasionally attended Mr. Catesby's bridge evenings on Tuesdays. He was not there on Tuesday, March 1st, but had been there on the previous Tuesday, on which occasion he had left his car in the drive, next to Mr. Chalk's.

"Had I suggested that you should ask Mrs. Burford if she knew Mr. Catesby, she would probably have replied that her husband occasionally played bridge at Mr. Catesby's house. This would have suggested to you the possibility of Mr. Burford's complicity. Upon such apparent trifles does the science of investigation depend."

"That's all very well, Professor," said Hanslet reproachfully. "But why didn't you let me in on all this?"

"For two reasons. The first a psychological one — that you were so convinced of Ellingwood's guilt that you would not have entertained an alternative theory which could not be proved. But I attached more weight to the second reason. Convinced as you were of Ellingwood's guilt, you hesitated to question him directly, owing to the handicap this would have imposed upon you. Even had I been able to convince you of the probability of Burford's guilt, you would have been in an identical position. I felt that I, the free agent, had a better chance of establishing the proof than you, the professional policeman."

"That's more than likely, while we have to observe these absurd rules," agreed Hanslet. "But, after all, Professor, have you established the proof?"

For the first time during the impromptu conference Dr. Priestley smiled. "I think so," he replied. "As I said originally, you shall judge for yourself. I prepared a trap for Burford, into which, in spite of a certain miscarriage of my plans, he has apparently fallen.

"I kept the preparation of this trap to myself, for I was not sure how far I was acting within the law, and I wished nobody else to incur responsibility. My first step was to approach a mutual acquaintance of ours, Superintendent-Doctor Brusek, the eminent graphologist. I told him that I wanted a letter written in a feminine hand, which could not, under any circumstances, be traced to the writer.

"He told me that could easily be arranged, and he sent his daughter to see me. At my dictation, she wrote a letter and signed it 'A friend of Mr. Lessingham'. You have that letter, I believe. Superintendent. Perhaps you will read it to us?"

"Well, I'm damned!" exclaimed Hanslet. "I'm not sure that you haven't rendered yourself liable to a charge of blackmail. This is the wording of the letter:

"'DEAR SIR, I have in my possession certain letters which reveal the familiarity that existed between your wife and the late Mr. Lessingham. I have thought of handing them to the police, but if you care to see them first, you can do so on Friday next, at ten pm., alone. I shall be walking along the road leading from Hedgeworth to Moorchester, close to the spot where, on the early morning of March 2nd you removed the steering pin on Mr. Chalk's car.

"If you care to meet me, we can discuss what is to be done with the letters.

"A FRIEND OF MR. LESSINGHAM.'

I must say, Professor, that's pretty neat!"

"I flatter myself that the letter is not without ingenuity," replied Dr. Priestley complacently. "It showed Burford that the author was aware, not only of the intimacy between Mrs. Burford and Lessingham, but also of the means by which Lessingham's death was contrived. Burford simply dare not neglect it. He was bound to attend the suggested rendezvous, at whatever risk to himself.

"My next difficulty was to find someone to impersonate this mythical female friend of Lessingham's. I foresaw the possibility that Burford might make a murderous attack upon this individual, and I was anxious to select somebody fully capable of self-defence. The name of Mr. Gateman suggested itself to me. I knew, from my previous acquaintance with him, that he possessed excellent histrionic powers. I thought that he would have no difficulty in disguising himself as a woman, sufficiently well to pass muster in the dark. And, finally, in case of attempted violence on Burford's part, I knew that he would render a good account of himself."

"I therefore asked Mr. Gateman to come to see me, and explained my scheme to him. He fell in with it enthusiastically. My instructions to him were these:

"He was to take a room at the Red Lion at Hedgeworth last night. He was to change into his female costume and walk along the main road towards the wood, timing his arrival there at shortly after ten o'clock. When he met Burford, he was to lead him to the spot where we found the spanner. If he did not meet Burford, or any other hitch occurred, he was to wait until half-past ten, and then walk back to his hotel. If he met Burford, he was to hold him in talk till we appeared.

"I had counted upon our being in position, surrounding the clearing in the wood, by ten o'clock. I guessed that Burford would arrive in a car and I was going to depute Mr. Weldon to put that car out of action. Burford, if he obeyed the summons, as I felt pretty certain he would, could not then have escaped us. But, owing to the unavoidable delays which we encountered, we were late in arriving upon the scene. Perhaps Mr. Gateman will recount his experiences."

"I had the time of my life, sir!" replied Richard enthusiastically. "I got hold of a girl's rig-out and took it down to Hedgeworth. The first thing I did was to explore the Red Lion thoroughly, and I found a back entrance through which I could slip out.

"Soon after nine o'clock I had got my fancy dress on, and found it wasn't half so awkward as I expected. Then I dodged out of the back way without being seen. I walked through the village, as bold as brass, and then an unfortunate thing happened — I was accosted by an amorous yokel."

A ripple of laughter went through the room at this admission. "What did you do?" asked Dr. Priestley.

"I took no notice of him for a bit, sir, but the blighter kept following me. I was afraid that he would come all the way to the rendezvous, and that would never have done. I had decided to wait for him as soon as we got clear of the village and give him a punch under the jaw. But luckily he gave up the chase after a bit.

"The road seemed deserted once I'd left the village behind, except for an occasional car passing, and there weren't many of them. I was a few hundred yards from the rendezvous, and it must have been about five minutes to ten when I heard a car coming up behind me. It slowed down as it passed me, then went on, turned, and stood with its headlights full on me.

"I guessed that this was Burford, and that he was taking stock of the young woman with whom he had to deal."

"Excellent," murmured Dr. Priestley. "Excellent! And what did you do then, Mr. Gateman?"

"I walked on and the lights of the car went out. I guessed that he had pulled up under the trees beside the road. I couldn't see the driver — it was pitch dark, and he kept in the shadow. There wasn't another soul about, and I confess I began to get the wind up. It struck me forcibly that, in Burford's eyes, I was a very inconvenient bit of evidence. If he had an automatic and decided to pot me without further investigations, I didn't stand much chance."

"Had I known how desperate a character he was, as revealed by his attempt on us last night, I would never have exposed you to the risk," said Dr. Priestley contritely.

"Oh, I soon got over that bit of funk, sir. I turned off the road towards the clearing without seeing anything of the fellow. But I heard footsteps rustling among the dead leaves behind me. I turned round and suddenly a torch was flashed in my face.

"I stood stock still and said nothing. I was afraid that if I moved or spoke I should give the game away. But Burford seemed to have no suspicions. After a bit he switched the light off. 'Good-evening,' he said, quite politely. 'I believe you have some letters to show me?'

"I was listening every moment for signs of you people. But I couldn't hear anything, and I realised that I must keep him talking. I wasn't quite sure about my voice, so I merely whispered, "Are you Mr. Burford?'

"'Of course I am,' he replied. 'You don't think I should show a letter like this to anybody else, do you? Here it is — that will convince you, I suppose?'

"He took the letter from his pocket, flashed his torch on it and showed it to me. I sort of nodded and began to fumble in my bag, waiting all the time for something to happen. Then he began to get impatient. 'I must ask you to be quick,' he said. 'I don't want to stay here all night.'

"At last I produced the dummy packet you gave me, sir. But I wouldn't give it to him. 'I don't like to part with the letters,' I whispered. 'I'm sure I could get a reward for them if I handed them over to the police.'

"This seemed to shake him a bit. 'What the devil have the police got to do with it!' he exclaimed. 'And, for that matter, how did you come to know of this place? I want a closer look at you, my girl!'

"I knew what was coming from the tone of his voice. I couldn't see much, for he had that confounded torch right in my eyes again. But just as he caught hold of my shoulder I hit out. I only grazed his head, but that was enough. I think he realised then that a trap had been set for him. Anyhow, he let go of me and bolted. I was pretty close to him, but I couldn't catch him. Then we came out on to the road, and the rest you know. The last I saw of you, you were in full pursuit. According to instructions. I went back to Hedgeworth, slipped into the Red Lion by the way I had come out, removed my disguise and awaited developments."

"I can only say, Mr. Gateman, that nobody could have played the part better." said Dr. Priestley gravely.

CHAPTER XXI

THERE was a moment's silence, and then Dr. Priestley turned to the superintendent. "You can have very little doubt now that Burford was the murderer," he said. "The very fact that he recognised the rendezvous from the indication given in my letter is sufficient to prove the case against him."

"Yes, it seems clear enough," replied Hanslet, rather reluctantly. "You've beaten me once more, Professor, I'm afraid. I'm wondering now how far Mrs. Burford was in the know. She must have lied to me about that wire from Boulogne."

"Not necessarily," replied Dr. Priestley. "In fact, I expect you will find that wire was genuine. I have no doubt that it was sent to suggest an alibi. I have studied the time-table, and find that he could have crossed to Boulogne and back within the day. No doubt he hid Mr. Chalk's car in the wood during the early hours of Wednesday morning. He probably removed the steering pin at once.

"By catching an early train from Hedgeworth, he could reach Folkestone in time to catch the first boat of the day to Boulogne. He would have plenty of time to send a telegram from there and then take the afternoon boat back to Folkestone. Thence he could return to Hedgeworth with time still in hand to drive slowly here. If he actually spent his day thus, you should have little difficulty in tracing his movements. Superintendent."

And with that, the conference ended. Hanslet hurried back to London at once, but Dr. Priestley insisted upon the others remaining as his guests at Moorchester over the week-end. He thoroughly enjoyed his holiday, and discussed every subject under the sun, with the exception of the murder of Lessingham. That he had dismissed from his mind as a problem solved, and therefore of no further interest.

Hanslet meanwhile lost no time. He secured a specimen of Burford's handwriting and found that it corresponded exactly with that on the telegram handed in at Slough. Orchard, who still remained faithful to his post, remembered seeing a parcel of maps on the table in Lessingham's room after Burford had called one day. Since they had disappeared when Lessingham started for the rally, it was probable that he had taken them with him.

Then Hanslet tackled Orchard upon more delicate matters. "Look here," he said. "That night when I found Mrs. Burford here, she told me quite enough for me to guess the rest, so it's no longer any use for you to try and shield her. She was here pretty often, I suppose?"

"Once or twice a week, sir, and always in the evenings," replied Orchard. "I used to hear a good deal of their conversation, sir, when I was waiting at dinner. Mr. Burford was a very keen bridge player and used to go out a good deal. She pretended that she didn't like the game, so as not to have to go with him."

"Mr and Mrs. Burford never came here together, I suppose?"

"Not recently, sir, though they used to at one time. From what I've heard, there was a bit of a bust up between them over Mr. Lessingham. Mr. Burford thought he paid her too much attention, or something. I heard Mrs. Burford say that he had definitely forbidden her to see Mr. Lessingham again. And that was some time last year."

"And yet you say that she came here once or twice a week. Now, look here, Orchard, you're a man of the world. Do you suppose that Mr. Burford didn't guess that his wife was disobeying him and carrying on with Mr. Lessingham?"

"Well, if he did, sir, he never showed any signs of it, as far as I know. But I often used to think that Mrs. Burford and Mr. Lessingham were playing a pretty dangerous game. Apart from her coming here so often, they used to go away together when Mr. Burford went abroad, as he sometimes did. And they were always writing to one another. What astonished me, sir, was that Mr. Burford, after never coming near the place for a long time, took to dropping in sometimes during the few weeks before Mr. Lessingham was killed. I heard Mr. Lessingham mention this to Mrs. Burford and tell her that it was just as well to keep on good terms with him."

"H'm; it is not a very pleasant business, whichever way you look at it," remarked the superintendent. "I fancy that you'll hear something about Mr. Burford in a day or two that will astonish you, Orchard."

Hanslet, armed with Burford's photograph, had no difficulty in tracing his journey to Boulogne and back. His movements had been exactly as Dr. Priestley had deduced them. Having established this point, Hanslet felt that the case against Burford was as complete as he could make it. But Burford was still in hospital, suffering from concussion. The Superintendent decided that for his own satisfaction he would pay a visit to Highcroft Poultry Farm.

Ellingwood was surprised to see him, and still more astonished when he understood the drift of his inquiries. "I only saw Lessingham once, when I called at his rooms and put a proposition before him," he said. "He was very decent about it and said he'd think about it and let me know his decision later. I could see that at the

166

time his mind was full of the rally. He told me all about it, and said that a friend of his, who knew all about maps and that sort of thing, was working out his route for him."

"I understand that Lessingham sent you a telegram, asking you to meet him at Hedgeworth on the evening of the 2nd. Didn't this surprise you?"

"It did. But I supposed he had some good reason, so I went down there, to a little pub called The Feathers. They turned me out of that at ten o'clock, and I hung about outside for Lessingham half the night, but he never turned up. I thought I saw him go through with another fellow soon after ten, but if it was him he didn't stop. After I saw there were no more cars coming through, I wondered what the dickens I'd better do. It was much too late to put up anywhere, and there were no trains at that hour. But I had a stroke of luck. A lorry driver hailed me and asked if I wanted a lift. He drove me up to London and I caught the 12.30 back here."

"Where had you spent the previous night, Mr. Ellingwood?"

"On the Tuesday afternoon I went to stay with an old naval pal of mine who runs a poultry farm in Essex. I wanted capital for this place, and I thought he might give me a tip as to how to raise it. He insisted on my staying the night; in fact, I went straight from his place to Hedgeworth on Wednesday evening."

By way of precaution, Hanslet took further details by which he was subsequently able to verify Ellingwood's story. Then, Burford having sufficiently recovered, he was formally charged with the murder of Lessingham and Purvis.

The trial was sensational, every point being keenly contested by the defence. But two points told heavily against him. The first was his recognition of the rendezvous mentioned in Dr. Priestley's letter and his own question to Richard: "How did you come to know of this place?" The second was his savage attempt to run down his pursuers when he saw that his line of escape was blocked. The jury returned a verdict of guilty, and sentence of death was pronounced.

Before he was hanged he made a full confession, in which he described his proceedings. These tallied exactly with the theory which had been enunciated by the prosecution. According to this confession, Burford, early in February, had learned of the relations existing between his wife and Lessingham, through coming across some letters written to her by the latter. He said nothing to her, but decided to kill her lover at the earliest opportunity.

He renewed his acquaintance with Lessingham for this purpose. He saw the opportunity he sought in the rally, and the car which Lessingham had entered for it. He knew exactly how to procure a similar car, and in Lessingham's casual mention of Ellingwood's visit, he saw a means of diverting from himself any suspicion that might arise.

The confession also cleared up a point which Hanslet had not succeeded in elucidating — the disposal of Lessingham's car after the so-called accident. Burford had repeated his tactics of the previous day. He had driven on until he reached a point some fifty miles from Moorchester which he had previously reconnoitred. Here there was a disused shed on an unoccupied small holding. He had run the car into this, walked to the nearest station and taken a train to London.

That evening he returned, took out the car and drove it to Slowford, which he reached shortly before midnight.

Having driven the car over the edge of the quarry, he made his way to a junction some few miles away, where he caught a night train back to London. There was no night porter at Shetland Mansions and he let himself in unobserved about six o'clock on Tuesday morning, to be found in bed by the maid a couple of hours later.

But, from Mr. Farrant's point of view at least, the most interesting part of the confession was this: Burford, when he arrived on the scene of the crash, had found Lessingham doubled up over the steering wheel, still alive, though unconscious. Purvis was already dead. In a sudden access of fury at the sight of his victim, Burford had dragged Lessingham from the car and flung him violently upon the ground beside Purvis's body, thus giving him the finishing stroke. He had then replaced the steering pin, in his haste putting in the spare one instead of the original which he had removed. As he took the maps from the car, he had seen in the far distance the glare of the headlights of another car coming from the direction of Moorchester. This, undoubtedly, was the Armstrong with Bob and his party.

It turned out that Purvis had made a will in favour of a life-long friend of his. But in view of Burford's statement, which proved that Purvis had predeceased Lessingham, this man did not oppose Mr. Farrant's application on behalf of Mrs. Ellingwood for letters of administration of Lessingham's estate. Highcroft Poultry Farm was saved and is now in an exceedingly prosperous condition.

The Armstrong was repaired and Bob proposes to enter her for the next rally. But he says that he will not be entirely satisfied unless he can persuade Dr. Priestley to accompany him as one of his passengers.

THE END

37054818R00105

Made in the USA
Lexington, KY
20 April 2019